Advance Praise for Jonathan Callahan

What we see in *The Consummation of Dirk* is a mind at work, a mind on overdrive, a mind that is relentlessly chasing down thoughts that tumble and slide and build and then circle back home only to be sent out into the world again, broken and beautiful. Jonathan Callahan's stories are twisted and hilarious and brilliant and announce the arrival of an extraordinarily gifted writer.

—Robert Lopez, author of *Asunder*

Jonathan Callahan's every strength is balanced by another strength: his fierce wit is matched by a righteous anger, his reverence for David Foster Wallace and Thomas Bernhard by an obvious determination to create his own literary ground to stand upon. He clearly worries his sentences but he does so with a sense of play, and while he often seeks to expose and illuminate the many indignities of life, he also clearly knows how a heart can be made to burst by better things than heartbreak. *The Consummation of Dirk* is the ambitious debut of a writer already powerful formed, one absolutely worthy of our full attention."

—Matt Bell, author of *In the House upon the Dirt between the Lake and the Woods*

Jonathan Callahan has a way of winding you up and, when you least expect it, hurling you into the beautiful unknown. *The Consummation of Dirk* is a raucous, cerebral, impassioned paean to youth, misfits, yearners, heroes, and art."

—Alex Shakar, author of *Luminarium*

Jonathan Callahan has a particular talent for that most high-wire of literary endeavors: the successful twinning of humor and woe.

—Katie Arnold-Ratliff, author of *Bright Before Us*

Stanley Elkin once said that all jokes are really about powerlessness. If that's true, Jonathan Callahan's various odes to failure, incom-petence, and want are among the funniest jokes possible. Narrated from the deep interior of misery, the stories in *The Consummation of Dirk* are desperately, pyrotechnically, apocalyptically hilarious. But they are also, in their strange way, tender. This is work that sings across the divide of consciousness to touch us in our cages.

—David Hollander, author of *L.I.E.*

Jonathan Callahan is a one-man literary three-ring circus. He juggles clauses like no one I know and stretches syntax into a high wire act. Also he wields a ferocious whip to keep his human animals - wild with traits ranging from monomania to self-loathing - in line. Callahan's first book, *The Consummation of Dirk*, goes where few authors dare in a high-flying manner few authors can imagine.

—Melvin Jules Bukiet, author of *After: a novel*

The Consummation of Dirk

Jonathan Callahan

Starcherone Books   Buffalo, NY

General Editor: Ted Pelton
Book Editor: Rebecca Maslen
Cover Design: Julian Montague
Proofreaders: Josie Martin, Florine Melnyk, and Jason Pontillo
Thanks to Steven Ansell for technical assistance.

The passage on page 171 is reprinted by permission of New
Directions Publishing.

Library of Congress Control Number: 2013933156

This book is made possible with public funds
from the New York State Council on the Arts, a
state agency. Starcherone Books thanks the
Council and New York State taxpayers for this
support.

State of the Arts

NYSCA

Better than nothing! Is it possible?
—Samuel Beckett

Contents

A Gift

The narrator was in pain. Neither the intensity nor the relatively abrupt onset and apparent immediate sourcelessness, nor even the narrator's dogged awareness of the pain was in any way out of the ordinary for the narrator, but these points did nothing to alleviate or diminish or even momentarily lighten or "ease" the pain. The narrator had not been drinking, nor had the narrator had too much to drink the previous night, nor had the narrator been unable to sleep the minimum number of prescription sleep aid–abetted hours the narrator knew failure to obtain would under ordinary circumstances produce an immediately apparent identifiable source for the immanent pain.

The absence of this sort of pain-conducing circumstance for the narrator to point to—and observe to himself that, for example, "I am in pain because last night I had too much to drink," and thus understand that the morning's monstrous sudden onset of nearly unendurable pain was merely a consequence of personal indiscretion or in this case not mere indiscretion but discretion exercised malignantly against his own person, as he knew all too well from relentless experience that for any respite, "artificial" or otherwise, there is always a commensurate price to pay—seemed to heighten or emphasize or at any rate clarify the pain, the narrator felt, in the way that the elimination or erasure of superfluous figures or elements from a central figure or element to whom attention is intended to be drawn's immediate context can intensify or refine the blunt impact of the now isolated figure or element painted on a canvas, alone. It was Christmas Eve. The narrator was not an as it were "religious man," but the narrator frequently found it difficult to withstand a yearning impulse toward some essential religious quality—an ascendance, perhaps, or a kind of supernumerary glow—he associated with days designated by the religiously inclined as sacred or holy and that he felt the chasm between himself and which with particular brutality during the long slow calendar trudge through the Advent Season, culminating in the all but unbearable morning of Christmas Day.

The narrator felt there was nothing worth liking in himself. The narrator felt furthermore that he possessed any number of qualities worth actively disliking, felt he was broadly worthy of condemnation and loathing, and in many respects, scorn, though the narrator's pain was such this Christmas Eve that the mere thought of enumerating even a vastly abridged list of these objectionable personal qualities or attributes would have been exhausting enough to compel him to duck out of the faculty lounge and return to the faculty bathroom's far stall and sit or "roost" on the toilet behind the latched aluminum door with his head in his hands for a number of minutes, had W—— F—— Memorial High School not this Monday commenced its Winter Break, but as just a single example he could identify an equivalent quantity of things worth liking in *other* people (that is, nothing), and could furthermore produce corresponding litanies of contemptible or condemnable qualities transparently possessed by every person he was forced to encounter daily, both teachers and taught, and with whom on particularly torturous if unavoidable occasions he was forced to interact, only the mere thought of the effort needed to articulate and compile even the most superficially glaring facets of each individual's loathsomeness was similarly exhausting, and as the narrator was in a more or less perpetual state of weariness and defeat he only rarely could commit himself to feel or think much of anything about the people he was required to interact with by the nature of his employment every working day, beyond the throbbing desire for each interaction's duration that the other person would just go away.

I reminded the narrator that he had felt pain like this before, but the narrator could not be persuaded that this was a valid argument against or barrier between himself and his present pain.

I pointed out to the narrator that in less pain-intensive epochs there were things the narrator cared about, things the narrator felt enlivened by, things that enabled the narrator to feel joy. Even things the narrator loved. However the narrator was unable to believe me, nor was the narrator swayed by my objection that the narrator had himself on any number of occasions compiled elaborate lists under various headings such as "Reasons to Live," "What I Love," "Odes to Joy," "Who I Am," and so forth, and filed these compositions away in a special folder he kept in the top drawer of his desk, or in certain cases gone so far as to post on high-visibility portions of available wall space of various apartments or "bachelor pads" he had rented in his younger days with the express purpose of resisting or combating subsequent onsets of precisely the sort of overpowering psychic pain he even now found himself struggling to wade through, but the narrator was of the opinion that the person responsible for these insipid lists had been operating under the stupefacient influence of a kind of fraudulent hope, had allowed temporary respite from the pain he saw now unobscuredly was his true or natural state to mislead him, guide him into taking the sort of now-humiliating defensive measures he could only perceive the hilarious feebleness of during periods when their effectiveness— had they the slightest chance of effect—became a desperate need, such as in the narrator's present hour of darkness and pain.

I attempted to argue, somewhat peripherally, that there were *people* by whom the narrator was loved, but this suggestion the narrator dismissed out of hand, even pausing in his approach to the still-distant bridge to chuckle and spit with contempt. The narrator's position was that since none of the figures or characters from the narrator's life I might cite as proof of his being loved knew the narrator *as he actually was*, it was impossible that he— that is, *he*—could be loved. Though it was perfectly possible that these characters might be cited as lovers of an approximation or projection or personal interpretation of the narrator, who after all provided the people he came into contact with every day an endless stream of projected impressions by which these other people might be reasonably expected to form certain personal conceptions of the narrator, none of these conceptions or impressions was the narrator himself. I asked the narrator the obvious question, at which point he abruptly began to sprint for the distant bridge, sobbing, but between sobs sputtering something to the effect that, Yes, this was precisely the problem: he *didn't* or more accurately *couldn't* know any of these peripheral figures in his own life's theatre any better than they could be counted on to know him, and that therefore the basis of his utter disdain and intolerance for and instinctive revulsion toward other people had its point of reference in precisely the kind of gross, superficial paraphrase of the man or the woman—the *who*—behind or perhaps more accurately *within* the projected impression that drove him on nights like this Christmas Eve beyond the limits of his usual or habitual pain down into a special kind of horror and despair—that is, knowing he could never be known.

Although, the narrator reasoned, easing off his sprint, there is of course at least one person to whom things are quite clear: the *narrator* had seen the narrator *himself*, and he now reiterated his position that there was nothing within the sum of this person's character or essential self to love or even not expressly loathe. The narrator hated the narrator, the narrator claimed, as we gradually approached the concrete bridge or overpass spanning the train tracks, hated with a pure and perfect hatred the full breadth and scope of who the narrator was, a kind of hatred exclusively reserved for the narrator himself, because the narrator was the only one allowed or forced to see or know the totality of what he claimed to hate. I had little to say to the narrator during this phase of our exchange.

And the narrator did not need to be reminded that his sadness (or "pain," in his insistent usage) was in no way unique or particular to him, he was in fact excruciatingly aware that any number of the people he passed, invisible in the cabs of their family sedans, or heavily bundled against the deep chill of late December, as the night approached its median, on his way to the bridge overlooking the metropolitan transit line's track, might be suffering in their own carrels of pain, in all likelihood many, perhaps most of the souls afoot this Christmas Eve had their own reasons for casing the darkness and withering cold, were correspondingly suffering, were themselves in serious pain—how could they not be—and he was furthermore aware of the strong odds that to many of these transient brothers and sisters in pain about the particulars of whose own suffering he knew nothing and could never know, the circumstances he had fought to keep from driving him to inward despair and ultimately a late night jaunt to the overpass overlooking the rail line on which countless express trains roved to and from the city's heart each night might very well present as favorable enough, even desirable; didn't need to be told about the material well-being he was able to secure for himself, having more or less successfully negotiated the educational warrens of his country's fading middle class, so that he was able to provide for himself the kind of material comfort and ease that the greater portion of every nation on the planet's populace, along with more or less entire *nations* in certain regions of the map about which he generally only knew what he was told in headlines, crisp and bleak and easy to forget, would and in fact often *do* kill to secure for themselves, and that he was able to have these things without having to as it were give himself away to work he particularly loathed, the narrator needed to be told none of this, and so these were among the topics about which I elected not to speak.

Of course it was inaccurate to say the narrator didn't loathe his work. He did—but not consequential to any inherent loathsomeness *in* the work: in fact, the tender incomprehension in the faces of students attending his brief explanations of algebraic fact, the young men's gray ensembles draped like ill-selected curtains from their bony frames, the nervous way certain crush-smitten girls would gaze up at the narrator as he manipulated systems of equations with his white chalk, waiting until he met their eyes to glance shyly away—these were a daily source of pinprickling joy, though there was little to be said in favor of the narrator's colleagues. It was more accurate to describe the utter loathsomeness *of the narrator* as he carried out his regimen of for the most part innocuous and in truth sometimes even enjoyable tasks that rendered the very thought of the work he did, the non-execrable source of his material well-being, so loathsomely oppressive that he passed the majority of his weeknights contemplating dawn in diaphoresistic waking horror, fore-feeling the inevitable tremor in his hands as he attempted to knot a sloppy Windsor in a fog of insufferable dread.

Nor was the narrator enfeebled by the excesses of his youth. The narrator no longer stocked his satchel with airport-sized bottles of whiskey or gin-brimming flasks, as it was no longer critical that he slip away from his desk every hour or half- for a quick boost or "jolt," to galvanize his cells before he could countenance the remains of the day (or, to be more technically precise, the successive interval separating him from his next quiet slip-away for a drink) and on this front I strategically erred, attempting now to persuade the narrator as our destination drew harrowingly near that surely this must constitute a kind of progress or growth?

The narrator's pain grew more potent still: If the measure of progress for a person like the narrator was a reduction in the quantity of intoxicant required to "make it through the day,"—and here he stressed "reduction," as opposed to elimination cold-bird—then surely no amount of progress or personal growth was likely to get him as far as the threshold of what it must feel like to be an ordinary man, at which point he would only be liberated at last to crave the ordinary cravings of ordinary men whose grim dissatisfactions with what *they'd* never had had of course been pure obscure fiction to the narrator to this point in his life, since his own pain's nature was such that he found it impossible to live like an ordinary man. I objected, correctly, to his delusive construction of this straw—ordinary bourgeoisie, but he had long since lurched beyond the reach of Reason's jurisdiction.

The narrator's wife was in their apartment alone. The narrator's wife was attractive, perhaps heavier than the narrator would have liked, but not by enough pounds for the narrator to feel much more than ashamed of himself each time he appraised some unobtainable slenderness accentuated by heels or revealed by the hiked-up blue skirts of female students, or resisted the urge to toss a casual soiled napkin over his wife's dinner plate after she'd clearly exhausted her appetite yet continued to pick. The narrator's attractive if a touch plump wife also left some space for desire in the department of casual discourse, about the narrator's day at work, for instance— not for any want of on her part of empathy or genuine interest in his quotidian affairs, but as a natural consequence of her own work, preferring as she did some evenings, after a particularly arduous session at her escritoire doing the work that the narrator secretly suspected was in its way far more taxing than his own (even if she did get to, as he had once loathsomely expressed it during a volatile lapse into enmity, "basically get to sit on [her] ass all day") but about which she seldom complained, to "veg out" with some food- or travel-themed cable television programming, on the sofa they'd inherited from her maternal grandmother, with whom the narrator's wife had since early girlhood nurtured an intimate relationship unusual for individuals hailing from such separate temporal climes, and whose massive myocardial infarction had not exactly been unanticipated at this late stage of life, particularly considering her absurdly high salt-intake, but whose subsequent passing nearly ten months back had naturally impacted adversely on the eudaemonia of the narrator's wife. The narrator knew well enough that he'd failed to support his bereft spouse during this acute tribulation, failed to "say the right things," sacrifice time he might otherwise devote to his own tinkering work, failed even to touch the grieving woman unless she specifically asked that he do so, though the narrator was of course amply aware that his wife was a fierce yearner for touch, always had been—her mother often told the narrator that as a girl the narrator's future wife's bedtime "routine" had incorporated a nightly request to be stroked along the inside of her arm expressed by silently exposing and extending this portion of limb to the narrator's mother-in-law, whose reported obligingness the narrator secretly blamed for the gesture's persistence through several years of marriage, and there was never a time he might touch her when she would not stop what she was doing to savor the ephemeral pleasure and emit a soft contented groan, smiling prettily up at him and even arching a bit like the enormous black cat to which she devoted undue affection and care and who harbored a patent aversion to the narrator, after all of these cohabitant years; this as opposed to the narrator, who theatrically sighed and pushed pages aside and looked up with an air of long-suffering forbearance each time she so much as brushed his shoulder in passing and inquired "how [it was] going" when he was grading papers or preparing lessons or exams, or, less often, pursuing his own faltering prose gestures toward a comprehensive survey of the cryptographic maths, what he had once conceived of as his *life's work* but was now merely amateur dabbling he needed to "squeeze in" when he could and was less and less inclined to do so on the remunerative main portion of his working life's margin or "side," and the narrator knew that this kind of monstrous disparity was in part a reflection or manifestation of the pain, but he could do nothing to prevent this insight into the sheer ugliness of his routine behaviors and ways from compounding or intensifying the already unbearable pain.

Nor could the narrator ignore the recent increase in visits on his wife's part to a host of professionals in the speciously flourishing field of mental health, about which whole apparatus of self-obsession and hyper-scrutiny of personal pain she had for much of their time as narrator and wife expressed acute distaste, but from the accredited representatives of which field she now accepted prescribed psychotropic remedies for her own variety of pain.

The narrator's wife often grew withdrawn or emotionally distant coinciding with the onset of the American "holiday season," an observable phenomenon she not only freely conceded was true but generally attributed to the ambiguous complex of feelings the season's unavoidable commercial festivities aroused, due in no small part to her having on the one hand distanced herself, not quite to the extent of estrangement, from the tight-knit family within which she had been raised devoutly—or, in the language she preferred when describing it to her husband the narrator, "fanatically"—Christian, and its Incarnation-centric host of seasonal rituals including daily readings of scripture printed on the back of cut-out cardboard figures or props removed from the glossy advent calendar presenting in mural fashion a pictorial narrative of the Nativity story as told in two of the Synoptic Gospels, culminating of course with the birth of Jesus, the Christ, which labor and delivery famously transpires in a stable or "manger," there having been no room in any of Bethlehem's inns. This climax to the season having been celebrated in the narrator's wife's childhood's household with a particular family tradition she had found so chagriningly ridiculous that she'd avoided all mention for several Yules before finally one day admitting to the narrator that each year her mother baked a small, generally though not always pumpkin-flavored confection, allowed either the narrator's future wife or one of her two sisters to light a single white candle protruding mid-cake, dimmed the wattage of the dining room's faux-chandelier, assembled the family around the oviform table and sang "Happy Birthday" to Baby Jesus, the narrator here courageously resisting the urge to laugh aloud or "guffaw" at his wife's obviously still-humiliating strange admission, though perhaps given inward pause to wonder who exactly this woman he was proposing to settle down for the long "haul" with really was.

And though the narrator's wife was no longer religious, she found herself annually beset with feelings of tender melancholy and a kind of faint regret or longing for the comfort and warmth she even now associated with the holiday season as spent with her since semi-estranged—as a perhaps unavoidable consequence of the nature of her work—family during what had been an honestly bittersweet youth. So though it was natural and itself somewhat of a ritual for the narrator's wife to slip into a kind of complicated nostalgia or slightly melancholic funk each year in the first week or so of December, the narrator's wife admitted that lately it wasn't only *her* childhood toward which the holiday season inclined her to feel wistful pangs and regret; in the context of the bittersweet nostalgia conjured by remembrances of family seasons past it was especially difficult for the narrator's wife to overlook, as she was by necessity able to overlook for much of the year, the longing she had for a family of her own, the child she had surrendered the opportunity to raise and love as an unspoken condition of her nuptials with the narrator, who had at the time kept the reasoning behind his disinclination to fatherhood unexpressed, but had not so long ago when she had tentatively wondered if having laid this foundation of a warm conjugal union together, seemingly only growing in stability and love, notwithstanding the undeniable difficulty of living with the narrator's pain, it might not be time to talk seriously about their unaligned views respecting offspring, at which point the narrator had preempted discussion with his unexpected soliloquy on the one duty he believed himself morally obliged to fulfill, which was to spare a potential next generation from being "plunged into the pain." That the one thing the narrator's wife had wanted all her life to be even more than a writer was a mom, and that every time she saw a mother for example helping her daughter consume a sloppy meal in a restaurant or shushing her candid assessment of some meaty co-passenger on the metropolitan train, she felt a kind of hollow warmth it was sometimes all she could do not to break down and sob over, and that she had willingly surrendered any hopes of fulfilling this dream, not for certain but of course she'd more or less known when they'd taken their matrimonial vows, was nothing to the narrator but a further compounding of his pain, and that she knew this and therefore did her best never to give the slightest indication of the sadness she would sometimes feel when walking past the store in the nearby shopping complex, for example, where it was possible to shape and fire and paint and glaze your very own pottery, the store being naturally aswarm with Christmas present–sculpting kids during the holiday season, some parents participating in the younger "tykes'" processes, others happily looking on, always tried to keep her sadness over the seeming death of this lifelong wish to herself, only intensified the narrator's self-abomination, since who but a monster would inflict this kind of pain on a, as the narrator's mother had uninventively designated her once, "peach" like the narrator's wife?

Then too, of course, the narrator knew that for the last two years at least his wife had faced a more imminent and potent source of this annual melancholy, since the narrator, too, though not the product or output of an upbringing that could be even loosely described as religious, frequently found himself in considerable pain during the season as well, had for as long as he could remember found the same closeness or affection or intimacy or cheer that his wife would occasionally recall in tones best classified as "wistful" almost unbearably sad, would experience the strung lights and snowmen and parcel-conveying reindeer as a kind of soul-wracking ache; and that the narrator's wife was by nature a more or less warm presence, regardless of what her emotional temperature might actually be, December being perhaps the one month of the year during which she permitted her spirits to modestly "flag" or "dip," and that the narrator had therefore usurped the one brief portion of the calendar tacitly set aside for his wife's inner or emotional life by suffering a "breakdown," as he'd called it, two years past, when he'd left his wife a shakily-handwritten note in the middle of the night on December the twenty-first, ambiguously phrased, but undeniably suggestive of intent, the seasonal festivity and joy's oppressiveness having at last exacerbated his perennial pain to an intensity he could no longer withstand, and that, ridiculous as it might seem to claim as much in the circumstances in which she would find and be reading the letter he was writing her in the middle of the night before he *left*, the narrator loved his wife, or wanted to love her, and wished he didn't have to cause her pain, but he was weak and couldn't bear his own pain anymore, [He] love[d] [her], Goodbye, the note said (the narrator never having had his wife's way with words, his typical discursive mode in discussions or "chats" or written explorations of theoretical math being a kind of pleonastic overkill that nevertheless always seemed to sweep past some critical nuance or shade, so that the narrator frequently seemed both to over- and understate his case, a point the narrator's wife was indulging and good-humored about, even though it was surely a pain in the ass to have to listen to him work out tangles of periphrastic syntax to get to a point he might have made in a single more carefully selected phrase, the narrator knew)—only to come staggering in early the next morning within minutes of his wife having been awakened by a need to pee, and on noticing the vacancy in bed, gone seeking the narrator, only to discover the terrible farewell note, which she now held, stricken, the paper fluttering in trembling hands, even as the narrator fell to the kitchen floor's hideously houndstooth-patterned linoleum and began to weep, and she knelt down and stroked his head while he cried for over an hour, and she said nothing whatsoever about the alcoholic stench, refrained from pointing out to the narrator that his note had essentially cracked open her heart or saying anything accusatory or angry, choosing instead simply to hold him and whisper that she would do whatever she could to help him make it all all right, this having been two Christmases back.

This December the narrator's wife seemed particularly forlorn, and one evening in an unusual access of concern for someone else, the narrator had unwisely pressed her to discuss the difficulties she was obviously experiencing as evidenced in the undeniable way she seemed to be "drawing away" from him of late, as he put it, pressed despite her entreaties that he let her work herself out of this "rut," for her to "open up" to the narrator, until at last she caved and proceeded to describe for him a dream that she said honestly recurred throughout the year, with variations, but which during the Christmas season visited her nearly every night, a nightmare:

Beside the narrator's wife in bed was a roughly narrator-shaped lump of blanket and sheet, motionless and supine, nonresponsive to a tentative nudge, or repeated queries of Honey, are you okay? nor even, she would abruptly apprehend, appearing to breathe, so that she would rip back the blanket or "comforter" in literally mortal terror, only to find the narrator living but with a kind of wire or cord wrapped around his neck in an apparent attempt at self-asphyxiation, his eyes each a globular bulge, whereupon she would wrest the cord from his hands (in the dream, she was his better in strength) and try to either chastise him or console him, depending on the variant of the dream, only here he would heave up from the bedclothes out into the traffic-dense boulevard that communicated with their bedroom door, and proceed to begin hurling himself into the paths of oncoming cars and trucks (in the dream these would manifest as fabulous hybrids of assorted motor vehicles and mythical beasts), but each animate automobile would skid and buckle to a halt, its operator sticking his head through an earlike window to berate the narrator or occasionally hopping out and catching him in a head-vise and bashing his face against a vehicular hybrid's mouth or hood—This part is silly, I know, the narrator's wife had interposed—but soon enough the narrator would lurch free and stumble into another car-monster's path, the narrator's wife all the while screamingly beseeching him to come back, but he slipped further and further into the vehicular sea, until at last she would understand he was irrevocably gone, and she would never know whether he was living or dead.

The narrator's wife had therefore with the onset of this year's holiday season slipped into a kind of speculative despair that she was sometimes able to subdue or repress via strenuous application to her professional duties, which this semester included

two graduate seminars at S————— College along with, it goes
without saying, in between lecture-preparation and -delivery, and
myriad meetings with students, emails the sheer weekly bulk of
which would stagger the pedagogical lay, having to hunker down at
her desk and resume once again the laborious process of "stitching
together" or "eking out" or somehow composing the works of short
fiction for which she was perhaps justly celebrated in certain literary
circles as a "dynamic" "master of syntactical metallurgy," who
"redefined the domain of the literary *avant garde*," and consistently
"exploded formal expectations" with piece after incendiary piece, yet
invariably imbued her "chaotic compositions" with that "rare, almost
preternatural" or "saintly" humanizing empathy that "part[ook] of
the suffering" of even the most "repellently vile" characters or figures
populating the worlds of her fiction, though recent critical attention
had sounded a note of slightly less unanimous zeal, the author of
one longish review in particular citing as worrisome the trend in
the narrator's wife's more recent output away from the observable
world so richly imagined in even the densest iterations of her earlier
work and into the helix and tangle of pure consciousness, as it
were "burying" the reader ever deeper in the Byzantine brainways
of characters the reviewer had honestly had just about enough of
after a handful of pages, in some cases a handful of words, which
criticism had affected the narrator's wife far more deeply than she
would admit even to the narrator, because the narrator's wife wrote
exclusively—the narrator knew of no more sophisticated way to put
this—*from her heart*: she wrote as an outpouring of the love and
sadness and confusion and pain that had always been her impetus
for composition, but where before this relatively straightforward or
artlessly *naked* approach to the creation of work that she was not the

only one to consider Art had been sufficient to earn the sort of rich acclaim transcribed above, it now appeared that this new impulse to transmute all the instinctual probing, seeking, path-carving into the subjects of her emotional preoccupations or even obsessions into something static and captured and whole was impelling her down a kind of rabbit or other burrowing creature's habitat, as she endlessly probed the labyrinthine suffering of characters with whose pain she empathized so fiercely it was not hyperbole to assert she felt it as her own, but whom her readers or at least impatient reviewers seemed increasingly not to like.

The narrator was of course aware of his wife's recent fading self-possession, her inability to pour herself into something or *someone* that readers would welcome into their own lives, her crisis of confidence, her inability to do the one thing she'd learned to do without hesitation or doubt after the long early years of failure and rejection, so that it naturally added still more tinder to the conflagration of his already considerable personal loathing and pain to learn that this winter the narrator's wife was only peripherally concerned with her recent professional struggles, because, as she put it, she felt she was being methodically *consumed* by dread of the day she confessed she was more certain by the passing hour would one day come when she would return from campus to find the narrator, whom she loved as she had never loved anyone else and couldn't conceive of a life without, gone, this time for keeps. It made her almost literally too sad for words, the narrator's wife admitted. She'd made a livelihood out of transposing raw sadness and pain into language that conducted or communicated this sadness and pain, only now the words had, as it were, failed her, it was as if the entire reservoir of language she had drawn from for so many years had simply leaked out of her, and she was left with nothing to say about or do with the pain, only the terrible pain itself, which she would simply have to withstand until the day she grew more and more certain was coming soon, when the narrator would end his life.

The narrator felt he had failed to tell his wife often enough that even a mediocre reader like the narrator was able, if only crudely, to sense the immensity of the gift his wife possessed, and more than the gift, the "saintly" generosity of spirit with which she seemed almost compelled or hardwired to apply it, the very same spiritual generosity of which he of course daily and liberally partook but only rarely expended the minimal energy or time needed to tell his wife he was genuinely thankful for, so that on nights like this Christmas Eve he sometimes wondered if she had even the vaguest suspicion that, all pain aside, this gratitude was something that he truly felt, even if it *wasn't enough* to extract him from his abominable foulness and pain. Naturally, the narrator felt inadequate to the task of fully appreciating his wife's literary work, the only "writing" he'd ever done—leaving aside the plunges into abstruse depths he privately had always known he wasn't smart enough to do much more than flop uselessly around in, hence the necessity that he teach algebra, basic geometry and, to students on the "Advance Track," trigonometry/alg-2 at the high school he'd come to think of as one iteration of an infinite variety of earthly Hells—having been in his private journals to which it had been some time since he'd bothered to add new thoughts, seeing, as, he'd explained to his wife one evening as they sat on the small wooden patio behind the apartment they shared just off S———College's campus, sipping rosé and staring at the light pastel cloudwork cast by a vanishing late-August sun, all the narrator ever wrote about anymore was *himself*, his own sadness and pain, that tedious pain, even *he* was repulsed by the prospect of hearing it further discussed, one of a number of reasons he declined to enlist the services of another mental health specialist, or "shrink," having almost immediately determined that the last of which was merely another clown in a longish series of such, and he didn't care to acquaint himself with yet another credentialed hack who would attempt to draw forth from the narrator yet again his whole tedious history of psychic pain, since *everyone* had his or her own "yoke to bear." The narrator's wife felt it was extremely dangerous for the narrator to close off *any* potential outlets for his pain, but also felt she had no right in the end to force this perspective on him.

Even now the narrator's wife was waiting in their apartment, "unwinding" after another day of failing to harvest literary fruit in her working alcove, probably watching a TV show about cats or international cuisine, maybe sneaking a piece of chocolate from one of the two stockings she'd hung from hooks on the wall beside the tree beneath which she'd earlier that evening set out a neat small stack of gift boxes crisply wrapped in shiny red paper printed with wreaths, reindeer, and candy canes, beside which sat the two presents the narrator had initially concealed in the previous Sunday paper's "sports page," but on seeing his wife's meticulous preparations had secretly unwrapped and located the roll his wife had bought and used the leftover wreath-, reindeer-, and candy cane–themed paper to inexpertly re-wrap, which gifts were books he honestly couldn't remember whether she'd said she wanted or had already read, and if she'd read them whether or not they'd been any good. The disparity in present stack–sizes rendering his abrupt announcement that he had "one last Christmas errand to run" at least plausible, which plausibility while she sat there and debated one more piece of chocolate from her own stocking and perhaps idly speculated about the nature of the special extra surprise the narrator had in almost heroic spite of his recently surging pain contrived to present her with this Christmas just as soon as he came back home naturally only contributed to and further heightened the narrator's *in extremis* guilt and pain. Some days the narrator could scarcely think of his wife's name without succumbing to a suffocating tenderness and regret over the immensity of the poor woman's compassion, and plunging into the kind of self-abomination there would be no escape from if it still held him by the time he reached the bridge.

Here I committed what I consider to be my first major error, as I seized the opportunity to suggest to the narrator that surely his wife's illustrious compassion and pain on his behalf were an indication of precisely the kind of narrator-directed love he had earlier argued against the very possibility of, yet simultaneously vehemently claimed to need, at which point the narrator as it were "wheeled" on me and literally shook his fist and shouted, Yes, she's in love with someone—*but it isn't me!* and now I began to feel the predicament of my rapidly waning time.

The bridge overlooked two sets of tracks. The metropolitan transit line ran as usual even on Christmas Eve. It was unpretty for the narrator to imagine the corporeal facts of the team of metro employees assigned to the late night or "graveyard" shift this Christmas Eve's unexpected additional task, so he endeavored not to dwell on the unavoidable stroboscopic visions flashing in his mind of the forthcoming visceral tableau or scene. I may have neglected an opportunity here, but my thinking involved the inconclusiveness of this kind of hesitation over the particulars of postmortem gore.

On the bridge the wind was naturally frigid, with light snow flurries swirling and twinkling like tiny windblown stars, just beginning to stick, so that the narrator's boots left faint tracks beginning just past the intersection with Vipadi Dr., which was a third of a mile from his home.

The moon was a preposterous sallow bulge overlooking the narrator as he gripped the overpass's cold metal rail and peered into an arctic gust downtrack toward the gradually dilating dual discs of white light. The narrator now revealed that he had either not been one-hundred percent straight with his wife earlier in the week when discussing the progress he'd been making this week regarding reduction in volume of drink or had determined ahead of time to fortify himself for the evening's mission or task, as he withdrew the familiar silver flask and swallowed several seconds' worth of rye. It was not within my power to stop him.

Here the narrator's thoughts took an interesting turn, as the express train approached. The narrator focused on a contradiction or paradox he found hilariously sad: The narrator's wife had made a name for herself out of inhabitation, understanding, empathy, communion with other people's souls; the narrator's wife was renowned for her capacity to put herself into the deepest pockets or cores of the kinds of people who seemed impossible to care for, let alone love, until she effected her special variety of miracle and through magic the narrator could never understand persuaded and enabled her reader to *see*, to know, to love the person and pain trapped in the depths of the monster; the narrator's wife transacted in a kind of compassionate possession—and yet it seemed to the narrator that the situation was more or less reversed in the case of himself: the person the narrator's wife had fallen in love with was a costume for the monster rampaging around within. If the narrator's wife were able to glimpse the true yellow-fanged virulence of his self-defining pain, the hopelessly festering horror that constituted the narrator as he knew he actually was, if the narrator's wife could just for one instant see the narrator's "soul," she would never again feel anything but loathing for the narrator, as the narrator felt for himself—would never have endeavored to share a "life" with the monster, would never have been able, even if in her strange goodness it was what she had wanted, to *love* the narrator, who, as he alone was able to see and know, was only monster and pain, unable to feel anything for anyone outside of pain, unable to feel or *be* anything other than pain.

What if the narrator's wife could go back to the earliest days of their courtship and see not the goofily dashing narrator by whom she'd been cinematically "swept off her feet" but the pain-wracked projectionist madly feeding film through the reel for each scene, if she could see his romantic efforts as mere desperation, to project himself out of the even then ever-present pain into a new way to be—that is, to *become* the narrator he was extracting all stops to persuade his future wife she could already look into his eyes over brunch at a South Village sidewalk café and see? How could she ever love someone who secretly knew of himself such horrible things?

On a pivotal night in the city she'd called him crying in frustration over a series of spectacularly hurtful interactions with patrons at the café over the course of a very bad day, culminating in an improbable four-missive stack of envelopes, each containing form-letter printed rejection slips from four different literary publications in any one of which she'd have been thrilled to publish a meticulously written piece, this being one of any number of difficult

days during an especially difficult stretch for the narrator's future
wife, before she'd published a word of the fiction she hoped to share
with the world and for which she would one day be enthusiastically
acclaimed, when she was routinely pulling double shifts at the
shabby café on D Street that was the only work she'd been able to
land during that period of memorably foul economic atmospherics
for just about all of us, a dark bleak time for the narrator's future wife
during which, as she'd often told him over the subsequent years, the
lone bright spot or beacon or guiding light she looked toward to
make it through each week's "grind" was the time she would spend
after-shift every third or fourth night with the narrator, who would
sometimes take the train into the city to cook dinner with her in the
kitchen of the one-bedroom she rented in the then-still-low-rent
apartment networks north of the river. That on the pivotal night
in question the narrator had immediately left his own place in the
little suburb north of the city where he was earning the secondary
degree he needed in order to teach high school math, abandoned
the several-hour study session he had intended to undertake in
deference to the following day's Pedagogical Paradigms: Old and
New course's big "mid-term" exam, arrived at the narrator's future
wife's apartment somewhat damp, as there had been rain, bearing
an excessive bouquet and a bag of both sesame- and poppy-seed
bagels, because he knew one of the two types was her favorite but
could stupidly never remember which, along with lox, and cream
cheese, and a bottle of red wine that didn't really go with the bagels
and lox but that he'd figured what the heck, and the two of them sat
at the low coffee table in her apartment's living area sipping wine
from coffee mugs and nibbling on breakfast food and mostly talking
about how dreary and bad everything felt for her at this difficult

stretch in her life, how she was beginning to wonder for the first time if she hadn't badly mis-assessed her own supposed creative "gifts," was it possible there was after all nothing so special about her? And he listened to her and told her as well as he could that he believed in her, as he called it, "dream," and he knew or could actually only imagine but, well, he could vaguely appreciate that it must be something like agony to feel like you've got something you'd desperately like to just give to the world only nobody's ready to accept the gift, and he urged her to "hang in there," and reiterated his ungainly appreciation for the pieces she'd shown him, taking care not to tread into editorial or even interpretive territory, as he'd come to understand this was somewhat prickly ground, sticking to the fairly bland appreciation, which anyway was all the narrator actually felt he was qualified to feel—and basically the narrator just did his best to help his future wife not feel alone that night, even staying over and rising nausea-inducingly early to catch the first train from the city and race back to his place and cram in a couple hours of study before dismally muddling through what was an honestly important test.

Surely these were the sorts of things, the narrator reflected, as he lifted his left foot onto the protective rail, that the narrator's wife thought back with fondness on when she sought to strengthen herself or make sense of a lifelong commitment to a man whose character's salient feature was pain. But what would happen to the narrator's wife's nostalgia's tender preservation if she knew that during that epoch of relentless romanticism and chivalry and sweets, the heroic self-abnegation, the tireless thoughtful concern, the elaborately tender and endearing, if crudely written compositions he would send to her almost nightly via electronic mail, the songs he'd write and perform for her on his spindly toned guitar, what would happen to all of it if she saw the whole extravagant charade as the crazed gambit it had been to construct a personage for his future wife to fall in love with, that the "narrator" she'd fallen in love with was nothing more than an edifice or bulwark willed into being to hold off the pain long enough to trap somebody else in it with him? So that all of the stories she returned to when she needed to remember why she had chosen to share a life with a man like the narrator, whose pain she had of course sensed from the beginning but had not anticipated annexing their entire shared life, were a lie. The narrator had furiously constructed a kind of fictional *character* for his future wife to fall in love with, and the narrator had no idea whether he had really believed he could one day become the person he'd persuaded his future wife to believe in or not, only that for in his opinion probably purely selfish reasons, he had honestly wanted to try. Of course he'd failed—here he was, the narrator laughed, crouchingly testing the slick wet cement—and though it was impossible even for the narrator to deny that deep down he did feel a kind of tender appreciation or admiration or gratitude or compassion or sadness and tenderness for his wife that others might call "love," only *he* knew the fraudulence of the entire construction, only *he* knew it was impossible for a "man" like the narrator to love, only he knew that no one could know the narrator as the narrator knew himself and feel anything but sickness and death, surely no one could see into the narrator's heart of hearts and, in spite of what she saw, love.

Because the truth is it's of course just not possible to know a fraction of what it's like to be, really *be*, anybody else. Even the pitiful, pain-crippled wreck that the narrator's wife knew slept so poorly that his sleeping pills had all but ceased to function unless swallowed as chasers at the close of a gin- or brandy neurasthenic onslaught, and once again upon waking sometime around the AM's one, even the narrator who held his wife hostage to the possibility that she would one morning wake up or walk in to find him deceased, even *he* was infinitely more worthy of love than the narrator as he actually *was*. And to the narrator it was this above all that he felt he could no longer face this Christmas Eve, that out of desperation a "man" like the narrator constructs on a lifetime of frantic impulses the semblance or projection or approximation of the kind of person he'd either like or believes other people would probably want him to be, and the strain of steadfastly, every day maintaining that projected mirage is perhaps yet another way of defining what the narrator ordinarily referred to simply as "pain," this tension between an aching unbearable need to just once in your life be absolutely known, by anyone, but more than anyone most dreadfully by the person you've persuaded to give herself to a surrogate "you" who is utterly unlike the subterranean man—*and* the knowledge that *no one can* ever *know him*, that narrator, the *real* narrator, the lying, unloving *thing*, because to know *that* narrator would be to abhor him, and the narrator could not stand the thought of his wife's withdrawing her love. The narrator *wanted* to love his wife, he wanted the freedom to give himself to her, the narrator himself, but he could never even begin, because to give himself the narrator would need to reveal himself, to be known by his wife, but the narrator could never be known and loved, it was impossible, there wasn't a way.

The train came on in a nimbus of radiant steam. The narrator had risen wobbling to his feet on the dangerous side of the rail from his perch atop the narrow ledge, and was trembling but seemed resolute. I had run out of time, so in little more than a whisper or breeze I said to the narrator: But what if there *were* a way?

The Witness

True story, more or less: On the morning of July 28, 1945, an errant B-25 bomber emerged from a thick fog hung low over midtown Manhattan and plunged into the Empire State Building's seventy-ninth floor. The explosion expelled elevator-car-operator Betty Lou Oliver from her car and left her badly burned. After receiving preliminary first-aid she was placed by emergency-aid workers on the seventy-fifth floor into another elevator—whose shock-weakened cables promptly snapped and sent her on a nearly-eighty-floor plummet to the building's sub-basement. She survived the fall.

April, 1945

—Still but okay: granting it's maybe your basic meat-and-potatoes ethical dilemma, concedes Oscar Oliver, Torpedo-man, Third-Class. He swallows, resets his stein atop the single wet ring its base has deposited on the unvarnished teak. —What's the difference? For me, ultimately. In terms of how I ultimately decide to act?

—The difference?

—Yeah. I mean, does it really *matter* whether these are not necessarily uncharted? In terms of as philosophical waters? I'm wondering.

—Does *not* matter. Matters absolutely nil, is exactly my point, O. Doesn't matter, and it doesn't matter whether it matters for you or anyone else whether it matters or if there's a fucking difference between whatever you even just said. Ultimately. Cept to the one person on the planet who gives a shit what you decide. Just pick *something* and quit blowing what still strikes me as a potentially salvageable night out there on the town, as they, as they say in other parts ... his over-the-shoulder gesture broadly indicates the bedlam just beyond the bar's patio, the beachside thoroughfare like some vast kaleidoscope projecting patterns of raucous young men in lieu of colored light, the bands of land-hungry seafolk who troop the boulevard in search of native treats... —if you weren't fucking set on spending the rest of it staring into your beer.

T-M,3C Richard Phurst shakes his head, vigorously rubs his nose, eyes a white-skirted waitress's dark legs as she sways past into the noodle-bar's deeper gloom. His stein is down to mostly suds.

—Look, says Phurst, —you want *my* advice? ... Pretend you do. I say forget the whole thing. As in don't think about it. Lose the memory.

Oliver shakes *his* head. —And what, he says, —just pretend nothing even *happened*?

Phurst's hand goes up in a later era's crossing-guard's traffic-halting semaphore.

—Not *pretend*, man. *Pretend*'s got nothing to do with it. You don't have to *pretend* shit. *Pretend* means you actively *do* something with your brain. What I'm saying is you're already doing too much. He leans back, runs a finger down the robust jutting eminence of jaw—I'm proposing more like the opposite of that. Do less. Don't think about this shit. You're already thinking too much is the real problem.

—I don't see how not thinking about it's gonna—

—Cause what's the point of thinking bout a problem you can't solve? Like remember how Floyd would, he'd be out there on the grounds at like 0400 every morning before PT doing the shit with where he's trying to jump up and touch the basketball rim only he's fucking as tall as my mom when she's not wearing shoes, and this is a small woman, O, Sicilian, maybe I never told you, the height's on my pop's side, plus she's starting to hunch, which I'm saying there's no fucking way he's touching that rim whether he jumps one time or ten thousand. Or a million. And plus too if you wanna talk about faithful, you *have* been serving God and Country with plenty of faith, is something to remember. If you you're looking for something to remember here.

—

—No need for that look, Oliver.

—What look? There's no look.

—Okay, there's no look. I'm experiencing, I'm getting fucking ecstatic visions of a certain facial expression—which is still on your face *as I speak*, by the way—okay now it's gone. But that was, that was a fucking *look* on your face there, a second ago.

—A look conveying what, did it look like?

—How the fuck should I know, it was *your* look: you tell me. Hey, Miss? Excuse me, Ma'am?

The hostess, half-empty pint-glasses perched and tottering, tray borne on one open palm, currency flapping from a pocket of her apron, pivots, squints back into the light.

—Nother round, the same?

She nods. Phurst returns a nuanceless wink.

—No look! All I'm saying is, seems like your advice is just to act like this isn't a problem that's kind of important to me, cause maybe in your opinion it shouldn't be, or it's, well, it's *inconvenient*. And you're saying because it's a problem with no easy solution I'm supposed to just give up or like quit trying to find one through the application of, of rigorous dialectic. Seems like an easy way out, you know?

—No. Wait, what? What I'm saying, it's a stupid fucking problem that only a panty pisses his first night away of shore leave on, is what I'm saying. That you should fucking exercise discretion when deciding what's important since let us eat, drink and be merry, for tomorrow we die, which this is the fucking Bible, am I right?

Oliver smooshes his face between both hands, puffs out a half-belch/sigh. Phurst reaches across the table as if to grip his shoulder or execute some similar fraternal gesture, prematurely withdraws.

—Just remember this, though. Leaving aside the fact you seem to be kind of blatantly overlooking—i.e. there's at least a decent chance she could *leave* you over this, right? This is something you've considered? And even if you work out some kind of understanding, the wife'll, well she'll be in a whole lot a hurt she isn't feeling now— shit she has no *reason* to feel, ever—if you do decide to open your mouth—

—Yes, but I detest a lie.

—And this is from the book too?

—Well? Marlow's got a lot of valid insights. Especially the further he gets up the riv—

—So you're saying, what you're saying is it's more important to *you* that *you* not be stuck with the discomfort of telling a lie than it is for you to spare *her*, the woman you supposedly *love* a little pain that she only ever feels as a result of knowing about *your* fucking up. And this is, this is noble, O? You tell her what you did, she's gonna hurt. The other hand, who hurts if you *don't* tell her? Only *you*, right? One way to look at it.

Oliver nibbles his left lower lip and watches nodes of pale bluish light shiver along the surface of what's left of his pint. Above him criss-crossed strings bearing crepe-papered lantern-globes representing the full spectrum of primary colors rustle in a light coastal trade. Higher, rows of tiny white light bulbs line the ceiling's bare beams. Phurst tilts the bowl to his lips, drains the last bit of broth, shoves the porcelain vessel aside, balancing his chopsticks on-rim. Out over the water to the north and west, a host of twinkling lights striped with a few deep-probing beams breaks up the dusk over Espiritu Santo's Big Bay.

Phurst grunts and shoves back from the table.

—Piss.

Oscar swallows what's left of his ale.

So then *never tell her* about that last stretch of opium nights before the *Tirante* took him north from Pearl Harbor for contested seas, because to tell her is to risk hurting her in a way that she has not been hurt before. To lie is to spare her some needless suffering. Is therefore an act of mercy, kindness—of maybe even *love*.

Except now, wait:

Supposing the situation were reversed, supposing Betty'd gone and done something like this to him (which, by the way: what if she *has*? during the lonely months Oliver's been away at sea? The notion burns, except how *could* it? How can he suffer with suspicion and still *dare* not to admit the hideous things he's done?), is it really true he'd rather never know? Seems sound to posit that, given the choice between hurt and no-hurt, he'd choose to avoid the hurt. Only that word "choice" is the problem, here, no? He wouldn't really *have* much of a choice, would he? The supposed "choice"'d already be made for him. *She'd* choose to spare him all the hurt. So that the question really seems to be, Would Oliver, in his betrayed wife's position, accept this deal whereby the choice *to choose* between hurt and no-hurt has been exchanged for the protection from hurt that is no longer his to choose? Oliver's viscera guess that, given the choice between pain and its absence, he'd rather take the pain than have the ability to do so taken from him. In which case he would rather know, now wouldn't he?

Only how can he *know*?

The Oliver who can sit here drumming the fingers of both hands in an obsessed tattoo along converging curves of his lingering stein—and where the hell's this hostess?—*this* Oliver, the Oliver who is here in the dingy little Filipino noodle-shop, facing north, lights of naval activity flickering out to sea, the strip aclamour with riotous R&R, *this* Oliver imagines two other, discrete Olivers in obverse situations:

First we have the Oliver who, upon returning home from an at-times harrowing but also *thoroughly chaste* naval deployment aboard the U.S.S. *Tirante* that took him from Pearl Harbor up the shallows off Kyushu's southwestern coast, through the Straits of Tsushima, patrolling the Pacific Theater's last hot spots in East China and Yellow Seas, navigating deep waters depth-charged and radared by maniac Nips with nothing left to lose at this point, death as honor, no surrender and so forth, returning to the wife he's dreamt of during what shut-eye he can snatch (his dreams unhaunted by opiate visions culled from a particularly epic shore leave in the *den of sin*), the young wife whose olive skin, if his memory's not embellishing things here, almost does *glow* in the weak light of the candle they'll sometimes place on the second-hand dresser set beside their creaky little bed, the woman, his wife, *glows*... this Oliver, returning home, is told the truth: that she has not been alone in this bed, *someone else* has breached their tiny sanctum, cramped and shabby, sure, but *theirs*, a shared sacred space for two; someone else has seen and felt and been enveloped in her glow... and the pain this Oscar would without question pitch into and keel about in, the bleak fathomless pain of *knowing*——

Well but then there's the second Oliver who returns home to this same beloved wife and is told nothing, tucks into the very same sheets (possibly even *unwashed*, though this seems unlikely, Betty Lou being fastidious to the point of light obsession), and comes together with the body (even the *soul?*) he doesn't know's been with somebody else, and so ignorantly reprises what he thinks is the very same joy and wonder of perfect intimacy, enters a euphoria of reunity that he can't possibly know is tainted and false—and so this Oliver, therefore *believes* himself still able to experience an unmarred bliss that the other Oliver will never feel again, and by so believing *does* obtain it—

But still, the original Oliver, old beerless ruminative Oliver, this Over-Oliver here in the Subic-Bay hole with his fingertips more or less pounding their accelerated pattern on the mug, this Oliver thinks he would *still* rather be the first guy, wrecked by the truth, than the happy incognizant fool.

But why?

Somehow Oliver, who shares neither his wife's Catholicism nor Faith, has this bizarre sense that the answer depends on whether or not there is a God.

A tap on-shoulder rouses him: the waitress bearing foamy ales. No sign of Phurst....

Depends on God, really. Well, not God. No such Being/ Entity/Thing. But say, an Eye, or a Ceiling, some sort of Limit that tells us whether a thing ultimately matters or not.

Because, now, hold on, wait a second, in spite of what he's just admitted to himself, Oliver is back to thinking that since there *is* no giant Eye/Limit/Ceiling or God—he sure as hell's never seen Him—no all-Seeing Third Party aloft to track the motions of morally purblind men, puttering through their choices and acts and blunders and lies, no one there to bear witness in the way that Oliver here has speculatively done with imagined Olivers #1 and 2—then what does it matter how ugly a lie might look?—There isn't anyone to see it.

No one to see or know except for the deceiver himself—who's accountable to Whom? And since *this* potential-deceiver's decision therefore comes down to a simple choice—to inflict or spare suffering, right?—can't it be argued that to take what he's done and stuff it down into a dark place where it might rankle and burn *him* for the rest of his years but never threaten to inflict anything on anyone else—specifically his poor little luminescent Betty Lou, who'd get to go on believing in their unblemished utopia, preserved and just as perfect as it had been then, before Sam dispatched him East to serve—well, wouldn't this be sort of noble, brave, heroic? … No?

Oliver drinks deeply, a long cool rich hoppy draught, and leans back, actually nodding a little to himself. Maybe old Rich Phurst is actually right: Betty will never know what he, Oliver, has done, and to tell her would be to make her hurt where she didn't hurt before. Telling the truth here would be indulgent, exculpatory for him, maybe, but a further wrong against his wife.

Except now—gahhh!—Eye or no Eye, even if there is no One to see—no God, no Over-Oliver, no Anybody—the scene of Oliver #2, ignorant cuckold, in bed with the wife who's suffering through excruciations of guilt in order to sustain for him the illusion of innocent bliss is *still* somehow grimed over with a stinking slick black muck that ruins the whole thing whether Oliver 2 or Anyone Else knows it's been ruined or not. Oliver's fist comes down on cheap wood, sloshes a bit of beer on his forearm. It *would* be ruined, he knows it would be. Who cares if no one knows or *sees*?

Oliver scans the dimness for Dick Phurst but still can't spot him. The wind's begun to whine out on the street, is that—yes, a sailor's cap has taken flight, swoops past, no bare heads to be spotted though: someone's out of uniform tonight. Humidity tinged with sudden chill. Oliver looks out over the dark water sequined with variegated light. The morning after next the *Tirante* will return to sea for one last northward patrol before setting course for Honolulu's Pearl Harbor, and after that, back home....

Not a month's passed since the night Oliver and his crewmates waited in vain off Oniki Saki to receive radioed response from the U.S.S. *Trigger*, with whom *Triante*'d been ordered to rendezvous, a ship on which many of *Triante*'s crewmembers, Oliver included, had served only last year. Verbatim from the one printed eulogy he'd managed to get hands on: *With surface ships there are survivors, messages, bits of wreckage, bits of memory to be stitched into cohesive last narrative; with submarines there is only the deep, the silence.*

And what had it been like, Oliver wonders, to feel the impact of that depth charge, torpedo, or mine, to feel the collision-alarm's siren-shriek knife through you, ship upending instantly, air pressure increasing, loose gear precipitation from what used to be below, eyes locked on the depth gauges even as needles yield to wheeling mania, the rushing floodwater's roar, the groan and creak of *Trigger's* caving frame, the pounding and the futile cries of eighty-nine doomed men... down, down, down, until the steel shudders and crumples in on you, the last few meters of consciousness almost too heavy to bear... and what would he see in those final seconds— what would he want to see? Beauty? Truth? God? Love? Nothing at all? Once more he envisions their relative positions switched, for a moment: suppose it were *her* dropping in the doomed sub, him safe at home in Manhattan, lonely during the long hours operating his elevator car in the Empire State Building, rising and falling gently through another day's listless wait, one more crossed-off calendar square, crossing his fingers against every newswire.... If Betty Lou were the T-M,3C, what would he want her, falling through those final darkening seconds, to see?

If a light shines down at spectra we're never given to see, secretly illuminating the labyrinths of our lives, if a hidden radiance gleams from every instant, motion, action, thought tunneling through time... an Eye, looking down, might witness something hidden from our eyes... but would it even need to see? If the light is there, does it ever have to be perceived?

What Oliver decides is as clear and bright to him as the colored glass twinkling from the surface of his pint, and he knows, when his ship returns to port, if he does make it home, if he's ever granted another evening in the little candle's flickering glow, husband and wife together again in their tiny quiet sacred space, well, he knows how he will choose.

Cymbalta

Much of this began when I encouraged renowned American fiction-writer and composer Rick Moody to pay me an extended visit at my place in Fukuoka, Japan. Or a little bit before this invitation. Rick, I said, eventually, in one of many similar electronic communiqués, the apartment is a bit run-down, but the *tatami* mats are new, or might as well be, the rooms are quite capacious, and you'll get to bathe in a traditional Japanese *ofuro* each morning at dawn, or whenever you decide to get up—or in the evening if you prefer to hit the *futon* for the night washed clean of the detritus of the day.

My first maneuver was to send him a modest tragic drama I'd composed the previous December and had my first-year high school English students perform for final projects at their abridged third trimester's end—a single act with only two dramatis personae: a celebrated fiction writer from America named Rick Moody and his unnamed interlocutor, a young scholar of contemporary literature who makes ends meet by teaching elementary English classes to rural Japanese by day, but devotes his nights *in toto* to note-compiling toward his epic academic treatise: *On Rick Moody*.

Rick responded favorably to this folderol—a mere few evenings' divertissement indulged in during a frustrating stretch in my academic work—just the kind of encouragement I'd hoped he might provide. Soon we were eager correspondents. He was too tied up with work and his most recent project, parenthood, to take me up on my offer, but was cordial, if rarely prompt in his responses to my not infrequent ruminations transmitted to his "inbox" via electronic mail.

The email doesn't seem to be the great man's ideal venue of expression. Where one encounters troves of verbal wealth on nearly any printed page selected from the Moody tomes, in emails all the garrulousness is gone, words to be read with emphasis are indicated in all caps, LIKE SO, as if that *signal typographical gambit* were the hallmark of some other prosesmith's work. Of course, one *earns* the right to make stylistic choices, as Moody has in fiction, song lyrics, scriptural exegeses and plays, and I have not, in either tract or monograph. Perhaps I was feeling a bit the breadth of that license-gulf between us, then, when I made the bladed reference to the similarly emphatically deployed italics that lacerate the pages of famed Austrian curmudgeon Thomas Bernhard—a spiteful ploy I now consider ill-considered, typed hastily in truculence one unpleasant evening when I couldn't overcome my indignation at his several-day-and-counting failure to respond to the friendly bit of literary small-talk I'd sent in response to his previous failure to respond to an email of mine.

That certainly got his attention! Within a half-hour I was rereading a forensically precise dissection of the specious but widely indulged misbelief that any connection might be made between the cantankerous Continental master's work and Rick's. Here I noted many of the stylistic tics of that famous Moody prose: the liquescent force of his rhetorical constructions, the supple but persistent use of what's known in literary circles as the "elegant variation," *and this.*

I apologized and said a mostly true thing—that I did not remember sending this email, as I'd sent it after many drinks, a bad habit of mine since making my trans-Pacific move—which soon transpired to constitute a second mistake.

Who was I to listen to a lecture on the perils of fermented grain? Who was he to give it to me? I scrolled through his response, dismayed at the generic similarity to a certain prominent Association's so-called Steps, that specious pseudo-scripture whose banality's been co-opted by almost all ostensive well-wishers in this therapeutically-inclined so-called culture and with which I was already naturally *all-too-well*-acquainted from earlier epochs of my life. And here is where I first questioned the authenticity of my "Moody." How could I be sure **rmoody** wasn't some impostor, maybe a small-time but ambitious writerly factotum with a knack for reproducing platitudes and imitating what's been spuriously labeled "purple" prose? Perhaps Rick had this fellow on his payroll—certainly a hired stand-in could save a busy fiction writer time. I thought I'd *test* him with a testy answer calculated to elicit a response that *only* Rick would write.

I opened my thesaurus, executed fifty closed-fist push-ups—my routine before each round of grappling with the page—then ignited the commercial end of a Marlboro Light, entered my email account after typing in my clever password, and started to audition tonally appropriate first sentences aloud—when it occurred to me that I might be *making a mistake*. Whether he had hirelings or not, I thought, Rick Moody was someone I wanted to have on my side. If he was less than prompt and diligent in his responses to my frequent, friendly missives, well, this was something we could work on. Instead of vitriol I went the other way, whimsically attached an mp3 of that rousing operatic ode to water moistening the sands of Death, "Love Reign O'er Me," to the note I wisely wrote instead—"Thanks, Uncle," I said.

I waited for two hours with my inbox open, watching peripatetic Japanese slump by on the street below my aging apartment complex till the sun was gone behind the minor mountains to the east, sipping cheap *shochu* in a state of developing unease; it's widely understood that Hiram "Rick" Moody's prowess is not limited to the composition of indelible prose—that while he writes incomparably *about* music, he also *plays* the stuff: I knew this from his Wikipedia page. What if he *hated* The Who? Many listeners do. Mistakenly, I'd argue, to the death, as I have *nearly* done on numerous occasions—but I dared not disagree with Rick! As he continued not to answer despite my *knowing* that he, fourteen hours back from me in his comfortable Brooklyn writing nook, was without question answering emails *precisely now*, so that I grasped at last that what was needed was a little clarification; I sent this email as a hasty follow-up:

On Thu, December 9, 2010 at 10:36 PM, <————> wrote:

When I'm grading the papers I want to be writing the book. When I'm writing the book I want to be watching highlights of the National Basketball Association's top ten plays of the day, or, on Sunday evenings, of the week. When I'm watching the NBA highlights I want to be walking the streets of Futsukaichi, engaged in inward dialectic with the works of H. F. Moody. When I'm alone with thoughts on

Moody, I want to be watching a movie with my so-called *fiancée*. When I'm stuck for the evening with the woman who is not my *fiancée* but whom I falsely described as such in order to ensure that we would be placed within reasonable proximity of one another upon being hired by the outfit that sends non-Japanese English teachers to teach English in Japan, the so-called "TRUCK Program," which proximity has resulted most often only in annoyance, as she has shown so little inclination to respect my need for long periods of intense concentration in absolute solitude without disturbance—in the form of thunderous knocks on my locked apartment or *jutaku*'s door, phone calls or texts, *fits of hysteria*—if I am to make any headway with the monograph, I want it to be late enough for us or at least me to go to bed for the night so that in the morning I can make more productive use of a full working day. In the AM, after I've checked both electronic mail accounts and finished my second cup of coffee but before I've undressed for the shower, I want the day to be over with so that I can start drinking *shochu* without risking imperilment of the modest but steady income I receive each month. About three quarters of the way through my third glass of *shochu* or second "tallboy" after work, I want to be just cracking my first beer, or actually *looking forward to* just cracking my first beer, an epoch of comparatively measureless hope, because after half an hour or so I've passed the state of intoxication at which it is possible for me to study pairs of Japanese verbs. When I'm studying pairs of Japanese verbs in the transitive and intransitive case, I am often forced to reflect that since I am able to do the work I receive a modest but by no means paltry salary or remuneration for to my employer's apparent satisfaction—certainly no one has complained, or if they've complained I haven't heard them, or if I've heard them I am not aware I have, on account of my poor Japanese—and that

I have no intention of pursuing subsequent positions that would require even the dismissible quantity of Japanese that I have thus far retained, and, indeed, the only work I *can* imagine myself obtaining on returning to the "States" being utterly contingent upon the completion of the *Moody*, which is no closer to completion than it was when we left—if *in the event of my failure* I am compelled at that point to find suitable or even unsuitable work, the only thing I can posit with some degree of confidence is that this work will have nothing to do with 日本語, that is to say with *Japanese*, so that my doomed attempts to master the long lists of verb pairs in the transitive and intransitive case are participants in or a contributing factor to a much vaster, indeed, life-encompassing failure that I will submit to if, in this pocket of material serenity, I am unable to complete the work that will once and for all establish my scholarly name.

Best,

—————

-----Original Message-----

To: rmoodycom@gmail.com <rmoodycom@gmail.com>
Sent: Thu, Dec 9, 2010 9:02 pm
Subject: Bernhard

Thanks, Uncle.

I'd not intended to end there, but had to stop mid-thought, just when my rhetoric was gaining momentum or as it were "steam," because my neighbor, Robert, wanted to go have a drink. He always wanted to go have a drink, a pathos-urging alcoholic, but I indulged him, recalling just how lonesome nights had been for me, before I'd adjusted myself to our comedic lives, here in south Japan. Now Bob, as I call Robert, does not read literature, a point I'd never held against him—he does other things. For instance, he snowboards. And, too, he brings a fascinating ebullience to his botchings of the native tongue, a trait I truly envy in him, as it's only fair to note that though *my* grasp of the native *Nihongo* is comprehensive, academic and precise, I all too often succumb to that dual bane of all introspective types: self-consciousness and -doubt, so that it's very difficult if not impossible for me to *strike up conversations* and I am not infrequently incapable of completing ordinary tasks such as exchanging suits in need of dry-cleaning for a thousand or so yen without initiating scenes of humorous ineptitude and personal chagrin. I can never return to the dry-cleaners I *first* patronized, a so-called mom-and-pop establishment whose proprietors were a friendly Japanese *Obaasan*, or grandmother, and her less friendly spouse, a Nagasaki-native veteran of our most recent World-splitting War, after an excruciating episode I decline to go any further into here.

So when I told Bob about Rick Moody's encouraging *response to my play*, his response was not exuberant at all ("Who's he?"), but I didn't necessarily mind. We settled on an *izakaya*, except almost as soon as we'd begun the twenty-minute trek to that affordable liquor-and-grease-concern I began to find myself wishing that Bob were dead. Now Bob is suicidal in his own right, and so I didn't air this sentiment, but one can only listen to elaborations on a single theme—in this case the desirability of middle-aged Japanese "muff"—before the deadening sets in.

—Of *course* you could, you idiot, I said, —I honestly can't
take this shit tonight: a bit of frankness I would one day, in light of
how things went with Bob, wind up coming deeply to regret. But I
didn't regret it at the time. I sprinted back to the apartment while
Bob presumably strolled on to have his *imo shochu* on the rocks alone
and started typing a new email.

I'm all alone here, Rick. You don't know what it's like—

I began, but then my "*fiancée*" came in.
    —What's going on, I asked.
    —Oh, hey, she said. —I saw the light. Thought you said
you were going out with Rob...
    —Not yet, I said, and made a mental note to change the
passwords on my various accounts. I had so far managed to deflect her
not infrequent requests for a copy of *my* apartment's key, primarily
by feigning the absent-mindedness that is in truth a lifelong knock
against me, but not to the degree that I sometimes *allow* people to
think when I infer that their fond condescension will serve me well.
Nevertheless, she routinely hijacks my electronic accounts and also
peruses my so-called "snail" mail anytime I leave it on my desk.

Alone again, I considered a can of lemon chu-hi. "Double lemon," it
said, in Japanese. This would be important to a drinking Japanese,
substance-abusive or not, this being the most *mathematical*
ethnographic group. There was a triptych illustrating the process

by which the lemons in question were chilled to negative-196,
centigrade, disintegrated or powderized, and then presumably
incorporated into the sixteen-proof sweet carbonated drink I have
come to so enjoy. Why -196, I wondered. Why not farther down the
thermometer—or *not* so far? And *Rick would no doubt understand*,
if not straight away, then after careful contemplation, research,
dispassionate analysis of all the relevant mechanical facts. I've
always lacked that quality—

I've always lacked this quality *you* possess, I typed: the easy
discipline, innate compulsion to simply *do things right.* I've never
done things right. My goal is always to avoid beginning things, in
order to avoid the final stage of having gotten them *all* wrong. Entirely
wrong, everything *precisely* as it never would have been done had
some *sane* executor begun from some sensible embarkation point.
Am I mad? I've often asked myself. I've been tempted to ask you,
Rick, for a while now, except you generally don't respond to what I
write—

The last line discouraged me. I got up to get a drink. Next
thing I knew someone was making noise outside my door—my so-
called *fiancée*. The sun was shining on her golden neck and I had ten
minutes to get suited up for work.

*

From: —————<—————>
Date: Tue, December 15, 2010 at 4:32 AM

Subject: Fingers of Death

To: rmoodycom@gmail.com

So here's what occurred to me at work today, Rick. Feel free to skim. But I had a comparably hard day. Obviously the assessment depends entirely upon whose circumstances we're conducting the comparison with, but if the revision option were available this is one twelve hours I'd go hard at with the red pen. I woke up at around two-thirty after passing out at ten. I knew with my first fully-formed conscious thought—which was actually to wonder what you'd have to say to yesterday's note—that I wasn't getting back to sleep. And I know this happens to other people all the time, but I really hate it when it happens to me. I got up, checked my email, drank a pot of coffee, had a beer, drank another pot of coffee, smoked three cigarettes, showered, took a shot of gin, geared up for work, checked my email again, took another shower, thought about another pot of coffee, smoked a cigarette, sipped a little on the gin, then left the heater running as I sprinted out the door to catch my train. At work I tried to focus my attention on some time-consuming tasks so that I couldn't think about how *bad* I felt, but what wound up happening was that I thought even more intensely about the feeling bad than I probably otherwise would have done, and I left several tasks unfinished, and the one thing that I did was poorly done, which obviously made things even worse.

I was scowling at some papers on my desk when I saw my friend Hirose Sensei go trotting by. She's always trotting, Rick, anywhere she goes she trots, I find it cute, even if she only does it to make sure that everyone understands she's working hard, which is of course pathetic in its way, but most things are when analyzed correctly, no? And so I followed her into the Reproduction Room where she'd gone to copy a few pages, figuring I'd work the phrase *Two-thirty in the morning!* into whatever conversation we would have, except when I said, —Hirose Sensei: yo! and she looked up from handouts she was sorting into stacks, I noticed that her eyes were wet. Well, it turns out that her mom had vanished over winter break. A suicide, they'd guessed: She said all weekend during celebrations of the new year—which are as important here as Christmas is back home, if not *more so*—her mom had just been acting *strange*. And then she went to visit relatives in *Saga,* a rural prefecture across the border to our east, and while everyone had been worried that she might not be in the best state of mind to embark on such a trip, she *was* the family matriarch, a widow, and if she wanted to see her *hisashiburi*[1] sister now, no one could give compelling reason why she shouldn't go. She snuck out from her sister's house at some point during the night. No one knew exactly when she'd left—the Japanese are known for stealth—but in the morning she was gone. A search party was organized, Hirose and her husband came, her sister, other relatives, converged upon this mountain village in which the matriarch had spent her youth. No luck. No sign of her that day, and when the night had passed and still no sign, they naturally began to steel themselves for whatever news would come, since this news would probably be bad.

It took a fortune-teller—so Hirose, in the copy room, still not quite crying, manipulating reams of paper as she always does when speaking to me in her excellent English, the only indication she'll evince of the inherent difficulty that expression of more than rote or pre-formed phrases in a language that you've had to stack on top of what you instinctively think in will naturally present—and

---

[1] The *Nihongo* catch-all that translates into English as "long-time-no-see" but is used here with considerably more frequency—*hisashiburi* beautiful cherry blossoms, recreational activities, regional cuisines, e.g.

this fortune-teller whose methods she omitted a description of had listened to the sisters' story, gone back into some space of private contemplation and then returned with his suggestion, which was that they investigate the site of her childhood home, a hut high in the mountains, no *longer* a home, the shabby architecture having been long since abandoned to decay, because he had a spiritual hunch he couldn't name.

I wasn't sure how to respond to this revelation, so I said nothing, but nodded my head as if to indicate that *in extremis*, I, too, might well regress to primordial disregard for empirics and reason. They *found* her there, she said, near freezing—pacing a patch of ice-hard dirt, absolutely ill-attired for the mountain chill.

So now Hirose had on top of punishingly trying preparations for her third-year students' future-determining college-entrance exams the problem of her suicidal mother, rescued from the mountaintop, but obviously not to be entrusted with any stretch of time alone.

I went back to my desk and didn't feel any better. *You* still hadn't written me, Rick, as naturally you know, and I was thinking about how good it would feel if, when writing the letter I subsequently wrote to Hirose conveying my pity, compassion, empathic grief and all of that, I could really *feel* the expressed sentiments as opposed to the actual felt motive that compelled me to complete several drafts of the thing before typing it up and slipping it under a paperweight on her desk, which would be difficult to articulate with perfect clarity but went something like this: in her pain I perceived an *opportunity* to reveal with the depth of my compassion something about *myself*. With one well-crafted letter I could win this woman's loyalty for life. Her mother's near-suicide, and probable successful subsequent attempt in the forthcoming months, had been my chance to remake myself in Hirose Sensei's eyes. Because the truth was I still felt quite shitty when I sat down to jot the notes I'd consult when composing the letter that later Hirose would tell me was one of the most moving things anyone had done for her throughout her life, and I was still conscious of how bad I felt, but was *glad* of the chance now to focus with enthusiasm on something else. Nothing could have been better for me that day than this news of my supposed good friend's mother's attempt to take her own life, and I exploited it, as no doubt any person would have done.

So here's what I'm wondering, Rick: You're on-record as being out to compose "fiction that saves lives," well:

Nevermind.

*

Bob came by again. He hadn't seen the inside of my apartment since I'd started making headway on my plan to "spruce" things up. The thinking was that if you're prone to certain patterns of behavior that will likely lead to undesirable states or "frames" of mind, and if you're not *completely* without brains, the first time you feel well enough to take some small preventive steps against future harrowing *encounters with the edge*, you will. I'd done a number of "little things" in the several days or so since I received Rick's concise but generous thoughts on my play, one of which was to compile a sensible compendium of words or phrases to avoid.

—So you're just *not allowed* to say "failure" or "weak" at all? Bob asked.

I poured us each another tumbler of potato *shochu* on the rocks.

—And what's the deal with "thirty-one"? Bob and I shared

birthdays, my second coinciding with his first. *He knew how old I was.* I asked him how his day had been at work.

—They did the thing about the smell again.

The thing about the smell was that Bob sometimes still exuded fumes of alcohol on mornings after particularly enthusiastic nights at the tumbledown *izakayas* and so-called "snack bars"[2] of our backwood town, and his colleagues, most frequently his "supervisor," liked to ask him if he'd been drinking in the AM before coming in to school.

—They're gonna fire you, I said.

—You think they will?

—They might.

I poured us more *shochu.*

—And if they do, what'll you do then?

—I don't know man. I honestly don't fucking know, he said.

On the one hand, I didn't really want Robert to keep his job—I've always liked to see a person pay for his mistakes, particularly mistakes *rooted in weakness*—but I would miss him if he left.

—Moderation, right? It's okay to have a drink or so at night: I do it, sure. But wait until the weekend for the heavy stuff, alright?

—I know, he said, —I know: it's just it's so *hard* when there's fucking shit else to do.

One thing I should mention about Bob is that he broke two of my ribs once, with a powerful blow I admittedly urged him to deliver late one evening at a dismal social event early in our days here in Japan. *I've* forgiven him, but *he* will never be without the guilt, and my awareness of this debt of conscience sometimes leads me into inadvertent cruelty when I wish I could remember that he's honestly

[2]i.e., caverns of lecherous sin

my only friend.

    —Well, one thing that's really helped the time go by for me has been my studying of *Nihongo*. Lately I've been putting in the legwork as far as trying to nail down verbs in the transitive and intransitive case. I'd be happy to loan you some of the flashcards I've finished up with, if you think that might be a little help.

*

From: —————<—————>
Date: Tue, December 19, 2010 at 4:32 AM
Subject: Fingers of Death
To: rickmoodylifecoach@gmail.com

I went outside to smoke beside my high school in the snow. The crows are fucking huge here, Rick: loud, absolutely unafraid of us, *I admire these crows*, as I think you would too, and I stood and watched a murder of them squall and crayon black smudges of chaos onto the ashen cloudscape until I'd burned out the last cigarette I had. I graded English Journals through third-period today, then spent a little time looking over sales figures for your paperbacks. It's interesting to note that they do so much better in the long haul than you might expect from initial sales. My personal sense is that the Back Bay Book paperback editions' aesthetic continuity really helps to emphasize the "Moody brand," not that this is something that you necessarily *need*, but let's face it: our readers are more fickle by the year, and whatever extra inducement you can slip into the sales-pitch certainly won't hurt, you know?

Two girls were going home early—I don't know why, I've been here eighteen months now and I still don't really understand what's going on each day at school. Actually I understand almost nothing. They gave me "A"s on my annual evaluation, a modest victory, to be sure, but I take my wins when I can get them, and was proud enough until a little subtle exploration turned up the interesting fact that, barring Bob, who has been put on something like probation, no Assistant Language Teacher has ever received less than a B+ on these assessments; the Japanese are by and large accommodating with us, though this is principally because they don't seem to believe in the humanity of anyone who isn't *Nihonjin*. Anyway, these girls who stood there quivering extravagantly in their silly dark blue skirts told me they liked my eyelashes.

It felt good, Rick, and my lashes *are* long, but it's in moments like these, *precisely* these moments, that I have to wonder how my life would be different if I didn't have the problem with my weight. I always was a chubby kid, and continue to struggle with the extra pounds—or kilos, here—as you've no doubt noticed in the pictures I've attached to emails over the past few weeks. So that the feeling I had while talking to these lovely native girls was that they were trying to find something encouraging to say to me *so as to avoid the subject of my weight.*

*

Once, a little while back, my "fiancée" came by and asked if we could talk. What about, I wondered, trailing her in to the

Moody Studies Office I'd converted one room of my *jutaku*[3] into. She said I *knew* what about, and, on reflection, this was true.

—It hasn't gotten any better. You've had several months *more* than what we said, I thought we'd agreed, and nothing's getting better. You need

—You're nuts! I said, giving her left arm a gentle squeeze.

—There's no comparison! Absolutely no comparison— think about the night in question. Or practically the whole month of June! If we were looking at a *June*-type situation here, okay I'd

—Please don't argue, she said, —I

—When as I've *willingly* conceded you were justifiably upset and I think our agreement was entirely fair, as I've also affirmed on multip

—How have things changed? You're never sober, you're never happy, I *know* you come to your apartment after work and drink until you've had enough to stand being with me for a few hours before bed.

—*Untrue! Untrue!* Come on now! Sure, I have the couple drinks or so after work, *you know it helps me* to unwind, I've never pretended to be, tee—to *abstain*—abstinence was *never part of our agreement*, and you know a little alcohol takes the pressure off the work when it's not

—But I don't think you're even *doing* the work anymore

—*Let me finish!* When the work's not going well, I was going to say, which I think I've been forthright about how it's hit a couple snags of late

—Okay, I understand that, but what's the timeline for this? Do we have a timeline? How long is it supposed to be, okay: the

---

[3]residence

Moody thesis

 —*TREATISE!*

 —The Moody isn't going well, so for *now* you're just, just going to drink? I mean, you haven't shown me new pages in how many months, you barely mention Rick to—you barely say *anything* to me lately, and this is supposed to be our li

 —Oh come on.

 —It's true! When's the

 —Come *on*.

 —When's the last time we had any kind of, meaningful talk, when's the last time we even

 —*OK! LET'S CHAT!*

 —*Don't* do that, Jo

 —*HOW WAS SCHOOL TODAY, HUN?*

 —Plea

 —*WHAT DID I MISS ON THE FOOD BLOGS?*

 I noticed that I'd left a glass of orange juice and *shochu* next to my computer. She stood and leaned against the wall beside my cork thumbtack board on which I kept my index of potentially useful arcane words. She was speaking in a very soft voice:

 —You wanted to do it your way. I've supported you. I've barely said anything since we talked about this in the summer. I've had to eat dinners I prepared for you *all by myself* watching stupid Japanese TV that I basically can't even understand or, fine, *reading blogs* while you lay snoring on the beanbag chair or wherever you passed out

—I've *apologized*

—I've turned down invitations to parties when you've told me that you couldn't be around *those people* without getting absolutely trashed… and then watched you drink yourself completely stupid while we sat at home doing *nothing*, or you played guitar or read aloud from one of his books.

—For fuck's sake! It's not like I *forbade*

—I've done everything I could to let you try to do this on your own, because I wanted to believe that we *could* be happier, that *you* could make things better for yourself, and all you've done is just continued to drink.

—Plus now we find out you don't like it when I play guitar?

—I'm telling you you need to get some help.

—I'm taking the fucking Cymbalta!

—I'm not saying cold-turkey, it doesn't have to be a *program*, I'm not even saying, you know—we're celebrating or you've had a long day, you want to have a few drinks on the weekend with Bob? fine: what I'm saying is it has to *actually* be like what we said this summer, or

—I'm taking the fucking Cymbalta!

—If you don't cut down the drinking I think it's going to kill you, okay? You're going to die. And maybe that's not a big deal to *you*, but it still matters to me. And if you can't find a way to see someone you trust here then we need to leave. I don't care if we break contract if it's between that and

—WHAT?

—If you can't figure out a way to get it under control, and I really think that means finding some kind of help then I need to go home. I can't just sit here and watch you drink yourself to death.

—WE FUCKING *LOVE* JAPAN!

*

Here's a quick plot *precis* of my play:

An unnamed character initiates a correspondence with famous American novelist, essayist and composer Rick Moody one night when he is intoxicated and discouraged, neither condition a particular aberration from ordinary patterns of nocturnal behavior and emotional state. The difference *this* evening, and the impetus for the brief dramatic narrative that it subsequently shifts into gear, being that at the very nadir of intoxication and discouragement, or thereabouts, this protagonist has been conducting simultaneous Internet searches, and while encountering some frustration in his primary endeavor to find fail-proof, painless suicidal modi operandi has happened upon a web site called "Rick Moody: Life Coach," and has interpreted this felicitous encounter as a kind of incursion on the part of Fate or at any rate some numinous Force too vast for reason to have easy dealings with, and in a Calvinistic spirit has interpreted this event as a *sign* that the one person on the planet capable of rescuing him from his nightly descent into deep discouragement and excess drink is this Rick Moody, Life Coach, with whose life his own was predestined to intersect.

Of course, it wasn't strictly the case that the Hand of God or Anyone had directed the protagonist to this web site, as he had just prior to clicking on its hyperlink entered the phrase "Rick Moody" into his web search engine's search window. While researching popular forms of felo de se he'd simultaneously been perusing one of the several of his new Life Coach's fictional tomes he kept stacked atop the book shelf beside his desk, hoping to find therein some compelling argument against Death. Because he truly admired Rick Moody's books, for the most part, though they were almost invariably flawed and even bad for stretches, all of them—this point actually *contributed* to the character's admiration, helped to "demystify" or "humanize" the Moody figure, so that he was not *only* the forbidding monolith that the undeniable success of his literary career might lead an admiring reader to construe him as, but was susceptible to shortcomings, inadequacies of talent, was fallible just like you or me. But these books, with their human verruca, blemishes and c., *spoke* to the protagonist of my play, moved him, and in a state of existential terror and genuine need he had gone to the Internet with the nebulous idea that in gathering still more information on Rick Moody he might feel a little less alone.

(All of this is backstory somewhat inexpertly revealed in a searching monologue just preceding the main action of the play.)

Anyway, the prime motion of the plot was that this nameless protagonist confessed to Rick in his capacity as Life Coach that if anybody was in need of a Coach at this point in his Life, he figured it was he—not necessarily because the objective circumstances in which he conducted his quotidian affairs were all that measurably bad, certainly plenty of people, many of them far braver every day than the protagonist could ever imagine himself in his best moments managing to be, confronted and overcame far graver and more punishing material and no doubt even emotional circumstances than what he found himself just about unable to surmount or deal with every day;

the difference, and in the play this little rhetorical gambit is what first wins the redoubtable author over to his side, between the protagonist and *them* being precisely that his own circumstances would be far from insurmountable in the eyes of many citizens of earth, so that the very fact of his floundering inability to get through most of his for the most part unremarkably unpleasant days would indicate his special qualification for receiving the Life Coach's professional services, since he'd be much more open to suggested self-enhancement strategies than would your average, adjusted, stoic, courageous, indefatigable woman or man.

To telescope: Rick Moody is moved, and he begins to coach his troubled young *protégé*, a long and mutually rich and generous online relationship evolves, which culminates in a granting of the unnamed protagonist's request that Moody come coach him *in-person* through this particularly difficult stretch he's going through as an English teacher in Fukuoka, Japan, eventually going so far as to mentor him through the grueling final stages of his *own* literary endeavor, an academic treatise on an unnamed author of American fiction, and then using his considerable leverage in the publication industry to help his grateful pupil find a suitable house for his work, which is set to be released upon the young man and Rick's joint return to the States, a journey for which the two are packing suitcases at the conclusion of the play, Rick playfully poking fun at the protagonist's ineffective T-shirt folding technique, and demonstrating a trick he learned one summer while working retail, slowly, then looking on to ensure that his pupil's mastered the trick, so that the general timbre of the drama as the curtains descend is one of fellowship and hope.

*

We were in a sacerdotal mood that night. I let Robert confess himself of certain crimes and peccadilloes he had perpetrated as an unpleasant youngster on the middling-rough streets of a certain neighborhood in Honolulu, the mellifluously ridiculous name of which I've already forgotten. In my assessment he'd been fortunate to escape prosecution—"consent," in particular, being a particularly thorny concern for many peer-constituted juries, at least in the Continental Forty-Eight with which I was acquainted—and while I naturally did not have it in my power to absolve, I also thought and stated that the Bob I've known has mostly stayed away from outright crime. Meanwhile I told him about the recent guidelines restricting intake volume I'd been failing to adhere to every night behind my *"fiancée"*'s back. We snorted a little of his Adderall and he found a few Valium to smooth them over with—it was Friday night, and my *fiancée* had already gone into the city to see an Oscar-nominated film.

—So we *don't* mention the candy to Abb tomorrow at any point then, is the plan?

—Right.

He flipped on a film about a famous Grecian conflict I'd researched thoroughly as a ten-year-old but now would not be able to situate in history with any certainty beyond its having taken place before the birth of Christ. The Greeks wore loincloths and were attractive. I thought about my high school's Sports Day, for which the young men stripped down to linen shorts and constructed interesting multi-figure human statuary in the indescribably humid heat. I reminded myself of the personal commitment I had made to being able to raise with my pectorals, and, in an auxiliary capacity, triceps and deltoids, a certain arbitrarily arrived at mass I'd decided on one unhappy evening after overindulging yet again on sodium-and-trans-fat-suffused snack products and *bentos* from the local *konbini*[4] but that I considered firm, having emailed this number of kilos to Rick Moody, on the "bench press." We crushed another pill to snort. I started to explain to him about Hirose, but a thought occurred to me that I wanted to express to Rick.

*

From: ————<————>
Date: Tue, Dec 21, 2010 at 4:32 AM
Subject: Fingers of Death
To: rickmoodylifecoach@gmail.com

I haven't pooped in several days. This isn't out of ordinary for me, but it isn't pleasant, either. I'd like to report on some anthropological nugget of fascination gleaned from my experience in pedagogical trenches with the youth of south Japan, but I really didn't notice them today. I was too preoccupied with visceral discomfort to think about much else. I'd really love to take a shit! This issue ever come up with you, Rick? I understand if not, but man. Talk about your day-assassins. I went outside at one point after lunch, free period, with this idea that I'd just chain-smoke until the nicotine compelled some kind of motion, but *it didn't fucking work.* I got light-headed and vomited some bile. I realize that you're already a busy man, lots of tasks to dispense with in a given day, so I guess I should

[4]i.e., convenience store

apologize for forcing you to think about my bowels for two minutes or however long it's been, but yeah: if you've got any Coaching that might pertain to regularity, let me know—I'm in a way of serious need.

About the drinking: I lied above when I suggested it was something that I liked. I hate it, Rick, as you inferred. Yesterday, after a dreadful showing in my second-period Speaking English class during which students openly revolted, certain baseball-club members going so far as to chant—with terrible pronunciation—the English word *shitty* at me, an imprecation I'd foolishly taught them, intending to emphasize the importance of correct pronunciation of the useful word "city," difficult for them because they have a phoneme for "shi" but no "si" in *Nihongo*, they did this for three and a half minutes until the chime sounded signaling the end of class, I had to fall back on my "emergency flask," from which I actually hadn't had to take a sip in several days, but the shitty chorus was too much, Rick: I sprinted from the classroom after returning their sardonic bows, retrieved my duffel bag and exited the building through clumps of students migrating to their next class like a fullback shedding tacklers in the open field (or in *Nihon* a rugbyer negotiating the pitch's scrum).

We have a kind of slope or elevation near our school. I've never bothered to acquire its name, assuming it has one, though I imagine it must—everything's got a fucking name here—but yesterday I climbed it, found a well-maintained grassy plateau looking out upon a *genuine* mountain's snow-drizzled peak and the *Nishitetsu* trainline in all its hideous industrial complexity, and quickly drank the contents of the flask. It's a large flask, Rick, and as I gulped its contents down I really was reflecting on your kind admonishments a while back, thinking hard about the success you've had as a sober, somber, capable man, and it sickened me, this thought that someone could *upend the flask,* or never need it in the first place, be potent, strong and wise, since *I* saw clearly in my class today that I will always *loathe* the hours of my day I give to whomever I've managed to persuade to give me money to perform some loathsome task, and if I had to face that loathsomeness without at least an hour, or on good nights, two, to anticipate of total if too-short relief I don't see what the point would be of doing it at all. I'm "hungover" every day, Rick: 10:30 is the cruelest time. My supposed antidepressant hasn't done its temporary work yet, and the dehydration has already completed its daily chore of reminding me why people die. Or why they shouldn't choose to live—what's that choice ever gotten anyone but dead?—eh, I think I'll probably hit the hay here, Rick, because I'm tired and I have to teach four classes in the morning and tomorrow's Friday and my "fiancée" thinks we're going out on Saturday when it's supposed to get a little warmer for the afternoon, which means she somehow thinks against all history and reason that I won't be too despicable to spend an afternoon with her eating *bentos* in some park she's chosen for its famousness with guidebook authors as an idyllic spot for us to spend the afternoon stretched out together under the forecast sun when any logical observer of our time together would confidently wager money on odds that I will be brutally overhung and so compelled to drink to ease the pain.

*

I went over to my "fiancée"'s apartment to help her build some shelves. Things went well for half an hour, I inserted screws and tightened bolts, she laughed at several of my jokes. I told her it was Saturday, so what the hell, I guessed I'd take a little nap, and this is when I staggered a bit while attempting to execute a simple backstep.

—You've been drinking?

—Come on, it's Saturday!—

—You're fucking falling over in the middle of the afternoon?

*

From: ————<————>
Date: Tue, Dec 23, 2010 at 4:32 AM
Subject: Fingers of Death
To: rickmoodylifecoach@gmail.com

When I wear the blue blazer I feel as if I've admitted defeat. When I'm stuck at work demonstrating tricky aspects of English pronunciation such as the extruded tongue required for successful execution of the phoneme θ, that voiceless dental non-sibilant fricative so critical for proper production of the initial sound in words like "thought" or "thing," I'm desperate to be working on the book. We want to do the things we know we'll never do precisely *because* we know that we could never do them. If I complete the monograph I want to write about your oeuvre, I'll wish that it was something I had never *dared* begin. If I don't finish the monograph I'll know—as I have *always* known—that I am an *essential* failure, that failure is the only constant character trait identifiable in my three decades here on earth, even as an infant I was ineffectual at getting the milk, for instance, or naps that I tended to want, my mother teased me during early childhood about my poor technique as contrasted with other siblings (I have six) at extracting milk from her breast, so that a feeding tube was eventually required to be inserted, or else I certainly would have starved, which feeding tube no doubt accounts in part for my *inability* to control my appetites in later life, as whatever mechanisms for caloric (or any!) restriction may have been in place *before* the tube-insertion were thenceforth overridden, and it is natural, if monstrous, that my eating habits now would disgust and in fact do disgust most people, as I am routinely unable to prevent myself from consuming far in excess of what any sane person would want, to say nothing of require for satiety. I try to eat in private for this reason, but as a working young adult I have no choice but to take my lunches in the company of colleagues and these luncheons are hideous affairs: I *try* to tell myself that supper isn't all that far away, and yet I succumb to what I've privately described as *my feeding mania* every day, the sweating starts before I've even unboxed the first of several *bentos*, and naturally increases in volume and aromaticness as the seizure crests, I begin by making relatively skillful use of the native chopsticks but they are dainty, care-intensive implements, and by the second or third *bento* I have no time for care, so that the fourth *bento* is without exception consumed by hand, and for ingestion of the fifth—on days when I've indulged in fifths—I am compelled to tilt the plastic receptacle at a felicitous angle and shovel the carefully arranged small portions of Japanese fare into my mouth, scarcely bothering to chew. Of course by this point the perspiration dripping from my face has collected in lagoons on desk topography uncluttered with *bento* boxes, napkins, or bits of food I've missed. You may wonder how the Japanese respond to these trencherman displays: "I'm not sure, but suspect they're not so much disgusted as impressed."

My eating isn't something that I'm proud of, Rick, but the Japanese are nothing if not dogged, and they seem in awe of my *capacity* to put away the quantities of food they see me eat. Of course, they cannot know that I am rarely in a situation to eat dinner, a point I've often reminded myself of, in vain, on days when some futile instinct toward moderation urges something like restraint. I jog for several hours every other day. I sneak off to the so-called "training room" and lift mass, purchase vegetables, read inspirational literature, *it doesn't matter*, it's my destiny to overeat. I drink too much because I want to get away, I eat too much because I must. In high school I would diet, every week's beginning was observed with a gravely constituted *chicken pita*, in which no more than a half-teaspoon of mayo was permitted. I ate my lunches looking on as classmates, enemies and "friends" consumed the ordinary male adolescent's caloric heap, desperate for more food, but still persuaded of that hideous conception, *human will*. On Fridays I did not attend the parties other kids caroused at but stayed home to polish off a pie or so of my Italian mother's homemade pizza and *whole twenty-four-ounce bags* of peanut M&Ms. Rare was the Friday night of sleep after such consumption; common was the Friday midnight five-kilometer dash, stomach in a state of enthusiastic opposition.

You may be wondering how such a creature could have found a "*fiancée.*" Well, she's kind of chubby too, Rick. Pretty, but not the slender one in any group of friends. Usually the middleweight, you might say, or very near the middle in the case of a more substantial set. And she's quite the food enthusiast, wanted to be a restaurant critic for a while, believe it or not, a failed endeavor I might have shown a little more interest in before she decided to teach high school English and just assess food as a hobby, on the side. She does maintain a food blog, if you'd like to have a look: I haven't checked it in a while—I honestly haven't had the energy or concentration to read much of anything at all during this difficult stretch in my work on yours—and I'd be happy to forward you a link. But she venerates food, loves preparing it, before that, shopping for ingredients, then snacking on a little something while arranging these alongside pans and cutting boards and measuring cups, and naturally she loves most of all consuming the extravagant concoctions, in ideal circumstances *with me*, nothing is more pleasing to her than a meal shared in front of a film she's selected, her so-called betrothed munching happily at her side, only as I've said the quantity consumed by me during my lunch break is most days sufficient to distend my stomach and cause discomfort, even piercing pain for several hours, I find afternoon classes almost impossible to teach, so that, knowing she will not be happy if I am unable to eat what she has made, I often exercise to near-exhaustion upon returning home, or induce vomiting—in the latter instance always reflecting that a more disciplined man would have done so hours back when digestive processes were still just underway—but even so the eating would be difficult without the appetite-enhancing side-effect of drinking to excess. Only who am I to etch some line in sand between moderation and excess, Rick—who's anyone? who are *you*?—for many men I've known *my* line would be drawn too far from the high tide's watermark, barely enough to soothe the toxic accumulations of the ordinary workday—take Bob, whose rampaging I find an almost numinous or *spiritual* testament to stamina; on the other hand, my friend Hirose tells me a single beer will wreck her for the night. Hirose's mother, by the way, hasn't been improving, this per Hirose—but the Japanese approach to psychiatric struggle is an odd coupling of primitive mysticism (a person's *ki* [5] is sometimes *heavy* here, which temporary mass-increase is often attributed to seasonal change, where in another nation this same patient might be briskly diagnosed with a variety of mood disorder) and irresponsible dispensation of mixed benzodiazepines and first-generation selective serotonin reuptake inhibitors of the variety that have largely gone out of fashion Stateside, along with relentless pressure to *gaman*[6] and that this aging woman hasn't seemed to benefit from such a phalanx of shoddy "treatment" is not much of a surprise.

Meanwhile she's been put into a psychiatric hospital or "home." I don't know how to feel about this information—*I* certainly wouldn't want to live in such a place, and it seems to me that if the woman went up to a mountain with the obvious intent *to die*, she should have been afforded at least the dignity of the time alone she needed to complete the task. On the other hand, I like Hirose. I don't know that this has sufficiently come through. In case it hasn't, I should emphasize that while in theory my position here is perfect for my needs—I have the surplus time and comfortable material conditions that I knew I needed to complete my Work—I generally hate my job, my coworkers are frightened of me, and though I have tried, intermittently, I still don't really speak much Japanese, in spite of what I may have claimed elsewhere. The only *pleasant* aspect of my working life therefore being that half-hour or so each day when Hirose Sensei, too busy as she already is, stops by my desk and chats with me in English, usually about some mindless shit. And while I realize that she's certainly intent on and perhaps invested in embarrassing her non-conversant colleagues, so that a wholly

[5]spirit, mind, heart, nature, disposition, motivation, mood, feeling[s], essence

[6]endure, or persevere

valid interpretation of our interactions would be that she's using my desperation for any kind of human intercourse to pound it home to whoever happens to be listening that no other *English teacher* in the fucking high school can actually use the language to converse, it honestly *feels good* to talk to someone without feeling like an alien at least once throughout the day. And if *she's* relieved to know that at the very least if she's not home to supervise her, her mother won't be shuffling off the mortal coil of her own volition, then maybe I'm in favor of it—except the woman obviously *wanted* death! How do we interpret such complicated things?

*

It's Christmas Eve, Rick. I'm in the *jutaku* alone. I may as well admit some things, I wrote. I've exaggerated certain points in emails, lied outright about others. My girlfriend left me on the first day of July. Two nights before, in a blackout after drinking and fighting about the drinking at her place I left her screaming and decided to *go out*. I somehow caught the *shinkansen* to Yokohama, an overnight. Obviously I don't remember this. I'd left my apartment locked, hadn't brought the cellphone, and was what's known in military parlance as "AWOL" for the night. I'm told my girlfriend suffered some form of "nervous breakdown" or "collapse." She thought I'd gone somewhere to kill myself, she thought she might have *driven me to death*, she lost her mind, for a few hours, and hurt herself, in unpleasant ways I'd rather not describe. Since being returned after a brief hospitalization on an emergency flight to her native New York suburb *she, too, has been living in a "home,"* though this is the extent of what I have been able to find out.

I put this information in an email more or less ungarnished, just as you see it here, and then I went out and bought a handle of *shochu*. I would have marked the birth of Christ with Bob, but Bob had gone back to Hawaii for the month. I climbed up to a lookout with a little shrine beside it from which most of Fukuoka can be viewed, and drank a lot of the shochu, and fed the cats who gather there some tuna from a can. My girlfriend has not contacted me since the night I left. I'd like to believe she *could* and chooses not to, but this is not something I've been able to confirm. I wish it didn't sound too monstrous to say that I hope she's somehow found a way to be all right, but of course it does.

I thought about her for a while, I drank a little more, *and then I started thinking about Rick*. I wondered if he'd write me back on Christmas Eve—how could he not—except the thought occurred to me I'd finally *said too much*.

I trotted dangerously down the low but steep-sloped mountain, half-empty handle slapping cadence on my thigh. If Rick was finished with me I'd have no one left. I bashed into my dark apartment and I inserted my portable Internet device into its slot and opened up my so-called "inbox" in a state of considerable unease.

The Great Challenges the Good to a
Duel: *Pistols, Dawn.*

The Good declines.

*

At the local Y the Great guards the Good in a competitive game of three-on-three. He makes liberal use of that disputed defensive tactic, the "hand check," but his size and forbidding aspect discourage protestation or complaint. He'll take the contest's final shot.

*

Tonight the Great's great thrashing bursts of semi-sleep are torn into by nightmare scenes of fecal combustion, disintegrating teeth.

By and large the Good sleeps through the night.

*

The armies of the Great pursue Good subversives across war-wrecked terrain, give chase through snow and hinter and up into the craggy passes of the West, along the outskirts of the Capitol, where burning oil derricks and humorous prose poems lampooning the regime—spray-painted over tasteful rampart-murals commissioned by the Crown—testify to the sheer calamitous *joie de vivre* of these resistless underdogs.

The Great marches on: in camp at night no fiddled airs lighten the mood of solemn purpose among troops seeking nourishment in tin bowls of campfire-scorched beans. There is only triumph—or the march.

But the insurgent element is innovative and sly; even the Great's heroic generals can't guess what guerrilla tactic will be used against them next.

*

The Great and the Good agree to settle this thing the old-fashioned way, with a sumo match.

*

Now the Good has stooped to truly juvenile pranks: the Great showers in the dormitory floor's communal bathroom, whistling *Allegro ma non troppo* a favorite phase from the first movement of the Ninth, but in the next stall the Good quivers with vindictive glee, knows it isn't *just* shampoo his suite-mate's scrubbing through his slick Prince Valiant.

*

The Great has constructed an indestructible super-station, spherical, with the dimensions of a small moon, a so-called "Death Star." At last the insignificant rebellion will be crushed, and order restored to the galaxy.

Onboard one small rogue starship, several important members of this ragtag band scrutinize deep space from a cramped observation deck, perplexed. What they're seeing simply doesn't jibe with what were thought to be un-compromised star-charts: for one thing, a whole planet's missing. And where on the map is that small moon?

. . .

That's no moon!

*

K—— has been on dates with both men, separately.

The Great is unrelenting in conversation, headstrong, brash, but masticates with cold precision.

The Good tends to banter with his mouth full of food. He enjoys a good joke—but also bad ones.

The Great suffers enormously with the selection of fare. If history is to be trusted, he may well fail to make the perfect choice. When their meals arrive he peers at K——'s plate with rancorous envy in his eyes.

The Good often cleans K——'s plate for her and needs help computing the tip.

*

The Great stops seeing K—— when he learns of past romantic history with the Good; the Good, in a subsequent telephone chat, proposes a conciliatory three-way or *ménage à trois*.

*

The Great stares at a single misbegotten sentence: He just can't seem to get it right.

The Good's hot-dog casserole went over well.

*

But then—unexpectedly!—the Good accepts the Great's demand to have his honor satisfied—merely the latest such insistence, the tone of which proposals having of late approached hysteria in their monomaniacal fixation on man-to-man combat *to the death*—by way of sung telegram.

This missive is delivered by a man costumed to resemble a large rodent—perhaps a hamster, or a well-fed rat. Following the brief acceptance-aria's final note is a coda of considerable length, incorporating an accordion for unexpected chordal modulations both pleasing and cloying to the listener's ear. The lyrics do not flatter the Great's avoirdupoisal mother, Mdme. G——; especially insulting is the overlong—if formally inventive—free-associative riff on the noble woman's dewlap. Her chastity, too, is unsubtly impugned.

The Great shoots the messenger with the very pistol he intends to dispatch his nemesis with tomorrow morning before dawn.

*

A Conversation with the Good (Interviewer's Questions Edited for Space):

Would you say that…?

G: Sure, I've got ambition—who doesn't? I think there's a part of all of us that would love to see his name in lights. But I think it's important to maintain a little perspective, right? Obviously this is something of a cliché, but, you know, we're going to be dust one day—one day pretty fucking soon in the cosmic scheme—and the unpleasant side of unchecked ambition is that it can amount to a kind of *dwelling* in whatever it is you've failed so far to do—a state that honestly strikes me as a kind of needless concession to death. In fifty years—probably a lot less, at the rate I've been imbibing certain inimical things—I won't be able to do *anything*; why let worrying about the infinitely smaller list of things I can't do now keep me from at least *trying* to do what I can?

I: What…?

G: My heroes were all a lot more successful than I'll ever be— though I'd like to think I've got at least one winner of a book in me.

I: Who would you say are your…?

G: Oh, you know, the usual suspects: Boethius, Falstaff, Howard Stern, early Who... big sports fan so actually a bunch of athletes, too: for example loved Randall Cunningham as a kid... really like Lebron James, the list is pretty—

I: Really? But what about...?

G: Well, a championship's only one measure of success, isn't it? A basically arbitrary one, too: I mean, does Lebron James really need a ring on his finger or a trophy to hoist for the cameras for us to accept that he's a terrific athlete? I just like to see him *out* there, on the court, the way you can tell he just loves playing the game, win lose or draw—I know: no draws in hoops, it's an expression—and the joy he clearly takes in getting out on the break for all those vicious uncontested dunks... meanwhile the thing I think people forget about *Jordan* is the size of his hands: a lot of the mid-flight maneuvering through traffic to get to the rim simply wouldn't have been possible without that kind of freak genetic gift. Which, take that away you can probably slash a title or two from his résumé. Meanwhile, couple shots bounce differently, maybe we're not even *having* this "Eye of the Tiger" as you put it there just now discussion, so I mean, how much of winning and losing comes down to pure chance, you know?

I: What do you...?

G: Paul Thomas Anderson is a fantastic film-maker. No question. But what about *Wes* Andersen? I thought that recent one didn't get a fair shake.

I: ?

G: The one where the kid dies in India.

*

No: *I* am your father!

*

An epauletted, seething Great leaves thirteen voice messages with the Good, demands an explanation for his lateness to the scene. At eleven he returns to the chalet, refuses the victory feast his servants have spread the table with, retires to his private chamber to pace, and think. He thinks about his new Stealth Bomber.

*

President Great urges a certain degree of moral accountability in his constituents, the citizens of this great nation. His "Pennsylvania Address" reminds us all of our collective *duty* to the commonwealth.

Comedic-pundit T. Good, on his popular satirical news program, jokes about the grandiose locutions, and the angle of the President's lifted chin in the throes of public discourse.

*

The Great is up at four AM. After a quick breakfast of five uncooked eggs, he's out on the streets of Philadelphia, putting in his roadwork. The title fight's two months away. There is no inspirational theme song: just Greatness and the empty streets.

You want the Good to take a shot? *O-kay!* He'll take a shot! Chuckles as he reaches for the Cutty Sark....

*

The Good has fought hard to secure a concession from a curmudgeonly Republican House: If tax breaks for the oligarchy won't be allowed to expire, then at least the modest breaks for working families will remain in place.

The Great foresees the failure of the Revolution even as the means of production are seized in factories across the land and gated communities go up in flames. *Meet the new boss,* he whispers to himself, and retires to his secret cave.

*

In the end, the canonical works of the Great novelist—those tales of fractured families, the peasant's burden, war and peace and lonely dying men, beloved by his nation and the reading citizens of the entire world—cannot save him from his fate.

And yet what does Christ ask, but that we give up *everything* to follow Him? The Kingdom of Heaven can only come when *all* men live as brothers, when noble and peasant join hands in the harvest fields, dance in communal jubilee.

Raving, convinced that he has thrown away his life on aristocratic drivel, wrapped only in a vulnerable cloak, he lurches into the punishing snow, that famous beard soon frozen stiff beneath his chin.

*

In one of his more whimsical short pieces, the Good describes a Museum of the Great that houses preposterous monuments to ego and bloated self-regard, humorous hundred-square-meter photographs of the Great scowling down from walls at visitors reduced to guilt and self-recrimination under the ferocity of the great moralist's stare.

*

In six quick but action-laden days, the Great has created a cosmos, from scratch. On the seventh he decides to take it easy; the Good, just rising from a nap, sees in these nubile naifs puttering around their vegetable patch a good-natured lark to murder the long afternoon with (the ball-game doesn't begin until eight). He'll ply the prettier one first.

*

The Great goes down with the whale.

And Never Can a Man Be More
Disastrously in Death Than When
Death Itself Shall Be Deathless

—The only men I admire are suicides, I repeated, as the Turk looked away, or not away but rather *past* me, the Turk was frequently looking past me, his thoughts seeming to drift like the wisps rising from his meerschaum pipe's slow burn—only to wheel back when I least expected and fix me with a gaze *of redoubled intensity.* In the morning on rising I immediately drank the cup of black coffee and smoked both of the cigarettes allotted me by the Turk, then lay back in my berth and stared through the porthole at the sun's perplexing diffractions for several hours before the Turk requested that I join him above.

The Turk was not satisfied with this answer. As a rule the Turk was not satisfied. This constituted the principal distinction between us: the Turk was in no way satisfied, nor would he be satisfied, even under the most satisfying circumstances, even if, for example, after untold adventure and hardship, he were to secure the object of a lifelong obsession, he would certainly find himself still more dissatisfied, his new dissatisfaction proportionate to the degree by which the consummation of a private ambition nourished over decades of unflagging if fruitless one-minded dedication toward this end *ought* to have left him absolutely sated—and yet even then, when the truth would have necessarily been most clear, he would have immediately convinced himself that he *was* satisfied, even while simultaneously initiating plans for the pursuit of some other objective toward which he might bend his considerable energies and, assuming eventual success, since in the end the Turk always succeeds, fail to concede to himself *then* that he was still unsatisfied; whereas I both knew that I was not satisfied and knew that I never could be satisfied and in this knowledge took my sole, perverse satisfaction.

Obviously the silver would make me unhappy. I would be miserable with the silver, as I was miserable without it; nevertheless I could think of nothing but the silver—or rather the silver *and the Turk.* The silver in a Turkish context. The success of the Turk. In the silver cache's untold scintillations I saw the terrible success of the Turk. For the Turk was a terrible success, as of course even a fool could see. It is only the terrible successes, the truly monstrous masters of their affairs, that dare present themselves as the saviors of vagabonds they find crawling naked and filthy through the streets of sub-tropical trading posts just before dawn, doglike (though this was an island with no dogs), emitting obscene growls and honks. I *don't remember* the weeks preceding my so-called rescue at the hands of the Turk. However I remember our first encounter with perfect clarity, I see even now the outsized Turkish face looming *all too clearly,* as he knelt and clasped a dusky hand to my shoulder and in accented but flawless English inquired after my well-being, so that I had no choice but to challenge him to a duel.

The Turk refused that duel, as of course I knew he would, only the favored, the victors, the gifted, the masters, the Turks, only those touched with infallible knowledge of their irrefutable will are permitted to refuse such a challenge, only a *man* dares refuse a duel, we sub-men are inclined, are even impelled, to *try our luck,* which will naturally be bad, in fact, it's even the case that the less likely I am to succeed in a contest, the more likely I am to take part in it.

For this reason I challenged the Turk to the duel, a single glance at his beard alone—that prosperous beard—was enough to confirm beyond any doubt that I'd be slaughtered the instant we withdrew our swords (I would of course need to be lent my weapon, from a squire or confrere), he would slaughter me with ease, without relish, it would be an absolute chore, a great inconvenience not to say a gross imposition on the efficient orchestration of his daily affairs for him to have to submit to the tedious etiquette governing such concerns and await ritual sanction to run me through. Without question I'd be slaughtered, and therefore I *needed* to propose the duel, it was impossible for me not to propose the duel, it would have been easier for me to resist the motion of blood through my veins than to fail to demand that the Turk accept my challenge to a duel, I would be nothing without the duel, I knew this from the second I saw the black curls of the Turk's copious beard encroach on my field of vision and I abruptly put an end to my gratuitous noise. Without the duel I would be even *less* than what I'd been when the Turk found me slobbering and insensate, wailing, clad only in smears of red dirt crawling among cockroaches of unusual size and brash disposition, in front of the Outpost of Progress, a saloon or tavern or *watering hole* I had frequented in the months preceding the onset of my debilitation, an establishment patronized primarily by a certain elevated cast of entrepreneurial men, among whose ranks I immediately took the Turk to be, though on this and not only this count I was of course to discover I'd been somewhat in error, as the Turk was many things but surely not a *mere* entrepreneur. I could only have refrained from proposing the duel if I'd possessed a shred of hope for victory. If I hadn't witnessed the athletic lope with which he altered course from across the quayside thoroughfare and approached me in my gutter, the casual grace with which his saber curved from his side, if I'd believed even in the possibility of a fluke or unexpected triumph, if I'd had the smallest hope of victory through some error or mistake I would have ignored the Turk, rolled back into the muck where the native insect rank and file was concentrated in still greater numbers, but one's first impression of the Turk, one's absolute cardinal impression, is that here is a man who does not make mistakes—so that I had no choice but to grope immediately to my feet, brush off the several large bugs still clinging to my torso, and challenge him, tell the Turk that on my honor— here I paused to consult the small timepiece I had lifted from a passing trader's unattended pack that very afternoon, the gears of which had frozen *some time ago*—he would not live to see another dawn, and to ignore the spreading concern on his face, and to insist that the cock would not crow before he stood aspectant with Our Lord, Heaven or Hell hanging in the balance, kneel and repent now, beg my forgiveness, I demanded; however the Turk *refused.*

Only a man like the Turk could have refused. Only a Turk is so authorized. In the end, if I desire a duel, even if I insist upon a duel, especially if I insist—one might almost argue *because* of my insistence—I lack the authority to enforce the duel, my desire is my guarantee against its ever transpiring, which is precisely why I am *compelled* to insist upon it, and I insisted even as the Turk took hold of me and hauled me bodily to the cleansing springs, at the foot of Oyama ("Mount") Oom, repeatedly dunked me under the waters that in dubious native lore are reputed to heal, with force but not untenderly bathed me with rich Turkish soap, and insisted on draping me in cloaks selected from his own private wardrobe, in which garments I still dressed each day when summoned against my will to join the

Turk on deck: I was resplendent under a burning sun, as we discoursed and paced, as we crossed wits, as we tested for weakness each other's defenses of ideological ground, while I inwardly added *wrinkles to my plan*, which already included the drowning of the Turk's wardrobe, in full, before absconding with the silver-cache, which latter task I have presently all but assured my successful accomplishment of as of the hasty draughting of these notes.

On the island, to which I came nursing private hopes of accruing a small personal fortune I would then use to achieve entirely selfish ends—which ends I will presumably accomplish this evening, in spite of my initial and protracted *failure*—it was not uncommon to come across a certain specimen of *conscientious objector* to the rapacious policies of the vast commercial enterprises engaged in systematic ransack and plunder of that plenteous island, the brutalizing of the native population, the naked scorn for civilized opinion, let alone Law, there were voices to be heard on occasion amid the general acquisitive tumult, crying out for justice, for the cessation of outrage, indignant objectors to the forces of oppression, who of course nine times in ten, ninety-nine times in a hundred, happened to be failed tradesmen *themselves*, in general the scale or intensity of an objector's indignation was commensurate to the size of the hopes for personal gain he'd had to abandon as a concession to his ineptitude or faltering will. Expelled via failure from the colonial business caste these envoys of justice gathered in the corners of nigh-empty salons to *discuss the native plight*, to shed tears over the fate of a population already decimated by foreign-introduced disease, crushed by the merciless logic of the very market on which they *aspired to sell* their anthologies of protest—assembled essays, screeds, pamphlets, tracts, composed in a generic tone of artless indignation—clustered in cafés round noon to orate with eloquence and grace, loudly, but not too loudly, refraining from all but the most absolutely necessary pounded fists, furiously praising the inborn virtues of the exploited native population they had as a rule been too weak or inept to exploit.

—Never trust a crusader, I advised the Turk, who, leaving aside the theatrical compassion of his rescuing me, was himself no crusader, was in fact a brutal man, a maniacal force, pure embodied Will, I knew the Turk well, I'd known the Turk a hundred times before I met the Turk, perhaps in less Turkish incarnations, but Turks nonetheless, the Turk was no crusader, he was brutal, though not necessarily cruel.

The Turk declined to respond with more than the gleam in his eye, only rarely did the Turk find it necessary to respond to my declamations, and I suspected he had little to say, although it was not always possible to tell what he thought or might say because the Turk's eye was frequently, almost *incessantly*, agleam. I had briefly considered providing him with one last *opportunity*, not even sure precisely of what this opportunity would consist, but the sagacity implied in that gleam squashed any last considerations of mercy, which at any rate had never been sincere. An old song came to mind.

—If I fall into the drink, I sang, —I will say your name, before I sink....

—What's that, asked the Turk, looking up.

—A ballad, I said, —of dipsomania.

—It's very pretty. Did you write it?

—No, I said.

—Well, not the melody, which I suppose I recognize, said the Turk, —but surely the lyrics…

—Neither the melody nor words are mine.

—I suppose you nevertheless make it your own, mused the Turk, peering out into the foggy iridescence that trailed the ship to port, —after all, who is this *You* whose name you propose to whisper with despair, as you sink, finally, into the drink, he asked.

—I'd never thought about it, I admitted, taking another pull from the flask the Turk permitted me to keep filled with water, —*myself* I suppose.

During our nightly tête-à-têtes, the Turk often asked me to clarify for him certain *facets of my psyche*, but never enquired after a direct explanation of or accounting for the state of personal dissipation, the loss of bodily-functional control evident in the scent I exuded as I wormed through ooze, never pressed me for the details I would at any rate have been utterly unable to provide pertaining to or accounting for the dramatically reduced state of my personal affairs, the corrosion I'd either endured or *inflicted on myself* prior to his coming across me, there in the sub-equatorial muck.

In lieu of ever requesting some factual accounting for the period anticipating my decline, the Turk had continually resorted to obliquity, cant, a pipe-smoking disinterest, one was inclined to feel, as he stood by the wheel (paying no heed to the pilot, a burly illiterate beast) and wondered aloud what I thought about, for instance, the teachings of Sir Thomas Browne, whose works I'd never read, or even been aware of, an imputation against my own scholarship that I elected not to disclose, casually pursing my lips at the mention of the name I had until that moment never heard, suggesting with that single dismissive mien an acquaintance with and utter disdain for the author whose birthdate I would have been unable to pinpoint within five hundred years, whose British—I suspected—lineage, I could only adduce by the titular Sir, and the Turk seemed content not to challenge my critical stance; meanwhile the Turk never once *asked my name*, never, which is in fact in part why I refer to him here exclusively as *the Turk*, even though this was not his name, or even a sobriquet bandied about by seafaring familiars, and despite his having immediately informed me of his *Christian name*, as he put it, as well as his abundance of titles, and in spite of his never once having provided me with so much as the slightest suggestion, not even a hint, of actual extraction, or even the vaguest reason for me to imagine that he or his people had once hailed from that venerable nation-state of Turks, or even anywhere *nearby*, even a distant country nevertheless lumped in with what we Occidentalists condescendingly term the Near East, for all I knew he was from Peking, or New Amsterdam, or my own hometown of ———————, though this last seems unlikely, given the niggardly tumbledown inconsequence of that supposed city; the one thing I could be nearly certain of, however, indeed the one certainty regarding the heredity of the Turk was that he without question could not have been an *actual* Turk by blood, I've known far too many Turks to be misled on that front, never in my life have I mistaken a non-Turk for Turk; however I steadfastly clung to my appellation, privately, and here, in these notes, he will always be *the Turk*, though in fact when we conversed I never once addressed him as *the Turk*, never let slip the slightest intimation that I'd privately christened him *the Turk*, and in point of fact, called him by his as he had it *Christian name* every time I addressed him, even going so far as to include several or all of the honorifics and professional titles he had accrued over the many decades of his considerable success in an assortment of ventures, enterprises, varieties of mastery over diverse industries, though he'd explicitly asked that I refrain from deploying the formal titles when speaking to him, had in fact urged me to call him only by his *Christian name*, though he'd never asked for mine, yet I was perversely impelled as time passed to rehearse the entire line of formal or honorary titles, so that in these notes a reader interested in strict adherence to the facts would need to substitute a nearly paragraph-long preface of titles which I decline to include for every recounted instance of Turk-directed speech, not limited to the times I claim to have directly addressed the Turk as *the Turk*, since these times naturally never occurred, but also any time I addressed myself to his attention, even in casual discourse, unless he expressly forbade me from repeating verbatim the paragraph-long sequence of honorifics for the third or fourth time in so many minutes, in which case I would temporarily acquiesce, subsequently *lapsing* inadvertently, as I protested, into further reiterations, but precisely to the extent that I have refused to refer to the Turk as anything other than the Turk in these notes, in person I declined to address him as anything other than the extravagant sequence of formalities that I have herein replaced with *the Turk*, and this may not be the only liberty I have taken with the facts.

However it is indisputable, the only *necessary* fact, that as I paced the quarterdeck with the Turk and we *superficially* transacted in relative banalities, I was simultaneously afflicted with the most strenuous suppressed compunction to *lay myself bare* before the Turk, to expose the *genuine* reasons for the failure of my manifesto, the work that was to have thrown the whole horrid enterprise into sickly light and my protracted failure with which anticipated and no doubt ultimately contributed, if indirectly, to my collapse, to my eventual drunken writhing amongst island vermin.

Of course it was not only the cockroaches I had come to loathe, though I did loathe the cockroaches. I had been apprised of the inborn loathsomeness of the native population, the cunning, the relentless untruthfulness, the senseless, petty machinations, the brutish dishonesty and heathen stupidity; however, *before I arrived* I believed these observed phenomena—if indeed they'd actually *been* observed and not concocted by sinister agents of the assorted commercial interests who stood to gain justification or credence for their rapine enterprises with every degree by which popular conception of the natives was reduced, which empiricism I naturally doubted—believed these loathsome attributes or traits could be written off as consequences or symptoms of the subjugated people's very subjugation—*before I arrived* I was entirely prepared to embrace *in toto* the culture even to the point of the idiosyncratic or exotic, perhaps even going so far as to embrace or even take part in customs I might otherwise have found inconceivably repugnant, as for example, the symphonic slurps and smacks to be heard at every repast; the disgusting food itself, which is as a rule slimy and cold, *they like it that way*; I was even ready, I freely confess, to participate in certain nocturnal rituals I'd heard rumor of but never been able to confirm in-flesh: I was ready to accept the whole panoply of oddities in a primitive people about whom, let us be clear on this point, I actually *knew nothing*. Because I was *on their side* when I came to the island. I disdained to frequent the cafés and ragtag colloquia popping up in support of the supposed revolution's foment, the pasty and unlikable assemblage of artificial anarchists who claimed a similar allegiance but were actually motivated or driven by precisely the same *voracity* that they vociferously decried, were outraged and appalled by, I eschewed their easy company and struck out on my own, on a solitary crusade against the forces of oppression, the venomous, wraithlike lurking commercial interests, but the natives, whose cause I'd come to the island to take up, *never liked me.*

Never, not on a single occasion did I once look up into a native's eye and see anything other than the loathing he or she would have ordinarily reserved for a roach, which creatures, parenthetically, on the island, were the size of small birds, and, like birds, *able to fly,* never was a young native able to resist the urge to snicker or look away with sheer gleeful disgust, absolutely unable to resist even for the sake of decorum the comedy inherent in my very presence, so that it was only natural that eventually I would come to *enjoy* the spectacle of their systematic devastation, their continued exploitation at the hands of the forces I had initially come to the island to oppose, only natural that where I had *come* to the island intending to expose the odious practices of the ruling elite lording it mercilessly over the (languageless, half-naked, crude barter-economied) so-called "barbarian" swarm, lay bare the full machinery of their insidious schemes to an otherwise tolerant, even favorably disposed general population at home, the public having largely been duped into believing these barons to be not only heroes but generous, compassionate, soft-hearted benefactors, philanthropists, the very souls of ruddy-cheeked paternal goodness, I soon found myself quite actively *rooting* for these monsters, the colonial kings, the very men I'd initially believed would be the antagonists or *arch villains* of the sordid tale I intended to tell of exploitation and incomprehensible greed before debarking from the mediocre vessel on which I'd come in *innocence.*

What did I care when I saw a native girl of no more than

sixteen dressed in the ceremonial *oothta*, a kind of full body–length sleeve, the ritual *hopstick* aslant through her finely bound hair, a single piece of bleached goat's fur bound with a bloodred sash so tightly round the waist that movement was restricted to a kind of acquiescent limp, ushered into a room to which I was barred access by the inconsequence of my station but from the gloomy inner dimensions of which I heard the familiar baritones and clinking decanters of genteel carouse, just as I was prevented access to any of the inner circles of the island's governing elite: how could I care for the girl destined for untold humiliations and sexual adventure of the most deviant, despicable kind, when the very same girl, or a girl who at any rate looked just like her, had not half-an-hour past ignored my repeated entreaties for service at the corner table I'd been ushered over to and ignored at for almost an hour, when all I'd wanted was to order a drink for which I intended to tip her handsomely and wholly unnecessarily, since tipping in this backwards culture is not merely unrequired but in fact can even be taken as a kind of grave offense to a service-employee's honor, parentage, even whole ancestry and, in some fairly exceptional cases, entire *race*, depending on the conventionality of the individual server, but I was willing to take my chances with this shy, graceful generously-legged barmaid in the hopes that she would appreciate the *gesture* of unpremeditated generosity, even if the cultural significance might be wholly lost on her or even at first something like a slap in the exotic face, only she ignored me and in fact when I finally, having cleared my throat and even gone so far as to whistle, softly, raised my voice and asked in the faltering phrases that constituted the sum of what I had been able after six months to acquire of the native tongue and she was forced to approach in order to avoid undue commotion, she *spat* in the sawdust before not so much acknowledging me or my patronage as occupying my table's immediate vicinity and indifferently loitering.

Of course it was with a certain trepidation that I'd taken up with the Turk in the first place. And on joining him in his *private berth* I was persistently vexed by his personal assistants: the Turk's assistants were perpetually appearing at odd hours, I'd occasionally awaken to find one or the other of these men shuffling around at the foot of my bed, once even smiling up at me from beneath the blankets I lay under for the first several unspeakable days of my purge... or perhaps this was merely an anecdote from a book I'd been reading before the onset of *my sickness*. However, at some point during the composition of these notes—which I decline to revise, if I've neglected to attend to certain petit-bourgeois conventions of punctuation, grammar, turn-of-phrase, then *qué será*, Reader, Enemy, Friend—I may have given the impression that I'd forgotten the weeks leading up to the moment at which the Turk encountered me at the height of my dissipation; I believe the exact phrase, or at any rate the phrase was similar, was that the days or weeks or months or even *years* (possible but unlikely) stretching from the moment of my first encounter with the Turk back to the precise moment of my collapse, the exact details of which I have also forgotten, were *a blur*. However, this was not strictly the case. It *is* true that I can recall very little in the way of particular actions or activities, conversations, or articulate patches of thought; however I can remember *all too clearly* the general character of that awful epoch, which was that I was continuously drunk.

Many years ago I was taken on as a young scion's secondary English tutor and I found that among the more taxing pedagogical tasks I was charged with performing for the urchin was communicating the subtle distinction between those sibling modifiers "continuous" and "continual," so let me be clear: I was not *habitually*, that is *continually*, at regular and predictable intervals during this period, drunk; I was *continuously* drunk, which is to say that there was never sobriety during the epoch in question—about which I have perhaps somewhat misleadingly suggested I remember nothing when in fact I remember *all too well* the full extent of my succumbing and despair, such as, for example, that I ransacked native orchards at the foot of the island's noble central mountains, illegally absconded with armloads—multiple armloads, because I repeatedly went back—of the sacred *wakawakyu* melon, the native fruit prized the world over, of course, one of the endemic commodities turning towering profits for the megalithic international institutions of commerce who demanded free and ungoverned access to them in the name of open markets and *fair trade* while the demolition of the island's agricultural bartering tradition left the native population little prospects for employment outside of service in the wildly proliferating inns, taverns, brothels and *cafés*, which I made off with to the provisional distillery I'd established in the small natural alcove carved out of the face of a promontory facing the island's northern coast before I was driven out by bats, intending despite my absolute ignorance as regards the distiller's trade to let the stolen fruit ferment in vats I had also acquired outside of the law and guzzle the resulting nectar, which spirit I *did* eventually quaff but was unable to hold down, so that the bats were more of an afterthought, really, I didn't mind being driven out by bats, those hostile local residents were in fact almost a relief since they made my presence in the cave and makeshift fruit distillery I'd established therein with nothing but my need and gross ineptitude to guide me inconceivable, so that

I now had no alternative but to return to my life of petty larceny, which in the end wasn't quite so petty, considering that the colonial news organ, a comedy, reported an alarming rise in bulk theft of high-proof liquor during the time (unless they reported no such thing and I am merely elaborating on a fantasy or dream I was overwhelmed by during the full force of my debauch), and it was speculated that a sophisticated syndicate or ring of pirates had made bold now to assert itself, declared to the colonial authorities that an upstart force would need to be reckoned with in the neutral waters just offshore... but there was no syndicate, no interpenetration of corruption and well-connected greed: only my insatiable *thirst*. I was a bandit, heedless, wanton, running amok, berserk, and it is no exaggeration to reiterate the distinction that I was emphatically *not* continually *three sheets to the wind*, the intoxication was continuous, the intoxication was absolute, even during my short apprenticeship as a private fruit distiller I kept my cave's bar well-stocked with absconded rum, there was never an instant during which the alcohol was not coursing through my veins, the term "continual" requires intervals of inactivity, which with me there never were.

On the other hand, what I remember most clearly about the period *anticipating* my collapse was that it was marked by *continual* drink. Toward the end of my dying struggle with the discarded manifesto, before I'd abandoned even the semblance of compositional effort, when I was still concerned with providing all observing parties (of which there were naturally none) with a plausible facsimile of scholarly diligence, but after I'd realized that the muse or spark of genius or mere competence was not with me, my manifesto would never shake the earth, in fact my manifesto would be insufficiently competent to qualify as a manifesto, not even a manifesto of inferior or even of absolutely shoddy quality, when I still bore in the ostentatious calfskin attaché I would soon thereafter pawn for rum the sheaf of uncoordinated pages I pretended together constituted the early stages of my masterpiece but which in fact I frequently padded the number of with slipped-in pages pencil-darkened with nautili or *spirals*, my favorite semaphore, etched in to maniacal depths, and I would spread some of this refuse before me in my corner of the café and peer quizzically at the chaos I'd managed to forge, a pen poised theatrically quill-over-pot, as if I intended to waylay or ambush the first stray thought or wandering clause to reveal even a hint of gap in its rhetorical mail, the first error to come bungling along at the fringes of my manifesto when in fact the *entire work was an error.*

The attention implicit in that authorial pose was moreover an inaccurate representation of my interior life, since I was no longer concerned with my own manifesto, by this time my principal preoccupations were with, first, the possibility that at another table in this café, or elsewhere, somewhere *someone else* was working at a *rival* manifesto, working harder than I, uninhibited by some of the factors that had doomed my endeavor from the outset, and that this man was even now arranging the torrent of insight and truth that came teeming resistlessly from him before forming into regimental lines, sentences marching into paragraphs dense with indisputable logic, an onslaught against the ramparts of received wisdom behind which the complacent or successful or stupid are wont to huddle and cling, and that this man in his fervor was utterly undistracted by the thought I could never chase from my head during my working hours after rising at noon, viz.: that soon—but *not soon enough*—the sun would have passed the point in its diurnal arc beyond which I'd permit myself to have a drink, since this was as I have noted a period of *continual* drink, and there were still several wretched hours stretched from late morning to early afternoon during which I'd sworn I would only sleep or work, a problem I eventually realized I could solve by simply drinking *while* I worked.

Of course, aboard the Turk's bloated vessel I was no longer a continuous drunk, nor even a continual drunk. This had been the single precondition of my involuntary passage, that I *leave the rot ashore* to use the Turk's own phrase, and the Turk's initial vigilance was such that continuous intoxication was absolutely out of the question, but in fact even continual drink of the sort I had enjoyed not only during the final few days of my sanity on the island but in point of fact for most of my adult life—I cannot remember a time, amongst "friends," hard at work, during the War, or in the subsequent deprivations of peace, as a young man with a future of some promise, if there had been such a time, never, I cannot remember a single occasion I was not either drinking deeply or in desperate need of drink, obsessing ferociously on the looked-forward-to savor of that first cool and permeating draught, inwardly coordinating a sequence of drinks to consume, a roster I would adhere to until such fastidiousness was no longer called for, I would resist a yearning to grimace when an interlocutor's wit urged congenial response, I would frantically work to provide the impression I was thinking, dreaming, meditating, paying attention to something—anything—other than the taste of that impossibly distant first gulp, and if there was a time in my life when this wasn't so, it has faded far beyond recall.

Because of the vastness of his generosity and his faith in the decency of men, it required the Turk several days, actually nearly a full two weeks, to discover that *someone* had been pilfering liberally from the storeroom's casks of rum, which were only onboard as a precaution—that is, as emergency bartering blocks against mutiny, or to be sold off in the event that our supplies ran short on the long voyage to *Nuevo York*. However he did not hesitate to act, a brutal man, in all things swift-minded, and every ounce of alcohol aboard the ship, including but not limited to the remaining nine casks filled with rum, and even the seamen's grog, the fo'c'sle was ransacked, at this the men nearly did revolt, which insubordination the Turk naturally could have crushed without resorting to the promised exchange of double shares for all men who *willingly* parted with their flasks, in the end every ounce went over the bulwarks, inviting Dionysius to some fortunate gathering of fish, (there is a man in black with a white-painted face peering in at me through the porthole, his eyes are red flames, God), and perhaps the Turk expected my *gratitude*, perhaps I was to be thankful that he'd disposed of the casks and not *me*, since in taking so much as a single sip of the *rot*, to say nothing of several full casks I'd worked through in a manner of weeks, as was actually the case, I had indisputably reneged on our so-called agreement, but I was *not* grateful, I wished it were me, begged the Turk to hurl me overboard before those round little oases of rum floated forever out of sight, but the Turk refused, he had me brought to his personal cabin as a kind of ship arrest, he saw deep into my heart, he said, saw the kind of man that even I could be, refused to throw me over, no matter how hard I pounded the shipboards and wept.

The Turk proposed to finish what he'd started, he would provide for my reform, as we made our way north, toward the sole motive for our journey. I was held captive in a hold of bleak sobriety. I was driven to absolute temperance by circumstances where the

Law alone had not sufficed, and now I may as well confess: sobriety has *driven me mad*, surely I would not have needed to compose these notes nor would I have, in a fit of insufferable clarity, found it necessary to devise a scheme for the theft of the plunder the Turk had spent the last twenty years of his life sailing the world's so-called seven seas in pursuit of, sometimes all but losing the trail, relentless, the silver *would* be the consummation of a lifelong quest, the key to which he'd had to barter for with blood.... *Men have died* for the tattered scroll, the map I secretly perused and memorized in a fit of panic and despair the morning of the day before last, when a sudden swell required the Turk's steady hand on deck, and I haven't had a drink in nearly seven days.

The Turk, I knew, proposed to be *like a father to me*, however I rejected outright this paternity. I declined to become his adopted or surrogate son, knowing well enough that the man already had any number of sons scattered round the globe, unacknowledged sons, perhaps hungry for the fatherhood they'd been denied by the dubious obscurity of their conception, perhaps not, but surely among the formidable evidence of the Turk's virility and brawn, there must be one more worthy of the lost father's regard, his weathered, steady hand, his love.

I was furthermore averse to the sole condition of the Turk's affection, as I have already discussed, his mandate being essentially that I live in Hell. Should I point out that only the ruthlessness of the Turk, the extremity of his patriarchal impulse—or rather his nature, since one needed only to watch the Turk's brisk potent strides to perceive that his Turkness was not cultivated but inborn—the Turk's remorseless surveillance, his refusal to leave me unobserved, the first time I was ever out from his gaze I'd been *locked in the cabin* while he attended to the squall, evidently he did not believe it necessary to secure the map from my eyes, only the Turk prevented me from flinging myself overboard, at least this is what I have long preferred to believe.

—The only men I admire are suicides, I repeated. To port were clouds.

—Yes, this is not a significant development in your thought, my friend, said the Turk. —Me: I have always admired the true pessimists who know the void, yet resist until the end.

—Those aren't pessimists, I said, and a rumbling came from below, where the men, as a concession for the discarded rum, have been permitted to wrestle and box (needless to say I was advised to avoid interaction with the crew) —they're fools, or cowards. Either they haven't apprehended the void, in which case fools, or they're afraid of it, and cowards.

—And what is it I ask of you every evening, he asked me, frowning, —the one thing, especially what have I asked you to refrain from doing *above board*, in plain sight, because it is bad for morale? Particularly since the episode with the men?

—Of the two it's certainly the former for whom I bear the greater disdain. Cowardice I can accept. Only a fool doesn't *fear the abyss*. On the other hand, it requires an even *greater* fool to suppose he *resists* when in fact he simply hasn't yet understood what he faces. You can't *resist* Nothing, can you?

—Please, hand me the flask.

I refused to hand him the flask, the flask, stayed with me, I *flourished* the flask, which was of course filled only with water, and I reminded the Turk as the flask *glinted* in the low sunlight shot across the endless continent *to the west* that he had promised me I would retain my flask, this had been his one, his only concession.

—But not aboveboard.

—And yet people do, I said. —People lift their chins like so, I said, lifting my chin —and *resist* under their sordid banners don't they? They congratulate themselves for the very evidence of the extent of their ignorance. What could be more repugnant than the twinkling-eyed idiot with head held high, striding around with fateful stomps, who has declined to look into the abyss, whose enlistedman's strides are in fact taking him *away* from the abyss, temporarily of course, because he is too much of a coward to face what's coming? What could be more disgusting?

—You are on occasion an unpleasant man.

—In this light we can begin to examine my hatred for women. When I say "women," I mean women generally, as a sub-species, but also individually: I've only once met an actual woman I didn't absolutely detest within seconds. Fat, buxom, jolly, sly, flirtatious, wealthy, wholesome, supple, sumptuous, crass, well-cultured, pretentious, pulchritudinous: I've hated them all, Turk. All but one: I once knew a young girl who'd *known* the void, a girl standing perpetually on the brink of misery, madness, horror—but she was the exception, an absolutely rare case, we shared the most horrific nights together, nights of sheer madness and dismay, *nights you couldn't begin to imagine*, I shouted, staring past the Turk at the reddening sun, —matching each other shot for shot, vodka, rum, whiskey, gin, scotch, tequila only rarely, a dirty spirit, absolutely filthy, I've always felt, we were essentially engaged in a standoff, a duel matching escalating howls—

—This one you will return to, bring home to her your share of the loot, to establish a shared life?

—She's dead. Fallen from a high rooftop. Under

circumstances other men might have questioned. If she was a suicide, however, she perished repulsed by *my* weakness. There can be no question there.

The Turk's eyes *wandered the poop*, flashing in the match flare as he lit his pipe.

—Listen, I continued, —here is a phrase I've always particularly loathed: *resistance is futile*—this phrase, doesn't it betray a certain allegiance *to* resistance, to acts of resistance, isn't there a latent wish *for* the non-futility of resistance, for struggle to actually mean something, as opposed to the actual case, which, granted, is that resistance *is* of course futile? Isn't there a pitiful resignation *to the fact* but nevertheless a kind of call to arms in the phrase's supposed fatalism? We'll *resist* because we have no other choice? ... But we *do* have the other choice of course—

The Turk fixed me with his pensive gaze, he was always fixing me with this very gaze, I hated the gaze, I would have murdered the gaze, not necessarily the Turk, perhaps the Turk too, but above all the gaze, the gaze alone, with its vaunted sagacity, I would have hammered that gaze to pieces, I would have drowned that gaze, but in men of the Turk's tribe, the gaze is undrownable, indomitable, an untouchable serenity, serenity *earned*, you'd have to murder the Turk himself before you could get at the gaze.

—Listen, said the Turk, and I craned back to take what was left in the flask, tried to imagine a deep acrimonious draught, even spluttered as if feeling that lost bracing heat, and the Turk fixed me with one of his other gazes, this one a twinkle, behind which briefly danced I imagined the fleeting image of some pair of slender legs, disrobed, wrapped around him in some smoky den of opiate indulgence that my *raw inexperience* would have prevented me from knowing (though I was actually *older* than the Turk, if it was perhaps true that he had frequented more dens than I) and without which I would of course be given to the kind of bleak juvenilia he dismissed my nightly fulminations as, especially as he believed I was not quite free of the grip of *the rot*, since to appreciate life one needed to *know* it, so that it followed that to *denounce* life one likewise needed to know it, and I was too consumed with a passion for denunciation, enjoyed *assaults* on life, in a philosophical sense, crowed too readily over my rhetorical broadsides to ever know life or appreciate it, I perceived this in the Turk's gaze as he blew smoke rings out over the lapping water and I leaned an elbow on the bulwark and watched the sun bleed into sea:

—But what else can a man do, he asked, —except resist?

—*Not* resist! I roared, —Resist the mandate to resist!

—Well, but the silver.

—What about the silver?

—The silver exists. And a man must live.

—

—And you admire the suicides.

—Yes, I said. —The suicides are our only heroes, the more ignominious, the more shameful, the more abjectly they *spit on* their lives, the more they shame their families, abandon their responsibilities, leave chaos in their wake, demolish the futures of those from whom they've been set free, I said, leaping onto a nearby spar, and swinging an imaginary cutlass through the wind.

—Who but a coward would *surrender*? the Turk spat.

—Who but a coward would surrender his *right* to surrender?

If we do find the silver tomorrow I intend to *abscond* with the entire cache, I've identified an island off the coast of Nova

Scotia, uninhabited, remote, pinpointed it on the Turk's weathered map, I will retire to *my island*, in the north, to a cold rocky barren land, pure desolation, a wasteland, humanless rock, desolate, an unpeopled waste, an island, en route I will purchase provisions and make for my final abode where, because I am a coward, I will not kill myself, I will live out my days, I will erect some rudimentary shelter to protect me from the absolutely *natural* elements, resist and survive for as long as I can: Because I am a coward, I will *live*.

The Consummation of Dirk

Dirk's Retreat:

Then came the summer of Dirk's retreat—into the mountains? The desert? On a single-sailed raft, adrift in uncharted seas? Dogsledding out over northern tundra? Or was it Patagonia, on austral ice, flocks of penguins drawn to him like angels to the feet of the risen Christ? Do we dare see Dirk fishlike, submerged with open eyes, gliding through turquoise waters, abask in the warmth of an equatorial sea? Picture him roaming rocky Galapagos, newfound avifauna arranged two-by-two, nestling placid along languid outstretched limbs? Or was Dirk lost in the rainforest, the Congo, Yucatan, pale titan throttling wet foliage, probing trail-less Amazonian depths, pausing, perhaps, to seek barter with native friends? Is he passing Canadian pines? Out of breath atop some arctic peak? Peering into pits of volcanic fire and ash? Sahara, Sonora, Siberian wasteland; across Australian Outback with long loping strides; Appalachia, Madagascar, aboard a private shuttle to the moon, spacesuited, on solitary pogos trekking lunar desolation? Could we have sought him out by telescope, if we had known to look, seen him bounding over lucent rock? Or an earthbound cosmopolis, in deep disguise on concrete sidewalks themselves partially concealed under the unseemly carpets of black splats of chewing gum, sandwich wrappers, crushed food cartons, transients with their salvaged goods, sidelocks and beard-sweep negating the chin's giveaway, covertly pacing our great nexuses of commerce, immersed in the commotion of complexly dubious finance, the stolid desperation, grim havoc after-hours, mortar, steel, glass, concrete, Mammon's sky-piercing citadels the garrisons through working hours to hosts of blind and hungry with their longing, vanity and noise? New York, Los Angeles, Shanghai, Seoul, Tokyo, Sidney, Rio de Janeiro, Bruges, Rome, *Cleveland*, London, Athens, Jerusalem, Unreal—into the wild, away from it all, to an isolate place, coordinates undisclosed.

On Horseback with Nash:

On horseback a young Dirk Nowitzki races teammate Steven Nash down a thin strip of floury sand along the lapping shallows of some sub-tropical sea, the duo's long hair flapping like matched manes in wind.

Dirk is clumsy on horseback, Nash skillful. Waiting at the finish line, Nash joshes his friend:

—Howdy, he says, doffing an invisible Stetson as Dirk's steed lumbers over the already-snapped tape.

Dirk chuckles, executes an ungainly dismount. A breeze flutters their similar white riding shirts.

—Steve, Dirk says later, the two of them sipping electric-blue mixed drinks through complexly-looped pink straws, their horses happily gamboling a little ways down-beach. —What could be better than this, Steve? We've got the whole world, don't we?

Nash stares out at the giant red sun, dipping down to graze the world's rim.

—Steve?

Skywritten over Dallas, December, 2010:

Marry me, Dirk!

Opposing Coaches address Dirk's tenacity:

Coach 1: If you look closely at Dirk, his tenacity really seems to pick up right there toward the end of his career, assuming this is the end—for the most part in that one final season, honestly. I'd say that he was less tenacious early on, more wide-eyed and excited to learn the ins and outs. Of the American game. Only in the end, particularly after the return from the, ah, the hiatus, did we really see a sharp increase in terms of tenacity.

Coach 2 (Retired): One instance really sums up the tenacity question for me. Late in a close game against the Pistons—or maybe the Sixers, similar color-schemes, doesn't matter, they both stank—J Terry gets fouled on a jumper, heads to the free-throw line. Couple of their guys lean into the lane, give him some of the typical shit, you know, get into Terry's head. Give him something to think about. Terry laughs—almost in a rueful sort of way, is how I'd describe it—then clanks the fucking free throws. Nice player, Terry, "The Jet" except for any time it actually fucking mattered. "Forty-seven," is what our guys always called him, in terms of his being mostly a stud for the first forty-seven minutes of the game.

So now anyway it's been back and forth all night, and the Pistons or Sixers go down the other end, and what do you think happens: they nail a three. Now they're up one. Timeout, Carlisle draws up the play, and so now under two seconds to go, Dirk gets hammered on an elbow jumper, heads to the line. Couple salient points here: first being this look of what I'd probably go ahead and call sheer malice or rancor—hate, even—all over his face. Needless to say, no Piston or Sixer comes within ten feet of him. Forget about running any interference. So Dirk drains the first one, all net, and starts screaming and beating his chest like a fucking asylum inmate, stares down the closest Piston or Six, who won't meet his fucking eyes, okay? and he's shouting right in this kid's face "Game over! Game over!"—shouts it roughly eight or ten times, I'd say—and then he *closes his eyes* and nails the second shot. Mavs win.

Mavericks Conditioning Coach: That last season, he just had this real tenacity in the weight room, I remember. One time finished a set of *extremely* heavy military presses and actually hurled the bar into the mirror. Completely shattered it, obviously.

Opposing Scout: We never took Dirk seriously as a physical presence—sure he could shoot the ball a little, but put a body on him and he disappears. Doesn't have the stomach or heart or whatever for contact, for physicality, for dirty work. Some guys just don't. Until he comes back with the bowling balls for arms and the fucking *nasty* attitude to boot. Off-record, I'd always felt the steroid question ought to be looked at a little more closely. But he tested clean—what can you do?

Dirk ponders:

At this time I began to ponder a question that had troubled me for some time:

As my status in the Association swelled, I grew accustomed to hearing the assembled American thousands thunderously chanting my name, causing it to reverberate from the rafters and shake the foundations of the arenas in which we would compete—

"Dirk"

"Dirk"

"Dirk"

"Dirk"

"Dirk"

"Dirk"

"Dirk"

—Yet increasingly the cheers failed to satisfy. So that inescapably I began to ask myself, Well, Dirk: What is it that you want? Did you not come to this country to pursue that somewhat vague referent you privately shorthand The Great? If a throng gathered to witness your performance and as one call out your name is not evidence of The Great fully attained, what is? What would be? Did I feel that until a championship banner hung from the highest rafters of American Airlines Center I would somehow not have earned those cheers? Perhaps this is the satisfying explanation. Except if it was truly a personal sense of merit and accomplishment I craved, not external validation in the form of those rapturous cheers, then why did I bother to perform? Might I have been satisfied making cabinets? Baking cakes, pies, and assorted pastries? Sculpting? Fishing the Chiemsee? If I am not so much concerned with the acclaim as with deserving the acclaim, is it not possible to do away with the acclaim altogether? Let the merit be all?

And yet I knew that this, too, was untrue. What man does not crave adulation? Appreciation, due recognition of his worth. Acknowledgment of success that has been earned. So what did I really want? Did I want to arrive, finally, at a point where I no longer needed to hear the mobs chanting my name? Or did I want to attain, once and for all, the ultimate, earned cheer? Or was it neither of these things? Did I want something different altogether? If so, what did I want? I found myself increasingly plagued and exhausted by the question. What is it you want, Dirk? What are you after? What are you striving for? What do you want? So that at a certain point I determined the question to be irresolvable, or that I would at the very least never answer it by looking inward. So that I began to look elsewhere. For answers.

Former lovers on Dirk:

H——: Well, for a guy who's seven-foot tall, his cock was actually surprisingly average.

B——: I always found Dirk to be a tremendously caring, tender lover. He would sort of gently cradle me against that mondo body of his, stroke my hair almost how like you'd pet a kitten, and just say these really gentle, really sweet, just loving things. I would always mark the calendar for Mavs road-trips to S—— and sort of count down the days till he'd come. I was always sad to see him go.

C——: Then one night back in the early days in Dallas, we're at one of the guys on the team's mansions—and I don't throw that term around lightly, "mansion," by the way, I've personally been in my share of extravagant private residences, leave it at that—and I think his little buddy, the point guard, Nash, the Nuck, he's with one of the girls somebody'd brought in, in one of the many bedrooms, my god, you should have seen the beds in some of these rooms—a couple being actually literally bed rooms, in terms of being rooms that were basically just one giant bed, you pull open the door and what you're looking at is, wham, just this huge sort of bed-pit, spread with satin or silk sheets, depending on which room, all kinds of music, but especially jazz, soul, funk, hip-hop, some of the better-known symphonies of a number of classical composers, including Wagner's *Ring Cycle*, in honor of Dirk was the impression I had, he'd shot the ball well that night and they got the win, coming from I assumed speakers hidden in the walls, since I never saw any, speakers, and also just lots of moaning and giggling, the odd slap and so on what have you, and so Dirk—who by this point is completely fucking blasted, just crashing and I guess you could call it careening from room to room, just picture this huge clumsy German guy lurching into doorjambs and walls, banging his head on like low-hanging lamps or chandeliers, sniffing constantly, nose now almost literally stopsign-red—and so anyway the funny thing is, he keeps trying to get me to come with him into the room where Nash and some other chick are already at. Saying "High time for all." Picture him saying this with the ridiculous German-inflections, this being back when the English wasn't so good, obviously almost flawless now but then... so Steve and him have this friend understanding, he goes. Tells me I should meet Steve, I'll really enjoy Steve, he keeps saying. Keep in mind this was before he went to the Suns, which we don't have to even go into what kind of heartbreak that must have been. Still. But so I don't think he even knows what he's saying at this point, you know? What kind of understanding's this supposed to be? But he keeps insisting, trying to convince me to go in there, actually getting a little flustered though not aggressive or anything like that, I never felt like in personal danger around Dirk, he's a gentleman, feel like I should make that clear, but kind of anxious or maybe confused the longer I drag my feet. So finally I said what the hell, and we went in.

Dirk discussed on Bill Simmons' internet podcast:

—Speculation of course being rampant: Does he miss the dunk on purpose? Maverick fans probably not about to forgive him either way.

—Nor should they.

—I think he plans to miss.

—Or at least chooses.

—Well, you watch the frame-by-frame, and tell me you don't see something bizarre happen to his face, midair.

—You're referring to the abrupt relaxation of the facial musculature.

—The infamous dropping of the scowl.

—Or grimace.

—The shift in demeanor.

—To sheer calm.

—Placidity.

—Zen.

—While still aloft.

—His team down by one, keep in mind.

—The final seconds ticking from the clock.

—Right: he's absolutely calm. Just before he blows the dunk.

—A two-handed dunk, he was attempting. Uncontested. Keep that in mind, too.

—Yeah, excellent point, Hal. Who the hell blows a two-handed dunk?

—That would have won the game, the series, and the Mavericks their first championship in franchise history.

—A perfect calm attained on the way to ultimate failure.

—The abandoning of the snarl.

—Giving up the ghost.

—Or the demon: the competitive demon.

—Right, okay, good. So now point blank: Does he miss the dunk on purpose?

—Well, can we really move beyond speculation, Bill? Realistically? In the end does the placid expression reveal anything?

—All right, look: let's say you're Nowitzki. All right?

You've failed just about every conceivable way there is to fail by this point in your career. You're already pushing the envelope, in terms of varieties of rejective experience. Couple seasons back, recall, you're voted League MVP the very week your top-seeded team gets bounced from the playoffs.

—With you so far, Hube.

—All right, so now here you are, a failure in every sense of the word, a gargantuan let-down, to your friends to your... keep in mind your best friend, sort of a mentor to you, fellow foreigner, confidante, etc., Steve Nash absolutely thrives as soon as he's traded away from your team, and you don't think this hurts Dirk, at some deep level? Nash being like a sort of adoptive older brother to Dirk, in addition to his closest pal? Plus now suddenly there's no one on the floor to get the ball to him at that foul-line extended area after those pick-and-pops... where were we?

—Huge let-down to family and friends,

—Exactly. So you've let down your family, your fans, your teammates, the organization that traded for you after you were taken with an extremely high—I believe it was the eighth?—

—Ninth.

—Thanks, Bill, the ninth pick, Mark Cuban having really put his neck on the line as an unproven owner in terms of grabbing an equally-unproven Euro-prospect at a time when they were considerably less in vogue, recall, and then let's not forget, maybe most painfully of all, you've also let down your friend and mentor, Holger Geschwindner, who's worked with you since you were an ungainly German teen, who you've come to think of as essentially your father—

—I've actually heard him call Gesh "Dad." In interviews.

—Absolutely, yeah.

—Ditto. "Vati," sometimes. In the Deutsch.

—And so, alright: here you are: mid-air, the basket's unprotected, you're about to undo in one fell swoop, as the poet says, every instance of shortcoming and weakness and incompetence and inadequacy and just basically not being good enough… all's about to be redeemed, in short. And you don't think it's remotely possible to let the thrill of anticipation cloud your concentration for just one split second? Enough to blow the damn dunk?

—

—

—Nope.

—Nah.

—No way.

—You kidding, H?

—Two hands on the ball, Hubie. He's not blowing a two-handed uncontested dunk, even with a little concentration lapse. Not possible.

—Unless he wants to.

—Less he's at least partly afraid of the other side.

—Fears slipping free of failure's grasp. At long last.

—Isn't sure who the heck he'll be. If he's not Losing embodied. Who'll he be without his failure? What sort of Dirk, if he's no longer the Dirk who always loses in the end. Fights hard, comes close, goes down, again. Losing's in his blood, his bones.

—Wants to blow the damn thing.

—At least on some level.

—Cause he sees it lurking or waiting for him. Something dark and unknown.

—Right there, he sees it.

—High above the court.

—Soaring on an uncontested trajectory for the game-sealing slam.

—Sees something somehow worse than failure, waiting for him.

—The gaping maw.

—Otherwise...

—Why turn away from what he'd been chasing all his life?

—Why now, when it's literally in his grasp?

—When all he has to do is flush that ball home?

—Nothing but a few collapsing feet of open space separating him from sweet, total victory?

—Who can tell?

—Who knows what lies in the hearts of men?

—Gentlemen, allow me to interject here.

—Sure, Bill.

—Your podcast.

—Just happy to be here, Bill.

—Appreciate that Gary. Was that Gary?

—Who cares?

—How many of us you got on here, Bill? By the way. I may have lost count.

—Alright, I just feel like we may be verging on, ah, philosophical territory, with some of these questions that you really can't answer, as House just pointed out, plus maybe starting to bore our listeners a bit here, potentially. No offense of course.

—None taken, Bill. You call the shots.

—Should we shift gears?

—I assume you won't want to go into Mark Cuban's suicide.

Irate fan contributes his two cents on an unofficial Mavericks fan-site comment-thread:

> My personal opinion is the [expletive] steroid-pumping Nazi [expletive] spent a whole decade biding his time just to [expletive] us over. [expletive]

Dirk reflects on his immortalization in fiction:

Of course that initial reading of the particular passage[1] I have already cited marked a particularly seminal or watershed moment for me—or rather I should say it illuminated for me precisely which attributes of a moment I had suspected must have been seminal or watershed but had not been quite able to identify or articulate for myself had conduced to the moment's being so seminal or watershed.

Essentially, I encountered or perceived or arrived at a truer vision of myself as I really am, or could be, in these pages than I had ever been able to come to on my own. A startling experience, to be sure—but also an intriguing one.

Excerpted from an interview with author Jonathan Callahan

Q:

A: No, I wasn't personally ever obsessed with Dirk Nowitzki. But I did perceive in Dirk fairly early on, uh, the, I guess you could call it the possibility for obsession.

Q:

---

[1]See Appendix A

A: Well, look, I'm sorry. That's the best I can do for you just now.

Q:

A: Allen Iverson.

Q:

A: Just liked his style, most of all, I guess. Plus he was small, too, you know? I mean, not as small as me, obviously. Few people are. No it's all right. I'm honestly not nearly as sensitive as I used to be, I don't think. But guess I always have admired plus also envied little guys who found a way to get it done. In spite of the vertical limitations.

Q:

A: Fine, yes. The subject is still sore.

Q:

A: Do I believe in god?

Q:

A: No, I heard you, I just, uh.... Look is there any particular organizing principle to these questions you're asking here? I don't really see the—no, I mean, of course I don't believe in god, certainly not a "merciful" one, as you put it. How could I? But I don't exactly believe in, you know, us, either. So I mean... what's a person to do besides head for the hills? Or the moon?

Q:

A: Or write a book about it. Ha ha.

Q:

A: No way I could get another cup of coffee or something in here?

Simmons revisits the seminal Game-Seven collapse:

—Let's revisit the seminal Game Seven collapse. We've had all sorts of speculation with respect to possible explanations, and I'd say it's never going to be resolved unless we get something from Nowitzki himself, and let's be realistic: it doesn't look like that's in the cards.

—You're saying you think he's, he's not coming back then.

—Look, there's of course no telling. Best we can do is indulge in a little speculation. Obviously.

—Of course.

—But when a guy drops off the grid. Disappears without a word. Vanishes into thin air. One night he's slumped at center-court after blowing the biggest game of his life, next day he's just gone. When a professional athlete of Dirk Nowtizki's stature just poof, exits—

—Right.

—Then I think you have to be pretty skeptical, in terms of believing there's any chance of good news coming down the pipe.

—You're suggesting he took his own life.

—Hubie cuts through the crap.

—One of the things I really love about the Hube.

—No dancing.

—No shuck or jive.

—Just the absolute chase he's always prepared to cut to.

—Well, all right. Sure. That is what I'm wondering, guys. You take into account the obsession with seppuku in the months leading up to the finals.

—The photographs depicting all varieties of suffering purportedly plastered across his locker room alcove.

—The obsession with Daniel Plainview of cinema.

—The refusal to meet with the press a month into by far the most successful season of his career.

—Which was of course all the more surprising, the success I mean.

—Coming as it did after the self-imposed hiatus.

—Following the latest in a series of playoff collapses that left him pretty vulnerable to questions of character and personal will to succeed.

—Right, but so not saying so much as a word to the increasingly-fascinated media as he racked up otherworldly stats, not to mention the greatest regular season record in NBA history, for the Mavericks.

—Who'd failed to even make the playoffs without him.

—The previous year.

—Yup.

—The incredible rise in every measure of productivity on the court.

—The steroid question of course therefore having to inevitably come up pretty frequently.

—But the NBA countermanding its own pretty strict policy and releasing tests demonstrating pretty conclusively that whatever was different, it wasn't roids.

—Nor HGH.

—Whatever it was, something was different.

—The guy's jumping a good eight inches higher, easy. Watch the tapes.

—Plus his arms went from that sort of floppy Euro-look to specimens of preposterous, just absolutely monstrous, muscularity.

—Shoulders the size of bowling balls. As has been remarked.

—Or at least softballs.

—Bigger than softballs I'd say. Plenty of guys in the softball range, if we're talking pro shoulders. This was—

—So one way or another, Dirk comes back from the hiatus ripped, springier, more powerful, shooting the ball absurdly well. Which was a forte to begin with, mind. You guys I'm sure remember, but I mean, people forget so easily, the guy was shooting a percentage that was out of this world.

—Ridiculous accuracy that year.

—Ungodly.

—What was it, ninety-percent? eight-five?

—There was that arc spanning the foul-line extended where I don't think he missed a single shot the whole damn year.

—Unholy, Jesus.

—Demonic.

—Eldritch.

—And of course steroids alone, if you're even willing to brook the steroid speculation, wouldn't have been enough to account for the shooting percentage.

—Valid point, Bill. But then keep in mind he also just starts dunking the heck out of the ball.

—Like a man possessed.

—Ramming it home.

—Throwing it down in people's faces.

—A lay-up-less year, practically. From a guy who, recall, at seven feet was known for putting up these pathetic little softy lays just way too frequently.

—It's true.

—But I for one can't remember a single drive or foray into the paint that season that didn't result in a dunk.

—Frequently a tomahawk.

—Two-handed thunder, as the Dallas press took to calling it, in a coinage of not exactly overawing descriptive ingenuity. Although it does sort of stick, doesn't it.

—Violence masquerading as two points.

—He'd put his head down and rumble for the rim with malice—

—Oh, lord, the malice!

—In his eyes.

—Broke poor Dwight Howard's arm at the wrist.

—Bloodied Blake Griffin's eye.

—Andrew Bynum lost a finger, don't forget.

—Oh my god. Drew, tell me you saw that live, you were at that game, were you not?

—Just a horrible, horrible sight. A sight I will truly never forget.

—No, afraid not. Long as you live.

—I shudder to think of it.

—Oomph.

—That's not a figure of speech. I'm literally shuddering here, Bill.

—Dirk Nowitzki.

—So but my point being, who'd of ever thought?

—Dirk Nowitzki!

—Didn't you used to get the feeling that early nickname, the Dunking Deutschman, was sort of a mean-spirited jab? Seeing as how he really didn't dunk too often?

—"Soft" was a word in pretty heavy circulation.

—"Soft" was bandied about.

—I myself said it a few times.

—Sure, who didn't?

—Nothing to feel sorry about.

—Dirk before the hiatus, or sabbatical—

—Or vision quest.

—Or mystic performance-enhancing regimen.

—Or journey into the heart of the silence, the light.

—Right: this prior Dirk being, we can agree, a totally different Dirk.

—Pretty drastically different players. Different men, I'd go so far as to suggest.

—And in the end?

—Same result. What a [bleep] tragedy.

—Whoa. Easy, Hube. Let's not give our already-over-taxed editing staff any extra work this morning.

—I apologize, Bill. Listeners. I apologize. Won't happen again. No offense intended, I assure you.

—Moving forward. But so is he really gone this time?

—Will we ever see Dirk in the League again?

—Will we ever see him, period?

—Of course you've got these Internet wack-jobs publishing their theories.

—Yeah, although there is the one set of pretty-widely-circulated photographs that would appear to be depicting Nowiztki, longtime guru–mentor Holger Geschwinder—

—And someone else.

—And a third figure, right.

—Who's the third figure?

—Can we say without a doubt that, (a) there definitively is a third figure, and, (b) that if there are three figures, they are conclusively Nowizki, Geschwinder, and this mysterious third, in a brown mantle, hooded?

—One answer to the third man question being provided on, ah, let's see, it's called Who Is The Third Who Walks Always Beside You dot blog dot net. Have you read this guy?

—Haha. Of course! Linked to him, couple columns ago. Looney but fun.

—The premise of this site being, for listeners who might not read the thing, that the blog's author is the eponymous third figure.

—That he was with Dirk, on this second reclusive flight from the world.

—Claims Dirk's still alive.

—And coming soon.

—As I said, I linked to a couple of recent posts sometime last week. Or basically "rants," is what you'd call them, maybe.

—Yeah, who is this guy?

—Hmmm. Can it be plausibly argued that Dirk's coming back?

—People are hungry, Bill.

—You can feel it in the air, Bill. The people want something. There's yearning everywhere you look. It's palpable.

—A palpable yearning or hunger or need.

—An empire failing.

—Money scarce.

—Falling towers.

—The people crave a light to guide them through the darkness, Bill.

—Wait.

—What's that sound high in the air, Bill?

—Maternal lamentations, is it?

—What, are you guys—

—Cracks and reforms,

—Bursts in violet air.

—Towers falling everywhere you look.

—

—Have we, I'm sorry, have we exhausted the topic of Nowitzki? Fellows?

Dirk examined exegetically

Stanford University's A. Horowitz rejects Litgenstein's essentially Oedipal thesis, viz.:

> We can no more readily presume Nowitzki's ambivalence to stem from the so-called "maternal lacuna" than we can suggest that the pretzel's savor derives from the absence of sugar withdrawn: the notion preposterously reduces and self-serves.

Ebstein on "mirroring":

> Certainly the mirrored lives become intertwined, beginning particularly with Nowitzki's self-imposed exile, increasing with astonishing rapidity—and to an almost preposterous extent—thenceforth.
> [...]
> The two real-world figures, Nowitzki and Callahan,

proceed to engage in a preposterously surreal pantomime of behaviors first enacted by their fictional counterparts in the novel (note: Several commentators have argued persuasively for a strong autobiographical link between Callahan and King, the fictional figure's notorious "staged suicide" notwithstanding; see in particular "The Mask Matches the Face: Memoir Masquerading as Fiction in *The Consummation of Dirk [The Once and Future King]*, Browne, Edna, 20—, Columbia Press), some of which behaviors, when charted chronologically, seem necessarily to have to have been initiated before the novel's publication—so that the possibility of consultation—or even collaboration!—becomes almost too enticing to resist....

Green, Franklin, et al. on how to approach the Callahan–Nowitzki case:

One necessarily approaches the Callahan–Nowitzki case with caution. Dare we write off the possibility of coincidence or chance? Is it beyond the realm of the plausible to posit the similarities might be circumstantial, merely? Nevertheless, given what we have on record from both figures, the parallels may prove too enticing to resist:

[...]

So that in a preposterous confusion of fun-house reflections[2], it may even be possible to assert that while

---

[2]In a bizarre sequence of life-imitating-art-imitating-life-imitating-art until it becomes a bit difficult to link eggs to an ur-chicken or chickens to an ur-egg, Lucas King, the protagonist of the novel's severely-depressed and Dirk Nowitzki–worshipping brother (who has earlier instructed his family members to refer to him thenceforth as "Dirk"), imagines a distraught and broken Dirk Nowitzki retreating into exile following yet another cataclysmic failure in the

NBA playoffs—
        Which (imagined) example Lucas or Dirk King subsequently
follows, sort of, as he stages his own suicide and hides out in the mountains of
western O`ahu in the hopes of arriving at some sort of satori-like revelation
or apprehension that he might then carry back with him on (triumphant?)
return to the life whose rushing pace he has found himself unable to keep,
being a grievously troubled, miserably depressed post-adolescent; or else, should
enlightenment elude him, actually carry out the previously-pseudo-self-slaughter
and dare a God whose voice he'd never heard pronounce his condemnation—
        Which fictional path the actual Dirk Nowitzki, having apparently read
and admired the book, following the calamitous '09-'10 season seems to have
roughly followed: while not going so far as to fake his own suicide, he does indeed
go off the grid, disappearing for over a year, during which time no one on the
planet can produce evidence suggesting he's still alive—
        Meanwhile soon thereafter the actual Jonathan Callahan, i.e. the author
of The Consummation of Dirk (The Once and Future King), also goes missing,
just as the media-frenzy surrounding the talented young author's audacious
debut (essentially an orgy of breathless adoration, book-reviewers, critics, and
even a few [in general, grudgingly] admiring academics across the country all
frantically rushing to anoint and then outdo one another in lavishing worshipful
praise upon the twenty-nine-year-old wunderkind) has at last begun to wane
or die down, and the author is purported by family members and his few close
friends to have sunk into a severe depression that rather surrealistically echoes the
depression the desponding, Nowitzki-worshipping Lucas/Dirk King imagined
the (fictional) Dirk Nowitzki, in a late passage of The Consummation of Dirk
(The Once and Future King), sinking into, just as he was at last on the cusp of
achieving his ultimate goal of winning a championship—which depression is
described (in prose the floridity of which has been rather egregiously given a free
pass by the wunderkind-hungry literary press) by Dirk King (who is revealed
by this point not to have killed himself, yet) in a brief nested "text-within-the-
text," manuscript composed in a wild-mushroom-induced ecstatic trance: D.K.
envisions a scenario whereupon the fictive Nowitzki, on the free-throw line at
the very end of the season that has marked his triumphant return to the League,
on the verge of at last earning the championship ring that has eluded him for his
entire career, realizes in a moment of devastating satori-ish total apprehension—or
sight—that it will never be enough, no cheer will be loud enough, no achievement
great enough, no ring's circumference vast enough to encircle his infinite desire,
this disillusionment obliquely literalized in the soaring, lyric, if saprophytically-
obscured passage (See Appendix B) and then elaborated on or further imagined
in a subsequent passage (C) during which the febrile Dirk King imagines himself
directly into the mind of a broken Dirk Nowitzki, who has at last achieved the
success he's craved his whole life and nevertheless found himself still empty, still
craving more, if anything even less happy than he's ever been (and he's always been
unhappy), which is why, Dirk King explains, in a lengthy soliloquy (delivered in
the disembodied voice of Nowitzki) to his sister (who is understandably unhappy
with her brother's decision to stage his own suicide some thirteen months earlier
and then haunt her otherwise-tranquil life at the small liberal arts college she's

decided to attend in order to get away from her tragedy-hammered family's stolid Christian optimism in the face of sheer calamitous Fate) that he decided to give up his pursuit of the basketball stardom he may have been on the cusp of back in Honolulu, (though the narrative implies that D.K.'s impression of his own abilities is drastically, bombastically, pitifully inflated, in spite of his insecurities: i.e. the fact that poor Dirk King thinks he's in possession of a rarely keen sense of self-awareness and insight into both his own consciousness's mechanisms and his capacity for self-delusion and therefore uniquely equipped to see through any capacity he might have to inflate his own estimation of himself only makes his still-falsely-inflated sense of his own worth [The book's front cover depicts what would appear to be a disembodied sneer] that much more tragic and pathetic) and retreat into the mountains in the hopes of attaining zen-like knowledge and peace—

Which example seems again to have informed the actual (i.e. "real life") Dirk Nowitzki's behavior, as, upon returning from his mysterious sojourn into distant regions undisclosed (the author Jonathan Callahan meanwhile still absent) as an absolute on-court machine, Nowitzki pilots the Mavs to the greatest record in NBA history (75–7—four of the losses coming during Dirk's self-imposed ten days of fasting and reflection, mid-season), and then meeting in the Finals a stiff challenge in Lebron James's formidable New York Knicks, culminating in the fateful dunk attempt described supra that would have won the whole shebang and that either went awry or Dirk intentionally missed, depending who you want to ask, after which Dirk (the real Dirk) goes missing yet again—

At which point the vanished Jonathan Callahan abruptly reappears, this time as the anonymous author (it is later revealed) of the quickly-immensely-popular Who Is The Third Who Walks Always Beside You web-log which begins as a sort of AWOL-Dirk Nowitzki Speculation-and-Gossip site but quickly evolves into a sort of Gospel-like account wherein the author (Callahan) simultaneously relates Scripture and casts himself in a John the Baptist–type role, claiming that he is not the light but comes to bear witness to the light, the true light, the light that shines in the darkness and gives light to all men, and that basically Dirk will return—

Which is of course precisely what Dirk King, the fictional character, does at the culmination of The Once and Future King, as members of that novel's considerable readership will recall: He returns to his father, the retired heart surgeon, now a broken man, haunted by a crushing remorse over his sense that he has failed his only begotten son, his creation, Dirk's return bringing the novel to a rousing emotional climax or culmination or consummation at which point the indication seems to be that the new life to be commenced beyond the book's pages will be defined by other-orientedness, genuine self-sacrifice, escape from the awful confines of solipsism or self-obsession—the implication being that Dirk, having come through the refinery of his personal quest into the deepest recesses of selfishness and, frankly, evil (in terms of having staged his own suicide and left his loving family in grief-wracked shambles), has emerged new and different and whole, having finally learned to love—which is precisely the message Kirk Nowitzki, having taken the new name so as to reflect the deep transformation undertaken in the secret distant reaches he has traveled to and sojourned through

Nowitzki first influenced the material assembled in the novel, that material has in turn influenced Nowitzki's life, subsequent to the events obliquely described in the novel, which subsequent Nowitzkian life has in turn influenced Callahan's actual life, twisting it to more closely resemble that of his fictional doppelgänger, Dirk King (once the real-life Nowitzki came to more closely resemble his fictive counterpart), whose seemingly farcical narrative arc either influenced or predicted or was influenced or predicted by the real-life narrative of his author, whose real-life relationship to the actual Dirk Nowitzki has been no less obsessive and strange than that of his fictional character's with the fictive Nowitzki—recent on-line pronouncements on the newly christened Kirk's messianic qualities, for example, having reached such a fever-pitch as to render the pseudo-suicidal protagonist's antics rather quaint or tame, in retrospect.

Speculation rampant on Maverick threads:

1: My personal opinion is that Dirk or Kirk or whatever the [expletive] he wants to call himself these days is gone [expletive] bat-[expletive] and that he's gonna need a whole [expletive] of a lot more than [expletive] love to get himself in search of understanding and peace with the self and its place in the world, will return one day to preach, the still-reclusive hermit-like Jonathan Callahan claims on his WITTWWABY blog—

At which point the *actual* Dirk Nowitzki returns from wherever he's been off the grid and announces he's changed his name to Kirk, and that he won't be playing ball anymore, no: what he'd like to do with the rest of his life is learn to give, learn to love and care for someone—anyone—other than himself, to find something greater, who knows what it will be, he's willing to spend his whole life learning how to do this, only where is a self-escaping man supposed to even begin?

right.

2: I think what Kirk's come back to say to us is really really important right now. When's the last time any of us ever thought about somebody other than ourselves?

3: Let's face it: the dude was on some kind of performance-enhancer, and in the end he just couldn't accept that he had to cheat to earn his success. Couldn't live with himself, basically.

4: Go to Sunday school, [2] and all you other sentimental [expletive], LMAOWROTFJTAHSYA!!!!!

[Etc....]

Dirk, who also is called Kirk

For in those times a great unrest had swept the land, like a plague, like a swarm of locusts or bees, an animus of shadow and blight, an angel of death grimly tolling the knell, afflicting the people with a dread without name, manifesting as doubt, inscrutable horror and fear.

And Kirk, who was once called Dirk, walked again among the people, bearing good tidings of great joy, peace to the strife-afflicted, communion to those who cried out from the pits of their solitude, hope to all who had abandoned hope, and the people received him with feast and dance.

In sackcloth and sandaled feet he walked the back roads and broken interstates, crossed the vast and barren spaces of this once-great nation, proclaiming a simple message of generosity, righteousness and peace.

And, lo, when they came unto him seated on the high modest dais beside the churches, before the synagogues, the mosques, the temples, wards, assemblies, congregations, synods, meeting halls; and also unto the great shopping plazas, strip malls, the great commerce-chains crosshatching the States of this disintegrating Union, flocked to him in multitudes, clamoring for audience with him wherever he went, when they spoke unto him of the sadness in their hearts, poured out unto him their grief and pity, as they pressed their small afflicted hands into his great open palms, when they sang unto Kirk lamentations calling forth in melancholic splendor all the sorrows of the world, and he looked into the eyes of those who suffered, and when he witnessed their suffering and heard their cries, Kirk wept.

Together all would weep as Kirk shook with an intensity of fellow-feeling, took into his own heart the pains lodged in this swelling legion of others, and he wept, and cried out unto heaven to have mercy on us, have mercy, o Lord, have mercy on your people, in our weakness and our grief, and to those who suffered and came unto him Kirk spake little, yet the tears streamed from his open eyes as the people cracked their hearts before him, stripped themselves of irony and sneer, peeled away the callused layers, removed their masks, exposed the naked pain, laid their armor down, that armor which defends feeling and in so doing crushes the soul, for the first time giving themselves over, with abandon, to sheer sadness and grief: for all have lost—

and all fall short of the glory of godhood which in our hearts we woefully crave; my people, humble people, nation of venture, nation of insatiable want, nation of the long loping strides across the boulevards of great cities, the desperate pacing from nowhere to nowhere, under the pitiless sun blazing down on the bowed heads of men.

And they asked of him, Kirk, What is to be done? How are we to live? and he said unto them, touch the water on my cheeks, taste this physicality of sorrow, for this is the true sorrow, the one sorrow that is life to bear and salvation to all who would break free of the torments of their own hardened hearts:

For Blessed are those who have emptied themselves of themselves,

Blessed are those who would stand before their brothers, before their sisters, before the strange people they meet in the overcrowded cities and towns, on the sidelines of vast suburban playing fields, as the chatter turns heated and ugly and the volunteer coaches are chastised for failing to provide sons and daughters with sufficient playing time, in the supermarket aisles laden with the mechanisms of want, gleaming under post-florescent light, in the megachurches where the righteous sanctify themselves, at the entertainment complexes where spectacle thunders and numbs, on freeways stagnant with vehicular clot, in the arenas, witnessing competitive feats, in the hearts of those who would soar high into the void,

Blessed are those who pause, who bend to give ear to the plaints of the fallen, who would listen to the cries of an other, taste the anguish of the world, reach out unto those too frightened to beg for touch, give unto these that which you would have them give unto you: this is the kingdom of heaven.

No greater love has he than he who would give his life for his brother in the full knowledge that there is no life to come, that his reward is no unseen paradise, for death and death only comes to all, and the kingdom of heaven obtains among us, here is the city shining in the hearts of men, no greater love than to dwell in the hearts of your fellow men, for this is the house of the Lord.

Give of yourself what is yours to give, that another might prosper, empty yourselves, o people, and you shall know God.

<u>Kirk walks the land, passing out tracts.</u>

In tracts he hands out to all who will take them as he treks across the benighted land, Kirk cites certain passages of his own particular inspiration, but stresses that each man or woman's path to comprehension of the light, each individual circumstance of seeing will be unique and unknowable save that it must come from the sincerest desire to know, to apprehend the light.

<u>Beginning to see the light</u>

But will we ever reach the light? Does the light shine only to be chased? If we know the light cannot ever be seen, Who can compel its eternal pursuit?

Appendix A:

[Excerpted from *The Consummation of Dirk (The Once and Future King)*, Jonathan Callahan, Smyrna Merchant Press, © 2011.]

However on the far wall beside the lone window and just above the bed's foot hung only a single poster, its dimensions approximately two-to-three times those of the posters forming a patchwork covering much of the other three walls' pebbled beige. The image, apparently captured from a vantage courtside at roughly the foul line–extended, would've been impressive enough even divorced entirely from context, Dirk had often reflected, a certain self-contained majesty seeming to obtain in the depiction itself—lithe body extended just above the glossy hardwood floor, the one jutting knee, the ball securely grasped in the involute palm of a pale flexed hand, the spectatorial tiers aglitter with camera flashes caught in various phases of frozen candescence, eight enormous on-court bodies statued in poses of desperate motion looking on as the snarling pallid airborne figure at stage-center cocks the ball just above the final defender's up-stretched fingertips—and didn't even necessarily *require* the additional symbolic heft or weight it acquired when you considered it with an appreciation of certain contextual facts: For example that the defender whose leap is by mere inches inadequate to the task of stymieing a to this point more-or-less-always-stymied-whenever-it-really-mattered Dirk Nowitzki from delivering the ball to the basket for a game-tying two points in the sixth game of a seven-game series that his team trailed three-to-two at the photographic moment is one Timothy Duncan, regnant MVP of the Association his San Antonio team is also the defending champion of, and that at least one plausible cause for the disbelief plainly evident on fellow San Antonian Robert Horry (who can be seen sprinting toward Dirk one second too late to have any impact on the play)'s face is that *until this very instant* pretty much no one in the arena has expected Dirk to do anything other than wilt under the singular pressure of a situation dictating that he either succeed right now or allow his team to be eliminated from competition, *win or go home*, even the TV analysts sound more or less resigned to the predictable outcome of Dirk heaving up an off-balance, prayer-less shot or else tossing the ball to a teammate so that he can't be blamed for blowing yet another game by missing the critical shot or dribbling the ball off his foot or in some other way *fucking up*—and so the chasing Horry'd been as stunned as each of the other players on-court, the desperate lookers-on from the bench, the crowd assembled at the Alamo Dome to witness yet another dismantling of the Mavericks (at this point something of an annual springtime tradition or ritual), television-watchers in living rooms and bars all across this sports-loving nation (and also in Germany, where Dirk was, in spite of his myriad failings, a near–national icon and still immensely popular among NBA-fans) and so the point being that you wouldn't even need to know the whole dismal history of Dirk Nowitzki's over-hyped and underwhelming NBA career, or even that the desperation apparent in the snarl twisting the Teuton's features was not merely physical but the equivalent of, say, a smoke-signal sent up from the deep roiling sacred reaches of the soul—none of this knowledge having been strictly necessary in order to apprehend in an instant the physical drama of the immortalized tableau....

But it certainly lent it an additional resonance or *depth.*

Dirk captured mid-flight, en route, at last, to a chance at that elusive ultimate glory.

Appendix B:

[Excerpted from *The Consummation of Dirk (The Once and Future King)*, Jonathan Callahan, Smyrna Merchant Press, © 2011.]

I saw Dirk Nowitzki acquiesce to certain facts about the true nature of desire, about the unmitigated consequence, cost, devotion, sacrifice of self to self; total gratification-as-annihilation, volitional mindlessness, the subsuming pain of true consummation; saw the horror of first knowledge shadow his face as a free throw rattled from the rim, saw him know futility—

Dirk, grasping perigee in its purest absolute, perceiving the unflawed beauty of centripetal collapse into the center of real Want; perceiving the inverted wrongness of all he has understood about pursuit, about life as pumping strong motion—upward outward aching expansion—succumbing to the clear-eyed sadness that accompanies true knowledge of Self-and-Other at its most bleak and Lear-like, embracing the truth unveiled after absolute de-circling, inward orbit-disruption, a plunge into the heart of absolute Need. I saw him know fear. Saw him understand.

Indeed, I saw Dirk, in the penultimate moment, literally enlightened—yes, illuminated, as by hot glowing filament, flaring up from some core-located nucleus of liquid fire that pushed beads of sweated luminescence through the pores of now-translucent German flesh. Saw his backlit eyes glow red, two tiny planets, hovering, the last of him to melt into light, dimming, loamish at the suspended last—twin lumps of shriveled clay—drained nearly of all light; frozen in time, space, memory, barely visible above the supernova that had been his muscle and bone at incandescent climax—exploded, imploded: who could tell?—and, diminishing, began to drip a glistening light that would pool and spread slowly over the charred-black hardwood maple floor.

Saw a crowd of 25,000+ literally enthralled: silence a sudden terminus at the edge of a violent and rapturous cheer.

Appendix C:

[Excerpted from *The Consummation of Dirk (The Once and Future King)*, Jonathan Callahan, Smyrna Merchant Press, © 2011.]

Dirk, whose post-epic-failure pilgrimage into his own self and consequently away from the League and the Nation in which it stands sent him trekking across the jutting plunging craggy terrain of a dry and perilously-mountained land, coordinates undisclosed, running dawn to dusk—pausing only for natural human processes of in- and egress (sometimes not even bothering to pause)—up near-perpendicular slopes garrisoned with considerable Dirk-deterring flora, fauna, and geophysical phenomena: ledges, overhangs, rockslides, cyclones, concentrated lightning storms, carnivorous Venus flytrap–like plants of a human-devouring scale, quicksand, pumas, pterodactyl-sized predatory eagles, *gnomes*—and beyond all of which, the ubiquitous sulfuric heat;

Dirk, having carried himself alone to a perceivably central— Centered—place, at the heart of a battered, scarred, murderously-hostile land, on high, which heart beat in the literal chest of an unbelievably sere- and psoriatic-skinned, phantasmagorically decrepit withered horseshoe-shaped wraithish hermit (Ω) who had willed his long-failing corporeal vessel to subsist for untold eons on the single handful of gray dirt he scooped and pressed to his tongue once every 172,000 beats of his heart (which cycle the solitary ascetic intuitively tracked with unwavering precision without the need to consciously *count*—a process that encapsulated precisely the sort of knowing-without-knowing that the pilgrim Dirk would come to understand as at the philosophical heart of what he'd come to See), scooping the nutritive dirt from a shallow pit he'd ages past finger-scraped into the ground behind the roofless rock enclosure within which he at all other times stood marmoreally stooped against the time-scraped motions of sun and moon and cloud and star;

Dirk, whose breath-deprived near-religious gasps of gratitude and relief upon having reached the destination he'd begun to find himself tormented by doubts about the actual existence of—this very Ω-shaped hermit's roofless hovel—bending down and prostrating himself in accordance with a decorum he'd sketched out for himself during the grunting weeks of rockface-scaling, silver-sand-pool skirting, clustered- (and somehow terrifyingly accurate, almost as if *aimed-*) lightning-bolt evasion, bare-handed puma slaying, eagle-beak crushing and -severing, gnome-punting, and general prolonged roiling struggle, since the last man who even claimed to have seen the Ω-shaped recluse was long since dead, and had at any rate encountered a far more youthful **r**-shaped incarnation of the being into whose pupil-less purple-veined eyes a prostrate Dirk unflinchingly gazed as he paid spoken reverence to the man upon whom he'd constructed a whole cosmic system of Hopes;

Dirk, who after a solid week (tracked via sun-and-moon circling) of increasingly desperate requests and finally pleas for an

Answer to what he'd trekked off-map to Know, doubting: at the end of the journey, in the heart of the mountains, in the center of the slightly-raised circle of hard gray dust upon which the hermit subsists, in the very center, a hole: black, temperatureless, bottomless, that travels into and through and throughout all time and beyond—

The hermit circling the hole, spiraling inward, each handful of teetering life-sustaining dust taken from a patch one feeble-hand-length closer to the heart of the circle, the empty space, the silence—

Swirling closer to a point beyond which, within which there can be no further inward progression:

Absolute zero—

Annihilation—

Nil.

The wraith a crescent closing in on itself—becoming, gradually, imperceptibly, a perfect circle.

Hamnlet Pursues the Black Unicorn

It is universally admitted that the unicorn is a supernatural being of good omen; such is declared in all the odes, annals, biographies of illustrious men and other texts whose authority is unquestionable. Even children and village women know that the unicorn constitutes a favorable presage. But this animal does not figure among the domestic beasts, it is not always easy to find, it does not lend itself to classification. It is not like the horse or the bull, the wolf or the deer. In such conditions, we would be face to face with a unicorn and not know for certain what it was. We know that such and such an animal with horns is a bull. But we do not know what the unicorn is like.

Jorge Luis Borges, *Labyrinths*

The black unicorn will be here, I said to myself, as the deeper shadows of what must be the Underwood reared up ahead. If the black unicorn can be found, here is where I will find it, I said. And I couldn't come back without the unicorn, this went without saying. The black unicorn, with its glorious gold trim. I'd told them I would return one day, perhaps soon, perhaps not—but when I returned, it would be with the black unicorn. Or on it. On the black unicorn, with its gold trim. An obsidian streak across the sunset's candy-striped sky. Why had I promised? Only a fool makes such a promise, I said to myself, as I paused to wipe more sweat from my brow, leaning against the broad trunk of some deciduous tree, as the light waned.

The hills that fringe Underwood Forest are populous with wild goats. Most are harmless. But I was raised among goats, know their fickle affections all too well. As a rule it's best to proceed with supreme caution and never to assume that a goat is docile or would care to be your friend, even if your first impression is of a docile creature inclined to be your friend. The goats are for the goats, and harbor no illusions as to others' allegiances. Wise policy, I said to myself, as I pressed on through these final outlying hills, casting frequent glances to all sides, searching the gentle slopes for signs of inimical goats. I bore before me my father's staff, gently thwacking my palm as I walked.

She'd never understood about the goats, I thought, as I approached one last modest rise. And beyond, what could only be the true Underwood's black vastness, far foliage crested by a bloody fingernail of sun.

—Gold trim? she had asked.

—Gold hooves, tail a tuft of sparkling fluffy gold. Horn, too, of course. A sleek golden horn inscribed with a helix rather than the traditional rings, I had said.

Few people in these remote parts have seen a unicorn. Much less a black one, with gold trim—which of course no one will ever have seen, until they see the one I cannot come back from my journey without, I thought to myself, as I once again shifted the heavy load on my back.

—I can't picture it, she had said, I recalled now, as I shrugged my pack higher and entered the forest, the surrounding verdure almost instantaneously dense.

—You won't need to, I had told her.

Arrogance!

In Underwood Forest, what paths there are seem to fold up under themselves, so that upon glancing down at the narrow dirt track beneath your feet you will often catch what would appear to be glimpses of lustrous pearl sky, far below. And above you? Through slits in the intricate branchwork? More sky! Of course it is insane, some skewed perspectival trick—and yet men have gone mad, I thought. Better men than I. Best not to look too hard. Keep your eyes ahead, I said to myself, peering into the darkness before me, seeing very little. No one could guide me to the black unicorn; the black unicorn would not exist until I found it.

The solar bear subsists primarily on sunlight, drawing supplementary nutrition from the lightsap found in gem-pines— "cocaine trees," in the traditional folk parlance—clustered principally in the Underwood's outer circles, I recalled, as the shadows seemed to deepen around me, silently reciting verbatim the brief account my father had found for me in his files—notes left by the last explorer to venture into the Underwood (a close friend; they'd sailed together in his youth), some several decades past. Now deceased. And what had he wanted with the Underwood? Difficult to say, exactly, his otherwise-elaborate field notes being muted, even cryptic on the subject of ultimate aims. Naturally there was no mention of a black unicorn; but in the man's crazed obsession with Ursula Solaris did I not detect a whiff of my own ambition?

As would be expected, the solar bear therefore prefers to roam during daylight hours, and between late morning and early afternoon may often be observed atop sturdier gem-pines, luxuriating in the nutritive warmth, paws sticky with plundered lightsap, growling his pleasure, I quoted to myself, surprised at the precision with which I could recall this ludicrous, possibly-fabricated text. I began to hum a tune I had not heard since the days when my mother wandered the house singing softly, poor woman, while my father chased his goatherds over the mountain range.

It was unclear what I intended to *do* with the black unicorn with the gold trim I had sworn to find and possess. Would I keep it for myself? Would I really want the black unicorn? If I ever found it? (Which I was bound by my promise to do.) Would the black unicorn be enough? Would I make it a gift? If so, to whom?

As sated solars, during said hours, will frequently roam the pathless forest seeking challenge or prey, the wise wanderer crosses outer Underwood in the dark. The solar bear is unlikely to attack after sundown, unless roused from its slumber, which is deep indeed, I recalled.

My father had rummaged through several storage trunks to find an old volume of bear-repugnant limericks.

—As a safeguard.

I told him I was not afraid of bears—or anything, for that matter. I would face whatever I encountered on the road, as a man.

—Take it anyway, he'd said, —just in case. Better to be safe.

—Safety is for cowards, I'd said, I remembered now with a wince. The volume's saffron vellum cover coated with dust, I recalled noting, as I'd slipped the book into my pack under his insistent gaze, waiting *like a coward* until I'd left the ranch's sprawl around the road's first full curve to throw the useless tome into a ditch. I shouldn't have done that, I conceded to myself, as I scanned the darkness to either side of the disappearing path, hoping to reach the interior before dawn. Even a limerick is better than nothing.

—With golden wings, I'd added just before setting off, as I stuffed the last bit of goat jerky into the pack, my father standing just behind my wife. —A black unicorn with golden wings.

—So a Pegasus, then, she'd said.

I didn't know what to call the creature I sought other than a black unicorn with gold mane, tail, hooves, and wings (and, in truth, I had only just decided to incorporate the wings—now it was too late to take them back—though I didn't necessarily regret their addition). No one had ever seen it except for me—and I, only in my dubious visions or dreams—so perhaps it had no name. Beyond "the black unicorn," which designation I'd stubbornly repeated—with unnecessary sullenness, I now saw all too clearly.

—Well, but what you're describing sounds just like a Pegasus.

Not uncommonly, however, the solar bear—particularly males of the species—will at once meet both dietary needs by quaffing sunhoney mead, brewed by stirring paw-kneaded lightsap ferment into vats of raw sunlight. Resulting crapulent sprees may stretch on through sunshine and darkness—traveler beware!

—The eyes will be emeralds, I'd declared—madly, I thought to myself, as an unearthly howl clove the indeterminate dark. She'd never tried to convince me to stay; I had steeled myself for theatrical weeping, desperate cries of —God, don't leave me! Not this placid nitpicking of my vision.

—Don't you know I'll probably die? or at least go mad? I could have shouted. I wished now that I had—though of course it was far too late for wishes. Instead I'd only described in further detail the sparkling silver striations of the beast's emerald eyes while she fixed the collar of my cloak, the cloak that even now was affording me laughably little protection from the Underwood's unholy gusts.

Of course I would have preferred to don the forest shroud, I thought to myself, startling at what was probably only the snap of a twig. But she'd *sold* the forest shroud. Along with a garden hose, some wicker chairs, beer steins, binoculars, most of my lepidopteristic texts, as well as several specimens I'd collected at university—all pawned away during that bleak late-autumn, as we scrambled for means, my vision of our shared life disintegrating. And was it strictly my fault that while her beauty virtually guaranteed her an easy succession of office-clerk appointments in that middling university town, I couldn't find work after Claudstein abandoned me? That for a season, yes, I took solace in the cup, before we'd at last conceded failure, returned to my father's ranch: in shame, certainly, I thought to myself, as another chill blast penetrated my cloak. My father had urged me to learn a trade, at the very least, if I refused to have anything to do with his goats, if I was hellbent on handing over my inheritance to the university in exchange for a useless, indulgent degree. Will your moths put a roof over your head, Son? Will they buy you your bread? Why not mail *them* your next request for an interest-free loan?

—You've never tasted beauty, Dad, *and you never will*, I should have shouted, I realized now—instead of choking this rebuttal back until I'd reached the sanctuary of my garret, where I spent the remainder of that winter interregnum muttering bitter variations on the sentiment, rereading favorite works of lepidopteristic theory, including, naturally, Claudstein's epic, The World as Wings and Representation (which I'd of course already scoured several times).

And before our return, she'd never even seen a goat, had she, I thought. Hadn't she laughed at the stories I'd told of my father and his ridiculous retirement, his faux-idyll, his belated embrace of pacific tendencies? She'd said the very least I owed the man—by whose alleged goodwill, whose extravagant grace in taking us in, welcoming me back (in shame) I'd been made violently sick—was to tend and keep his flock as he advanced through his middle age. Middle age? I'd scoffed. Middle age implies a decline, an ensuing downward arc, an end: that man will never die, I'd said.

I watched her learn the work, watched her apparently learn to enjoy it, laughing and whooping as she chased the mindless creatures down the mountain, riding Sheryl, our pony, flanked by the exuberant dogs, the goats' flight an ensemble of hideous bleat. I still see her smiling up at my father, her skin a luminous bronze in the fading light. Of course the labor fulfills her, I'd thought many times, I recalled now, tugging at the loose flesh beneath my chin (a near-unconscious tic accompanying serious thought): she hadn't learned over a lifetime to loathe it and fear its inevitability. She'd never known desperation, had she? Never wanted more. What did she want? Nothing! Nothing but what joy or contentment could be found in each insipid day: the rush of a crisp westerly wind, the satisfaction of a newly mastered task, freshly churned goat-butter on her tongue. *Why can't you just be happy*, she'd often ask, offering me a languid smile, while the goats grazed vapidly out over the receding pastures. Perhaps she would understand what I had always been waiting for when she saw my return—like a late-anointed king, high overhead, astride the black unicorn, I'd stupidly hoped, I reflected now, smiling, bitter and sad. Owls or some other nocturnal birds hooted nearby. She wouldn't be watching the skies for me.

Three days ago, under that late-morning sun, I strode down the walk from my father's estate, my carriage erect and assured—but even then, I remembered now (peering up at what stars could be seen through the Underwood's reticulate canopy of branches and leaves), I'd been plagued by certain questions and doubts.

For instance: how would I find a black unicorn with golden hooves, a tail like sprayed fire, horn a glinting spear, eyes like emeralds, seraphic wings, when I couldn't be sure such an animal existed? Did such an animal exist? Why should it? Where had I first got the idea? From a picturebook? A nursery rhyme? A dream? Evenings I would sit on the rounded wooden beam of the ranch's vast pennery, staring up at my father, his staff raised high above his head, arm an unwavering rod, as if to scorn the winds shrieking down the slopes of Mount Boom, whipping up his great musky cloaks, a cavalcade of goats rushing past to fill the lush feeding fields—the entire tableau filling me with nausea and despair. Imbuing me with a bottomless dread so absolute that I would leave behind my only golden one (will I see her again?), the only woman who has loved me, the only woman I will ever love... here in the Underwood, utterly lost, chasing a conjured beast, a dumb salmagundi of some slow child's dreams.... I was a fool! Should I have heeded my father? Learned ministration to the goats? Settled down on his capacious ranch? Would she have been happy? Was this all she had wanted?

I will never find the black unicorn, I thought. There is no black unicorn. If there is a black unicorn, it isn't for me to find—but most likely there is no black unicorn. I will die in the Underwood, alone and without hope. Exhaust my supply of goat jerky, fall from the treacherous path, plummet into the heart of whatever strange phenomenon casts its mirage of nacreous sky underfoot, I thought. I'll be eaten by a solar bear.

Why carry on through this lugubrious gloom? For a vision? But what a vision! I see her on the slatted porch—her long blond hair aflutter in goat-scented breeze, she gazes skyward, wistful, forlorn, searching a cloud-obscured horizon... and then: an iridescent speck, glinting high against a cobalt sky, slowly swelling, at last assuming half-familiar form: yes, me—atop the fabulous steed, borne back on heaven's roads, the beast's wings refulgent, a glorious blaze of sable and gold, we swoop down from above, skim the vast pastures that feed and fence in all the goats of my father... and I return, in triumph.... But supposing I were to turn around. Would she take me back without the black unicorn? (Certainly my father would, with a vindicated grin.) If I found the black unicorn, would I let her have it? What if I wanted to keep the black unicorn. What if I wanted to fly right past my father's ranch—Westward a young man must always go—

—Why won't you just lie down and die? I shouted, wildly addressing the walls of dark foliage, looking for I wasn't sure what. (A witness?)

As a boy I would lay my head in my mother's lap, and she'd sing to me in a doleful minor key a lullaby about the end of all things—

Nothing is coming, she'd quietly sing, Nothing is coming to bear us away... Nothing is coming to carry us home....

Goodnight, sweet prince, she'd whisper as I drifted off to sleep——

Bats!

Mindlessly, as if acting out another fool's vision of lonely valor I withdrew my father's sword, and with it began to carve clumsy arcs through the fluttering night. My antagonists' eyes glowed like droplets of blood, casting their rustling forms in faint, unreliable light. Their screeches were the wails of the dead. They came in twos and threes, flapping like wet cloaks given unholy life, swirling round me like a clotted wind, avoiding my axlike heaves of the paternal blade—because I was *never any good with the sword.*

Few in this far-flung region now recall, but my father did not always herd goats. In the days before Elsinore Ranch no man but a fool would dare challenge him to a duel. My father, now a quaint provincial authority on the upbringing of goats, distributor of the district's best milk, renowned healer of farm animals, a presence quietly venerated for his patience and hard work. Once master of death. A man not to be trifled with. A legendary consumer of rum. The quondam Pirate King. With eyes like hellfires and a rage without likeness. Lord of the Night. Scourge of the Eastern Provinces. The Power and the Glory. The Thunder and the Rain. Hamnlet the Blade. In the end, retired to dismal distant mountains, to raise his herds (and me) in peace.

He was too kind to me, I thought, as the borrowed sword seemed to swing me, instead of the other way around. Too easy. He thought he was sparing me something. Saving me from something he'd taken on, so that I would never have to suffer—but all he did was leave me unprepared: Unprepared for the battle. Unprepared to fight for life. Unprepared for unexpected combat, with bats, in the deep darkness of a mysterious forest, on a vapid quest now for the moment all but forgotten as I struggled to survive, frantically fought off the rodential scourge as well as I could, which was not so well at all. (Aware all the while that these were only bats; what would happen when the bears came? Let alone the thunder wraiths?) He left me unprepared, the old bastard, for anything but goats, I thought, crouching low as the bats left suddenly of their own accord, for now, a sob welling in my throat.

At the university I was a man of science, a thinker, an unassailable intellect, lepidopteristic savant, the land's most promising moth scholar, collector of incomparable samples, intuitor of hidden migratory trends, the discipline's rising scholarly star—I was respected—revered—for my considerable (but theretofore unacknowledged) cognitive gifts. And Professor Claudstein was *like a father* to me, dispensed unto me alone all the wisdom acquired over decades of tireless labor in the service of our shared passion:

At sixty-seven he could still be found, afternoons, careering down emerald hillsides, slicing his custom net through perfected patterns of ensnarement, a hale physical specimen in spite of his advancing years, and in spite of the decades of nightly lucubration well into the lightening pre-dawn. I trusted Professor Claudstein. I was his chosen favorite, his only true pupil, he was meant to mentor only me—Claudstein, *why have you forsaken me*, I thought to myself, the whole of Underwood Forest seeming to deflate and collapse around me, quivering like a pinned specimen at its hub.

Of course, I might not have been the student he'd said I was. He might have been deceived, gradually disillusioned with my ability. I might have shown more promise than I could keep. Or perhaps he'd never harbored such illusions: was it I who'd been deceived—duped into grandiose notions of my own worth, deluded by my beloved Professor C, who had never really reciprocated my veneration—or love—but had merely allowed me to believe what I would? Because he was *too kind to give me the truth?* Had he, too, meant to "spare" me—only to leave me ten times as vulnerable to the inevitable apprehension of my limits, the folly, the sorrow of weakness, under which I would eventually be crushed? No! Claudstein never would have hurt me! I would have died for that man. Given over my choicest specimens, all (excluding, perhaps, my cherished Crimson Luna). Ceded almost all glory to him. Served him to the end, asking in return only that on the day I finally deserved it, he might put his hand on my shoulder and say,

—Well done, my boy: well done indeed.

In those halcyon days I foresaw a scholarly dynasty: I would follow in the master's footsteps, as he made his inexorable ascent, attained heights of unimaginable achievement. I foresaw brilliant new species, with wings like spun gold or shattered gems, sparkling as they fluttered through the weak light in recessed pockets of the earth. Our names ornately embossed on the pages of all the best butterfly-and-moth periodicals. Fanfare. Symposia. Fortune. Fame... Claudstein!

Of course I ought to be grateful for the time I'd been given; Claudstein was only a man; to expect more of him was to invite pain. Pure misery to indulge those foolish visions of Professor Claudstein and I carousing from tavern to tavern, deferred to wherever we went. On the porch of his on-campus manse—endowed by a wealthy baroness—where we'd smoke tobacco-wheat pipes, seated on stools he'd hand-carved (and that I'd helped to varnish in mahogany and inscribe with letters of bronze, silver and gold)... later, with lyres on our laps, improvising melodic loops for hours on end, caught in an endlessly metamorphosing scheme, twin intrepid sensibilities loosed to gallop off on harmonic expeditions into the unknown—where all true endeavor must lead, as he'd so often (rightly) insisted. We might have visited his favorite brothels together. Breathed the fumes of boiled gem-pine sap. Watched the prismatic sunsets of his private butterfly collection's wall morph in hallucinogenic light. He would have proudly witnessed my own nocturnal collection multiply in lunar grandeur....

On the Underwood path I sat with my legs folded, knees to my chin. As a boy, I reflected, I was useless with the bow and arrow.

—Pop, I'd say, —why can't I hit the bull's-eye? No matter how hard I try?

—Son, he'd respond, a twinkle in his own graying eye as he looked fondly out over my shoulder at his massed goatherd, all that marshaled fleece casting a faint silvery sheen up into the dusk, —you come close enough.

But he never emphasized that I might develop my technique; never suggested that I might strengthen my feeble arms; never pointed out that I failed to sand or polish the shafts of my arrows, as all the other boys my age did, that I heedlessly left them lying around the cottage while I, too, lay around, *like a vegetable* staring stupidly into the radiant flames as they danced on the hearth, even during daylight, while there was work yet to be done. I had always been a slothful, fat, pathetic child, I could admit it now. The village boys had been right to call me "Goat's milk," I'd deserved that, and the beatings, and each of the schoolmaster's lovely daughters' scorn, and everything else (he never *told* me I should be better), I understood now, and would continue to deserve it, I'd never made a promise I could keep, I saw now, feeling weak with self-knowledge, as the fatigue began to settle into my bones, into my heart, I could never go back without the black unicorn. My father would expect me back soon—without the black unicorn, with nothing but further failure and shame, which he would unquestionably *forgive*. I could never go back.

The forest seemed to shudder or heave, and I collapsed on the rutted path and sobbed for some time. My father's sword lay beside me, blade unblemished with bat (I hadn't actually so much as grazed a single one). I could take it, thrust it through my heart, could I not? The bats would eventually be back. Perhaps this time with a clearer sense of purpose. And if not the bats, then the solar bears, assuming there were solar bears. And if the solars, too, were mere fantasy, then I would starve to death. Or die of thirst (my goat-hide canteen already having grown disconcertingly light). I couldn't leave the forest without the black unicorn, and the black unicorn (it was time to face it, someone ought to) did not exist. I was going to die in the forest.

Sooner or later, I was going to die, I thought to myself, pausing for a moment, to let the truth settle, before continuing to sob. I could lie here and wait for the bears or whichever other forest element would eventually be my doom... wait for death to take me, as death surely would.... Or I could take up my father's sword, raise it high—and with a shout thrust it home, through my ribcage, into my idiot heart. Or I could chop open my throat. Detach my own head, if I was strong enough to do so (probably not). Slice open my wrists, if I wanted it to be easy... or plunge the saber deep into my stomach, carve through the bowels, twisting the blade within viscera, as I'd heard was the fashion among despondents in the East.

—Death will take care of me soon enough; why should I wait for it, I wondered aloud, staggering to my feet now, though still hiccupping and sniffling, my eyes not at all dry. What an amusing malapropism "can't hack it" (as the village children were wont to say of a weak boy who could not keep pace with what was daily expected of him), might prove to be if I were to retrieve my father's sword from the dust where it lay, glinting a bit in what was presumably moonlight, though I certainly couldn't see the moon, and hack myself to death, I thought, laughing aloud. —Who decided, I soliloquized, —that it is more noble to go on fighting, to go on struggling against an ocean of woes, to take ridiculous arms against them all, when you might with your father's bare saber or bodkin (I'd brought with me both, though the bodkin was near-uselessly blunt)—reject the fate you've been given? ... —I could do it right now, I affirmed, nipping in the bud my loquacious propensities (no doubt a lingering academic affectation, I supposed, pausing once more to curse my beloved Professor C.).

I could end it——

Only what if the sword were not the end? What if I were to wake from one nightmare to find something worse? Did I dare really believe this folly was a nightmare? (Hadn't I heard tales of *real* terror? Hadn't my own father looked into the red depths of *real* nightmare, pausing for a triumphant moment to peer down into ocular wells he'd uncapped with a flourish of the legendary blade I now uselessly bore at my side, the bodies that were not yet corpses of enemies left screaming, writhing, blinded in his booted wake—his, as it were, *signature* he'd once sickeningly revealed to me late one evening toward the close of the only prolonged discussion of his infamous past we'd ever had.) Perhaps it only seemed such to me now, at the height of my weakness, or the nadir of my "strength." Did I dare? Would I ever dare?

I lay back and considered: Perhaps I simply hadn't penetrated into the forest far enough. Perhaps I ought to rest a while. Perhaps a solar would come to kill me in the morning, I thought, my spirits now beginning to lift a little, as I sheathed my father's sword in its leather scabbard and laid it down by my side (noting the twenty-three tabulatory skulls notched into the grain). No need to act, but merely carry on. Whatever would be, it would be.

For some time I lay, quiet, on the forest floor, perhaps even briefly nodding off. When at last I stood up and resumed my clumsy progress farther into the aphotic Wood, I felt entranced by a clarity that was almost hypnotic in its focus. Deeper into the darkness: where death or the black unicorn lay in wait.

Near dawn I came across a silver piano with keys of emerald and glistening jet. On a small throne or dais sat a knight whose armor was like wax, a corrugation of rippled gold, burnished and gleaming with hints of rose in the day's first light, fit to the contours of his body as if it had been poured molten over him and allowed to cool, hardening as a gleaming cascade. Beside him, upright, was a great flaxen bear.

The piano stood beneath a stately cocaine tree, from the trunk of which corkscrewed a segment of tubing with its terminus in a hole punched through the rear of the knight's helmet. This cannula must have been of some clear, rubberlike material, as it seemed to pulse or throb with the flow of the gem-pine's viscous white sap.

I stood still, until the knight, as if himself keyed into motion, with his gauntleted fingers decrypted from those emerald keys a circling melody, simple, pure and sweet, and yet intricately glazed with such spectral flourishes that the enchantment, I imagined, standing rapt, transfixed, must entrance, not only me, but eternity—bearing hearer and creator aloft, away from witness or memory... and I saw myself in my own suit of gold, my fingers lifting the emerald tones, braiding the sweetness in an everlasting round, endlessly augmented, twisted, fluted, finessed, a kaleidoscope of fragile harmony bursting, relentless, like a lattice of sparks in the night.

And I thought I could see, poured through the motion of my fingers over the glittering keys, my own soul made bright, given chiming form, in the music permeating the depths of those haunted woods.... And it seemed that the knight played for neither me nor himself (nor the pale sentinel bear), nor for anyone, I understood, but he continued to play, and meanwhile I was under his spell so that I came to suspect he had been there forever, or a very long time, and likewise would remain... and here was a place I, too, could stay, I felt, for a moment undiluted by words—my breath caught, I disappeared for an instant, vanished like the silence in this sudden startling gap in the forest, I was swallowed by the interlude, and dissolved into the knight's honey-fueled song that was itself like a kind of honey, suffused with some pale amber glow, pulsing like the white sap that seemed to be its furious source…. Could it be that the rush pumping into that knight of gold was passing through him unabated—but transfigured, entering the dusky bower's air as radiance, as a shimmering, mystic transubstantiation of sound? A miracle song on which the hungry might feed, from which the thirsty might sip, under the canopy of which the beleaguered chaser of a black unicorn might lie down to rest… an aural vision passing through this strange figure, so that he was not the light, but an echo of the light, as it shone through the endlessly uncoiling variations that were his and were not. He was a conduit of the forest's light… and the thought stirred in me: Could I be a conduit too? Deeper into the forest: might I find my own piano? A different instrument? An enchanted lyre? Would the song take a different form, just as this knight's liquid light seemed transposed to song? Would my own light or song take its own, separate shape—for instance, that of a black unicorn? But what about the black unicorn? Would the black unicorn even *be* a black unicorn? Might it come as something else? As a lightpost? As a moth? As an echo (of an echo)? As a cloak? A piano? As layered whispers on a chill breeze at dawn? Had I *already found* the black unicorn? Who could tell me? Whom could I ask? Claudstein! Father! (I saw her standing on the porch at dusk, waiting, arms across her chest—but with shining emerald eyes upcast, as a mountain breeze wisped golden hair.) I walked on.

ボブ
(Bob)

—

あ

By the time the two ALT-bearing taxis coast to a halt alongside the Kyoshokuin Jutaku and disgorge their weary passengers, Bob's already been out in the lot for a while, pacing, serially dispatching Marlboro Golds, shirtless in the late-summer sweat, thoughtfully palming the amiable bulge of his bare paunch, waiting to welcome everyone aboard. Greetings! says Bob, I'm Bob. Bob's been in-country a solid year now, Bob explains, and while he wouldn't go so far as to class himself an "expert" on the myriad socio-cultural vagaries his new jutaku-mates can expect to face on a pretty much daily basis now that they've committed to a year of Assistant Language Teaching here in the Land of the Ascendant You-Know-What, and while Bob'd be the very first one to concede that there are all manner of nuances and subtleties he hasn't quite got figured out yet, and that, sure, even after a whole year of residence among these odd but usually good-natured people, he'll almost every day be faced with certain quantities of honestly small-potato inconvenience and frustration that nonetheless often suffice to induce deep discouragement or even fits of rage, he's certainly qualified and frankly excited about the opportunity to help out with whatever aspects of settling in and getting themselves totally acclimated to and comfortable with their new home country away from native home countries anybody might find daunting or stressful during this critical and potentially stressfully daunting—but exciting—first phase of their expatriate lives.

Bob ventures a guess based on his own experience with the odious sequence of virtually identical New Assistant Language Teacher Orientations and Pedagogical Seminars and Culture Shock Colloquia that they subject every incomer to for a character-trying weekend of tedium up there in Tokyo, which he likens their mandated presence at to what being rolled flat by the foremost vehicle in some kind of military procession moving at victory-parade speed and then inched over repeatedly by each subsequent HUMVEE, Bradley, M1 Abrams Battle Tank, Striker and so forth while somehow managing to stay not only alive but excruciatingly conscious as one after another of the autocade's vehicles' treads and IED-resistant tires ground you into the asphalt or tar'd probably be like, that he'll just bet they're feeling some uncanny combination of over-saturated with info on some topics—for instance the harrowingly complex-seeming instructions for sorting household waste and recyclables into the appropriately hued transparent industrial-grade-plastic bags that can be purchased on the cheap at just about any establishment hawking domestic wares (or, as the Japanese prefer to say, "goods"), which Bob swears on his *keitai* does not require the strenuous cerebration the Tokyo clowns make it sound like it will once you've got the system down, plus the occasional honest goof won't land you in the local pen or anything—but also simultaneously scared shitless about certain ground-level facts, like:

What'll my first day on the job be like? Will they ask me to perform some kind of self-introductory speech? If so, will I have to deliver this speech in front of the entire student body, segregated columns (girls in back, some with their little doughy legs tucked up uncomfortably beneath skirts in the so-called *seiza* seating posture—don't even get Bob going on the treatment of women here unless you're in the mood for moral outrage) arrayed in docile rank and file on the school auditorium's well-preserved parquet, some of the less inhibited san-nensei (—"third-year students," seniors here in *Nihon*'s final stage of secondary school) girls blowing clandestine kisses in a gesture you definitely should not interpret as anything more than just casual coquetry, no matter how foxy the series of blinks or salacious the moue? If so, they're not going to ask me to do the thing in Japanese are they? Even if I don't actually speak word one? Is it going to be this fucking hot all summer? Will the kids make fun of me for how much I sweat? Can I furthermore expect the faculty to welcome me with a standing ovation when I first step into the teachers' lounge, then stare at me with faces waxed in fascinated grins until I say something, which: what the fuck am I supposed to say? Given the obscene heat and humidity is it really necessary to wear a suit each day? Even when you don't foresee having to dispatch any official pedagogical duties, in other words when you've got zero in the way of classes scheduled and nobody's asked you to do anything or even so much as looked you in the eye, although you know they're watching, and you're basically just cruising Net, trying not to get caught perusing sites stocked with questionable content, generating hot springs of aromatic sweat? (Yes, except in regards to the attire: nice slacks, a shirt and tie are fine for guys, though Bob himself is into blazers; ladies: no strict guidelines but you probably don't want to show too much skin)... and so forth, no doubt you've each got your own personal concerns—but this is where Bob comes in. He sees his role as that of a field guide or liaison.

A seasoned vet. Ready to help out at the drop of a ten-yen coin, or hat. Anything you can think of, anything whatsoever. Fire away. Shoot. *Keitai* is what they call their cellphones, fyi. Don't ask Bob why.

The new language instructors retrieve their luggage and sundry travel effects one parcel at a time but with haste, thanks to the courteous industry of their cab-driver–porters, who bow when the task is completed and resume their starboard positions behind respective wheels untipped— tipping a Japanese service employee would basically be like dropping your pants and loosing a steamer on something highly important to him, for instance in this case his vehicle's dashboard or hood—circle the cramped lot before heading back to the streets of Futsukaichi. Which repatriation squared away, the five have their first chance to get a good look at and assess their new digs, and the common feature of these separate appraisals is that the Murasaki Kyoshokuin Jutaku have pretty obviously seen better days. One's initial impression is that these days were probably a number of decades back, their heyday perhaps even predating the War in which either "we" or "the Yanks" kicked this country's ass, depending on which ALT you ask, though, take it from Bob, this isn't something you want to bring up with Natives over drinks. Veranda railings sclerotic with rust; stucco flattened out by weather and time or visibly crumbling away; sliding screen doors that your thinking jutaku resident will not be relying on as any kind of reliable front line against the *gokiburi* ("cockroach") legions' annual summertime offensive, though at this point Bob elects not to address himself to the matter of the bugs; even the scattered satellite dishes look like shit, weather-soiled and dangling superfluous cords. Jutaku means basically "government employee subsidized housing," Bob inserts, and while these particular projects might lack somewhat for aesthetic charm, everybody would do well to bear in mind how much worse he or she could do in the States—or, Bob presumes, the UK's conurbations or whatever the hell you call them in Australia, assuming anyone here's from Down Under, if so, the kids'll really dig your vocal tics—for what works out to roughly two hundred American bucks a month, when you convert from the yen.

Bob figures aloud that now's probably the time his new neighbors will want to shuffle on off to their respective quarters, unpack, settle in a bit, scope out the new living conditions—don't let your first impression discourage you: "run-down" and "squalid" are two different things, and history's replete with case studies of down-at-the-heel or even brutally persecuted groups of people in places like internment camps and ghettos making the best of living conditions much worse than this, after all, the mind is its own cosmos and can make a Heaven of Hell, although vice-versa, too, no question—maybe take a quick nap, but don't clock out for the night!, as Bob's sure he doesn't have to remind everybody what a poor jet-lag-coping stratagem this would be, but before everyone can disperse to go do his or her own private thing lets it be known that as veteran jutaku foreign resident, he's made it a personal goal to take them all under his wing and act as a kind of senpai a la Pat Morita of Karate Kid film-franchise renown, God bless the departed, for as long as they feel like they might benefit from a little mentorship and guidance through their first experience with expatriate life, which, by the way, show of hands, for how many of you will this be your first experience living abroad? Believe it or not, Bob had never set foot on foreign soil before deplaning in Narita at around this time last year, but he's acquired an incredible quantity of data ranging from the quotidian practical such as pertaining to the before-mentioned system of waste-collection and -disposal all the way up to wide-ranging if still sort of nascent anthropological theories about The Japanese, though Bob would be the last person to describe himself as an intellectual powerhouse or anything like that: Most of what Bob's picked up—both locally here over the course of his ongoing international experience in Japan, and more broadly, as a man—has come through trial and error, more of the second category than Bob likes to admit, Bob is ruefully willing to admit, with what's quickly been established as the signature Bob laugh, a vocal emission that sounds less like ordinary human laughter than someone serially shouting the word "Ha," but maybe if anything this is the single one thing that in Bob's view is probably the most critical to bear in mind during the first tumultuous months when daily life may well be frightening and otherworldly and sometimes even liable to trigger fits of rage, but Bob does truly also believe and hope, fun: you're going to make mistakes, if you're like Bob you might even make a few *really bad* mistakes, and, sure, there will probably be times when you latch the *jutaku* door and switch off the lights and sit down on the edge of your bed with a bottle of gin and stare motionless into the terrible void, but the important thing is that everybody's got each other now, which is how they should stick, i.e., together, no one can beat loneliness alone, and Bob is definitely here to help everybody out, in whatever way he can.

By the way: Bob bets nobody's made dinner plans yet, right? Who's up for yaki-tori? It's basically just sticks of grilled meat, but you can choose from all kinds of other options, too, if you're working from a restricted dietary palette for whatever reason, be it medical or ideological or just some other personal circumstances you'd rather not disclose, or if you're the type of person who after a whole lot of travel just doesn't....

い

Inside the *yaki-tori* place it's raucous and smoky and full of Japanese. To a woman and man these patrons enjoy a long stare at the troupe of *gaikokujin* as they follow Bob into the vaporous gloom, and the interesting thing about this collective assessment is that it's virtually impossible to decode. Are these local *Nihonjin*, for example, *impressed* by this spectacular incursion on their Friday evening of beer and succulent meat? Are they *excited* by the prospect of cross-cultural exchange? Do they *welcome* the newcomers' presence in their otherwise uneventful town? Or is it more like *they're afraid for their lives*? Could it even be that they *hate* these non-nationals who speak with gusto and at high volume in their abrasively nasal foreign tongue and almost without exception smell unbathed? Perhaps some are still bitter about the lost War. Who knows? The starers are vacant-eyed and neither smile nor scowl, though it's safe to say that no one looks unequivocally thrilled. Meanwhile the meat-grilling proprietors or employees—it's not immediately discernible which—of this establishment greet the new guests with a chorus of something that sounds a little bit like "Here the shy must stay!" and also take a quick break from their food-preparation at various stations to indulge their own long stare. Bob appears to be on friendly terms with these energetic young men, who are on the whole pretty vigorously enthusiastic about their work back there behind the counter, keeping alive a perpetual call-and-response of high-volume reiterations of guest food-or-drink requests and synchronized *Ey!*s of assent, and at least seem to be in high-enough spirits despite being so absorbed in the concentration-intensive work of pan-frying to perfection salted skewers of meat. *Irasshaimase* means "Welcome honored patrons," basically, Bob hollers back to the group, as he waddles up to the counter to engage in some friendly banter that he either declines or neglects to translate.

Fortunately at least one new ALT happens to have brought to Japan a respectable academic background in the Japanese tongue—it transpires he co-piloted the campus Japanese Language Quarterly, as a mere undergrad at a moderately well-regarded East Coast university whose name he's already worked into conversation close to a dozen times—and when Bob is preoccupied at the bar in the midst of an especially impressive-sounding *Nihongo* disquisition on some unspecified topic, this small, unwell-looking guy whose unconvincing gesture toward the sub-bottom-lip vibrissae vernacularly referred to in some quarters of the U.S. as a "soul patch" does little to countermand the unsettlingly detectable psychic emanations of either a virgin in his mid-twenties or a young man whose successes haven't come in savory circumstance, and who has introduced himself as "Jake," appears to sense an opportunity and inserts that, as far as he is able to tell (which, even taking the inevitable travel-wear into account, is frankly more than enough), Bob, while enthusiastic, and high-volumed, and generally genial-seeming on this everybody's first night in their new international digs, is not producing what any neutral-but-acquainted-with-*Nihongo* observer would describe, even in a charitable mood, as particularly accurate Japanese. In fact, it's borderline impossible to tell what the fuck he's talking about, notwithstanding his amiable interlocutors' agreeable miens. And here Jake quickly, perhaps as a kind of credential-establishing gambit, translates a sample snippet of *Nihongo* from one of their hosts, as he regales this apparently regular gaijin patron with conversation, and then notes the really egregious lack of any kind of germaneness to their new cultural ambassador's reply, which is not only grammatically unparsable, as a speech utterance, but is in fact semantically unrelated to the sentence to which it's presumably intended to constitute a valid response.

While a quick survey conducted by the revenants or wraiths observing this as-yet-difficult-to-perceive-the-wraith-relevant-significance-of episode of cultural relocation gauging group opinion on Bob and Jake at this early stage would undoubtedly indicate a measure of gratitude for their garrulous senpai's hospitality, as well as a vague but rapidly increasing distaste for Jake (whose revelation strikes everybody as pedantic and basically kind of mean), it's hard not to note, upon closer observation, that the smiling Japanese guys actually don't appear to have any idea what the fuck Bob is trying to say. Mostly they just laugh and attend to the sizzling gristle and brawn. The interesting question raised hereby being perhaps whether or not Bob *knows* that's he's not participating in a successful cultural exchange.

Smoke-greasy slices of pork, each bite an unhealthy dose of *Na*. Beef-and-onion kebabs. Fried *mochi* that's gooey but good. Whole fish whose eyes Bob says you can go ahead and eat. Mushrooms, which are a little different in Japan. All on thin wooden sticks you stick in a convenient cup after you've stripped them of sustenance. These jovial Japanese meat-slingers turn out to be no joke: Alyssa, the retired ballerina, is already predicting calamitous weight-gain over the course of her stint here, if all the food is this good, which Bob assures her it is. Jake mumbles something obsequious and creepy about her figure being in no danger of something or other that makes everyone uncomfortable. At a table in the place's right rear deep pocket a cluster of sleek-suited salarymen with facial pigmentation traversing a spectrum from pinkish through scarlet and mauve to in one disturbing case what looks almost like aquamarine have spontaneously risen and linked arms and begun to sing, kicking up their legs in synchrony as a kind of unappealing chorus line—they do that, notes Bob—and at the far end of the counter, in front of the skewered raw beef chunks and intestine of pig, are two young Japanese girls in what the group will soon come to recognize as the ubiquitous high school uniforms: the white blouses, the navy-brown checked skirts hiked up to reveal rather generous expanses of thigh above dark socks stretched to mid-calf, and these two have been enjoying themselves mostly without ostentation, engaged in a little light flirtation with their patrons that's probably a bit sketchy in view of the discrepancy in age, but never gets especially out of hand, picking at the offerings dished up before them, emitting the occasional spirited fit of high-register mirth; and now, having quenched their apparently modest appetites for meat, examined their faces in their *ketai* cameras' reversed displays, brushed up their false eyelashes, gathered their handbags and tugged up their skirts another cm or so, all set to settle the bill, have passed, on their way to the register, just by the alien-resident table. And given *Dylan* an extremely favorable once-over.

Of course, just about any wager-inclined wraith looking in on this evening's first Futsukaichi outing might have put money down on tall, cinematic Dyl taking an eventual pass at Alyssa, given the way he'd positioned himself to the rear at roughly 0730 with respect to the former dancer on the twenty-minute amble over here earlier on, from this advantageous perspective conducting a survey, almost academic in its detail-attention, of the long, toned ballet-molded twin-offerings of the former dancer's gams. Then, too, given the way he doesn't say much but when he does speak—as for instance in response to a long-term-hopes-and-aspirations question posed during one brief round of Bob-less banter, in his faintly Appalachian twang, simply: Figure I'll get into film—Jake's not the only one to get the sense that this is a young man who does not particularly wrestle with the quintessentially Jakeian problem of getting girls to bed. So this duo of underaged native flirts had apparently also picked up these effortless amorous bandwidths, as young women will, and the slightly naughtier-seeming of the two had caught his eye and slyly batted the artificially enhanced lash: a wink.

In itself no big deal. But what no one at the table but Bob happened to spot was that Dylan returned a subtle wink of his own, truly devastating in its impact on the J-girls, whose exeunt devolved into stumbling giggles and several looks back at the foreign table where Dylan was cool behind his pint, the bolder one proposing an entirely inappropriate group activity in youth-inflected Japanese that's fortunately too demotic to be parsed by any of the *jutaku* contingent but its wraiths, though Bob has witnessed the whole mini-cultural exchange and can pretty much guess they weren't inviting him out for parfaits, and thus perceives a valuable teaching opportunity:

One of the more challenging aspects of the job, in Bob's view, is the constant moral vigilance required to resist the urge to maybe probe the dimensions or ramifications of the constant coy attentions you're bound to receive from *Nihonjin* jailbait in their revealing little tartan skirts and peppy blouses, with their blemish- and hairless skin (they shave pretty much every visible surface, including knuckles, Bob confirms) and their adorably chunky little legs, which if you're not tempted to peek up at the naughtier regions of from down at the base of the train-station stairs or to hope a little gust of heaven doesn't help you out with as they coast by on their goofy bikes, Bob proposes a dearth or possible complete absence of vital fluid in your valves, and, okay, no big deal, but you know it's really only a matter of steps from this kind of harmless flirtation and good-natured appreciation of what it's absolutely natural Bob believes for a red-blooded male to admire and enjoy into territory that Bob describes as morally perilous and legally vulnerable, I mean, this is a country in which it is possible to purchase high school ladies' panties from vending machines, and you'd better believe that's not the only item available for purchase if you're a savvy consumer with excess cash to burn and downtime to disperse. Bob prescribes forbearance: it's just honestly a potential rabbit-hole of bad news and unhealthy Lust and all of that Deadly's attendant self-loathing and guilt. A bad business you truly don't even want to get into and would be exceedingly well-advised to nip right in the bud, take it from your new buddy Bob, this advice obviously only applying to the male contingent of our new social set here tonight, though you females might want to think twice about letting one of these forty-something supposedly married male colleagues get you one-on-one, too.

Quick pause, here, followed by:

—What do you mean by "rabbit hole," exactly? (This is John: Asian-American, friendly, unattractive, and, somewhat embarrassingly, pretty much not on wraith-radar, until now.)

—Well, let's just say...

二

What was Bob's life like, before he caught his big break, viz., this plentifully remunerated gig abetting the Japanese Ministry of Education's perennially unsuccessful endeavor to equip the future members of its corporate workforce with a rudimentary comprehension level of that famously international language of global commerce? Before he was suiting up each morning—literally donning a slightly too close-fitting cream ensemble, the fabric of which was sort of permanently damp during the brutal summer months, which are thankfully not too far from finished, though he wishes he'd had his own Bob to step in last year and clue him in on how the suit was overkill—and facing the daily adventure of expatriate life in Japan? Not so bad! Bob hasn't had the chance to talk about it much, he tells Jake, whom he lucked out and bumped into on their separate return commutes from their respective high schools this still-hot late September PM, since last year he was the only *gaijin* abiding at the *jutaku*, you know, but he's certainly had the opportunity to give it some thought.

Granted, he confides to his new friend, just like any young American who hasn't found his vocational calling yet and thus still isn't embarked on a challenging but ultimately fulfilling professional career, he was probably drinking a bit too much, and certain of his colleagues at certain of his less-dynamically-stimulating places of employ had on occasion taken him aside and floated the possibility of some kind of diagnosis and/or drying-out treatment, just maybe giving it a try, if Bob were the sort of person to go in for psychiatric horseshit, but you can't let yourself dwell in negative things. Also granted, the situation was your typical dead-end, he continues, smiling down at Jake, who is openly assessing the trimly-attired OL heading up the hill on the other side of the street's derrière and bare thick legs (Bob's a leg man as well, always has been, which works out in this country of predominantly breastless chicks with ample lower halves—by the way: they actually do call the office ladies "OL"s, Bob points out) the specifics of which dismal situation are too boring and mundane to even bother going into, he apprises Jake, beyond it sufficing to say that he'd been twenty-seven, pushing twenty-eight, and a little worried that he might spend the rest of his life selling women's shoes.

The thing they don't tell you on the front end, when you're thinking about getting into women's footwear as a possible long-term career choice, is that it's not all getting to look at and sometimes, if you know what you're doing and can pass it off as just a routine part of the general customer-assistance shill, actually touch women's feet, though if you're a guy like Bob who's ever since the faintest stirrings of interest in the fairer sex just honestly had a thing for ladies' feet—the whole leg, to be sure, which by the way, are you seeing this across the street? "Mount me," am I right?—the calves, the thighs, give Bob a pair of smooth legs in plain-old cutoff denim over the most rococo concession to Fashion just about any day of the week, there's no question, but just between him and Jake, he's always had a particular, at times honestly almost painful fondness for women's feet. So you'd think that the associate sales clerk position's opening up just when Bob and Bob's manager at his previous place of employ, Pizza Pete's, had been unable to resolve a difference of opinion on certain quirks of Bob's pizza-delivery methodology, such as the occasional harmless beer or two enjoyed in private out back behind the dumpster between delivery runs, and then the sporadically flexible interpretation of start-times for certain shifts that were inefficiently scheduled to commence during the practically Guest-less interregnums well before his presence at the tiny take-out-and-delivery-only establishment would be more than a waste of Pete's resources and for Bob a tedious pain in the ass, so that Bob and this manager had conferred and put heads together and mutually determined that their perspectives were just too divergent to harmonize, and they'd amicably agreed to part ways, so that the foot-loving Bob wandering up to the sales desk in this department store's shoe department the very morning an unhappy twenty-year man had declared his intention to put the several-inch-long stiletto heel of the women's footwear article he brandished like an instrument of war through the eye of the recently-promoted-ahead-of-him new Head of Sales, a cocky kid whose MBA wasn't yet two years old, with what a fellow salesclerk named Randolph subsequently filled Bob in on was a truly maniacal look in his eyes and gone rampaging out into the front and chased this green manager around the cross-trainers' rack several times, upending boxes of white Nikes and Addidas with their feminine trim in pink and aquamarine, now swinging the stiletto more like a cudgel but still threatening to do the thing with the eye, until a platoon of security had vaulted several sandal displays to come to the young kid's aid—it had almost seemed like destiny, Bob reveals, stars arranging themselves auspiciously to provide Bob with this opportunity to earn a modest salary plus commission by spending his time around women's feet, only what they don't tell you up front is that it's not all pink toenails and hairless sweet-smelling skin, because they obviously want you to serve: what they never tell you is how lonely it can get, pacing the aisles, jockeying for sales-opportunities, balancing the purely commercial considerations of which gals look like they're actually liable to do more than try on a few pairs so that you can pull a decent commish vs. also obviously wanting to chat up a few young specimens with well-maintained feet; lonely because the intimacy you share with these customers for the fifteen-minutes or so during which you are the only man in the world with sole and exclusive access to these soft groomed pedicured *objets d'art* is strictly business and what strikes your typical womens' shoe salesmen at first as a stroke of almost radiantly good fortune almost without exception devolves very early on in the game into a kind of daily torture, as you'll never get closer to these women and their feet than you are during the brief interval of the pitch and transaction, and, Bob leans in to ask Jake sotto voce if he's ever even considered... but Bob's confidence is cut short here by the intrusion of a small commotion, a rather boisterous scene for *Nihon*:

Clustered on the sidewalk, obstructing Jake and Bob's homeward path is a parcel of teenaged boys, in baseball gear; presumably these are students from the sports-focused high school across the street. If these youth don't seem to realize that they're in the way, interfering with the regular traffic of pedestrian flow, it's because none of them is paying much attention to what's happening down here on the pavement. To a young man, they've got their heads craned way back and are hooting and shouting encouragement in the manner of a raucous cheering section at, say, a baseball game. And it transpires that they *are* spectators, for when the two obstructed *gaijin* in turn crane back their heads they too are able to descry the locus of this adolescent upheaval. Up around the building's fifteenth floor, a young man's bare torso is visible above the concrete parapet of his apartment unit's balcony. Most of his bottom half is unseen, the view interrupted by the low privacy wall, but what is available for spectation, protruding gamely through balustrades that form the balcony's stage-left border is the spindly erect shaft of his phallus, which he is attending to with a kind of grim two-handed wrath. Atta boy! bellows Bob, clapping Jake on the shoulder and shaking his head as they nudge through the baseball players, who for once when presented with foreigners are staring at something other than them, though a couple do glance away from the balcony to smirk up at Bob and down at Jake and greet them: *Ha-ro!*

三

あ

It's party time at the *kyoshokuin jutaku*! Welcome, everybody, a bit belatedly (it's already October) to Japan. ALTs from all over the prefecture have made the trek. The native neighbors are unhappy. These apartments might be shitholes, but they're fairly capacious, and they'll accommodate plenty of drunk. Also, there's a grass apron out front for barbecue and small-group performances of bygone

FM radio mainstays, American football-chucking, and general neighborhood-calm disturbance.

Bob is not at his best tonight. For one thing, there was the saké-festival a few hours ago, at which Bob drank a lot of saké. Then the interregnum during which Bob got to hang out with Alyssa in Alyssa's apartment and drink beer while Alyssa played vintage video footage from her balletic heyday, during what she calls her Continental Phase. Bob meanwhile thinking: a) Alyssa has really nice legs (and feet—although the unexplained ankle-bandages he's never seen them unmarred-by do diminish the allure); b) I just bet Dylan's already hitting this.

Also, c) the current pace of beer suggests one of two possible Bobcasts for the evening: 1) The Bob everybody likes to be around, or at least feels like everybody likes to be around him; or 2) The Bob who makes mistakes.

So the leg-assessment on the sly between comments on his time-encapsuled host's graceful execution and precise technique, which color-commentary her blow-by-blow explication of the action is fortunately breathless enough not to leave exposed for more than a second or two to substantive examination (Bob'd never actually seen a person dance ballet before today), was tinged with some foreboding. On the other hand, you can't slow down; nights like these, to slow down's suicide.

Nevertheless, this break in the pigskin action beneath the back balcony of Chez Fondu (John's reluctance to divulge his surname makes retrospective perfect sense, now that everybody's up to speed) is precisely the sort of circumstance in which teaching opportunities are bound to arise, and, since Alyssa's asking, in Bob's view, your best bet in terms of getting off on the right pedagogical foot would probably be to enter the classroom without any illusory expectations of success, because these are unrealistic and will only lead to your feeling crummy about yourself, as both an English-language instructor, and, as the failure continues and the discouragement piles on, as a man—or of course woman, as would be the case for present company.

But why not aim high? Give these novitiate English-learners as much as you can? Swing for the propaedeutic Green Monster out in right field—or is it left? The one in whichever MLB ballpark that's all but impossible to homer over, but's thereby extremely good for credence if you do, a mark of true power hitter bona fides? Make your timid students' progress toward fluency a kind of personal quest? Trust in your own competency and enthusiasm for the task?—Well, because English is just not something the Japanese can speak.

To be fair, Bob has encountered any number of English-speakers who can't form one solid sentence of Japanese, so it's not like Bob means anything derogatory or offensive about the collective mental capacity of their host country's citizenry—"host" being a word Bob would urge just about any foreigner to save right out in the open on the desktop of the old personal hard-drive, as he's found it almost invariably useful to recall that we're basically all here as guests—but the fact is, nobody here really speaks English at all. And why should they? They're Japanese! Sure, they've made it an official priority to acquire some proficiency with the so-called global tongue, but approximately three-fourths of the students you're supposed to be improving the "oral communication" skills of in class have no intention of ever leaving the country except for maybe as part of one of those huge gaikoku tour groups that come with guides and interpreters and get shuttled from one sightseeing trap to the next to hop out and take virtual reels of digital photos of themselves standing in front of whatever they've all shuffled off the bus together to gather around and admire and see, photographers counting off "*Hai*: one, two, *chee-zu!*" while young and old *Nihonjin* alike flash the nearly universal hand-glyph indicating "peace."

The abrupt resumption of gridiron competition trims the audience for Bob's discouragement down to two humans: Alyssa and some girl whose name Bob didn't get. Alyssa keeps looking up at her own *jutaku*, on the fourth floor. There's also a cat named Kaki skirting the action behind the cooler and an empty case of Asahi, waiting for these pungent bigcats to wander off so that she can spend some time in the box. Kaki's loved boxes since as long as she can remember, at least as far back as the other *jutaku*, the small one that had more bugs to play with and less sunlight to curl up in, where she remembers her bigcats were always using the loud voices with each other and the stupid voices with the infant, and she couldn't have been more than a kitten then. Loved being in boxes, specifically. Possibly the most poignant quality of kittenhood lost being how as a youngster Kaki'd been able to fit into just about any box. Sometimes she'd hop into one and scoot it off into a corner or behind some heap of the stuff there just wasn't enough space for in that eight-tatami domicile and curl up for hours while the cast of the female bigcat's plangent Kaki-chan!s steadily eddied up toward panic. Though the pleasure of the box runs deeper than its functional capacity as hideaway, Kaki reflects: there's something elemental, a nameless pull, some secret boxness that in indulgent moods Kaki has even fancied spiritual, a kind of divine encryption, Mystery.... The giant bigcat with the salmon face is at it once again, embarked on some elaborate pontification she'd probably only be able to parse the gist of, if she were interested in anything other than the box, Kaki's English being only so-so.

Bob clues these two in on one important cautionary point to bear in mind in case you're the type of ALT inclined to take the minimal and frankly laughable from a pedagogical vantage sum of instructional duties associated with the position as a transparent invite to swing for the recreational fences, most nights, and in particular if your recreational performance-enhancer of choice is some variation on fermented grain—which, as a foreigner in Japan, you're not looking at a buffet-table (or, as they say, *viking*) of readily obtainable choices, unless you're willing, as Bob is frankly this year 100% unwilling to risk, the very real contingency of time in Japanese incarceration, which is, Bob has personally heard second-hand, unimaginable, primitively indifferent to basic Western principles of just jurisprudential conduct or humane treatment of the detained (so that your typical apprehended suspect in, for instance, a case of alleged aggravated assault will agree to almost any degree of long-term financial gouging by way of settlement out of court in order to avoid a stay for any length of time; plus if they actually jail you you're out of a job, shit out of luck, out of the country forever, that's it)—though we're certainly gaining ground of late in the context of our various imperial-democratic adventures abroad, Ha! Ha!—somewhat analogous to being one of those eight-year-old kids in some Victorian sweatshop as depicted in practically any Dickens novel you want to pick up (*Bleak House* being the one

Bob recommends starting with), to suggest just one crest of the horror-story iceberg—so if you're going to play it relatively safe and stick with the legal poison, then be advised that it's kosher to drink regularly and with gusto, your colleagues will admire a certain degree of consumptive stamina, since nobody in this country can hold his fucking booze, Ha!, but one thing you definitely want to stay away from as far as you can is showing up for so-called "work" one morning, clad in your already-sweat-sopping shirt, tie, beige jacket, and so forth, exuding a detectable alcoholic scent, because they'll definitely bring it up with you. Or more accurately, they won't bring it up, but will let you know in their no-uncertain-passive-aggressive terms by posing some ridiculous line of indirect inquiry that is clearly designed to let the sub-hominid know he's not supposed to show up for work reeking of drink. E.g.: Smells like you were able to enjoy last night, weren't you?

It's just Alyssa and Bob now, a circumstance Bob is just getting around to appreciating and pondering decision trees with an eye toward escorting her back upstairs, when along comes Jake, who, if possible—and Bob would not have believed it possible had he not witnessed the looping stutter-stride and pixie-blooms on cheeks—might be in worse shape than Bob, but our Jake-tracking contingent confirms that while off on his own roistering-vector he has indeed been roughly trading ounces with Bob, whose body mass index comes out to like 1.5 Jakes.

The label pasted to the empty bottle clutched in Bob's left hand indicates that it once contained forty ounces of something called Enjuku. Bob frankly can't remember how he came by this artifact, and certainly has zero recall of the good times and fine quality promised, in English, beneath the illegible crap, to partakers of this beer-approximation, which is cheap because hop-less in a country where it's hard to come by hops, that critical beer-constituent replaced with the abundant local crop, soy—and thus tastes a bit like soy, but not much like beer. In the empty Enjuku bottle Bob perceives an indication that it's high time for the transition to Chu-hi, that deceptively fruity endemic libation, 8% alcohol, and sweet, as without a can of this reliable standby occupying a fist or two at all times, there's no telling what he'll put back. Jake punches Bob in the chest.

What are you doing, Jake, asks Alyssa. Yeah, please don't do that, Jake, says Bob, though nothing hurts. Jake proposes a reciprocal strike to the chest, which Bob hasn't had time to run the full decision-tree on when all of a sudden a far-off Fondu bellows something about taking this thing upstairs, impressively initiating a slow mass migration almost at once.

い

There's a hillock of sandals and sneakers stacked high in the vestibule, plus one pair of the perforated foam-resin clogs internationally distributed under the trade moniker Crocs, which you just know have to be Jake's. Inside, about thirty malodorous foreign residents cram together and spill assorted liquids on the *tatami* mats (Jesus guys, they're brand new! a recurring reminder from the apparently still-unimpaired Fondu).

This being the tail end of a party that wasn't all that great to start with, the smells aren't all that's bad: There's bad guitar-playing, bad singing, bad explanations of all things Japan, bad-liquor consumption, bad jokes, bad motor skills, badminton, improbably, briefly, in miniature, out on the balcony, until the birdie flutters irretrievably down to earth. And overall just some bad vibes. Still no sign of Dylan being really the only positive note.

Somehow there's a small arrogant-eyed gray kitten of indeterminate provenance and that tuft-tailed indigenous breed prancing around by the last carton of Asahi, rubbing up against the cardboard edges, circling the box almost like it wants a beer. An O-lineman-sized Alabama ex-pat pours a bit from his own bottle into a little saucer, which the stupid cat doesn't even bother to sniff.

Bob locates Al in a corner, improbably alone, and in his friendliest bellow remarks that now that Bob and Al whom he hopes she doesn't mind his calling "Al" have reached a point where they're at ease around each other, Bob would love the opportunity to open up to her about a somewhat personal matter tonight. Bob's sentences seem a lot more syntactically sound to Bob than they do to anyone else, but the thrust of his remarks is that it must be really hard-going for foreign women here in Japan, for the simple reason that while *gaikokujin* males of all persuasion, but generally speaking the lowliest geek-type guys you'd ever come across doing complicated internet shit in American coffee shops and cafés, the same ones you might have thrown the odd good-natured shoulder into on the occasional high school hallway *en passant*, are for some reason highly sought-after here: visit any modest metropolitan hub and witness for yourself the whole demographic sub-set of hot-blooded J-girls, habilimented like stylish whores, wobbling through the commerce-warrens on treacherous heels, seemingly hell-bent on tracking these losers down, or more accurately attracting their attentions by limping past the local Starbucks or other likely *gaijin* haunts with their cultivated toes-in gait, offering brazen displays of naughty legs, and feet. (As somewhat of a lower-body connoisseur, with special attention to the toes and feet, Bob's always found it fascinating that the Japanese deploy one word—*ashi*—for the whole shebang, although the written characters are different.)

A literal caterwauling erupts, as some clown has taken seriously another's blithe proposal that the darkness-curtailed football game be recommenced indoors, with a non-porcine, meowing, makeshift pigskin, and poor Kaki is being well-protected with both arms just below the chest—this fullback benefited from some quality coaching somewhere along the developmental line, Bob predicts—and not seeming to care if she deviates from that noted Japanese proclivity to keep one's feelings of discontent contained inside.

It's one reason Bob has never pursued romance with the Japanese: he wants to be loved as a person, qua Bob, you could say, not savored like some generous helping of *yakitori* meat. Sure, the common perception is that these transplanted fringelings are living the Oriental Dream, honoring that great Western tradition of unfavorable home conditions abandoned for adventures in exotic climes, where unsatisfying former identities can be shucked as painlessly as old wardrobes, with no one the wiser since how the hell would anyone know? and, sure, Bob's been tempted to test the local waters all right, maybe stretch the action at a "snack bar" (you know what these places actually are that they for some reason call "snack bars," right?) some night, see where a little purchased flirtation might lead, or else just work up the nerve to settle in next to some cutie heading in to Tenjin on the Nishitetsu train; but wouldn't it be lonely? Suppose you felt a specific something, something potent and acute that you would need to draw on all your articulative powers in the native tongue to really get across, something that you logically wanted to share with this, your closest friend, something that meant a lot to you: wouldn't it be wearisome to know you couldn't ever do it? To live in a permanent interpersonal fog? Always searching for some fumbling approximation—or else just courting resignation to a pair of separate lives? Anyway, Bob's ambivalence notwithstanding, the common theme of conversation with these admired ALTs tends to be how easy the girls are to get into the sack, a point Bob hasn't personally confirmed but certainly believes.

Whereas—and Alyssa should feel free to contradict Bob here if this observation is in any way off-base—Japanese men by and large seem to locate foreign women somewhere between ungovernable ogrettes and obese pains in the ass. Even the prettiest (and thin) *gaijin* seem to draw nothing but disgust from these guys, and Bob theorizes there must be more than a few lonely foreign gals who'd love to get to know a big, jolly, well-intentioned, accommodating foreign resident, a guy who, sure, would naturally find them physically appealing, and would certainly devote ample attention to such a woman's legs and feet, would almost certainly if given opportunity wind up being one of these guys who when he's watching TV the girlfriend's legs are stretched across his lap for him to stroke, gently cup contours of calves, backs of knees, knead tender little ankles, give every toe a gentle tug, and so forth, but who would also want to get to know the girl, the Who, would want to dive right into her, to know where she comes from, where she's been, what she misses about being a kid, how she'd come to dance ballet, what she dreams of, after Japan, would never tire of kicking back and listening to her talk... and who doesn't want to spend some time being really heard? why, there must be some lonely gaijin out there—maybe even right here in Kyushu, or even in this room tonight, unpersuaded by the artificial chaos (the cat was briefly airborne during Bob's bit about the feet) with whom Bob'd develop a friendship, first, of course, and then sort of see where things might lead.

Bob carries a towel with him at all times for the purpose he now applies it to, mopping up sweat from the pink forehead and neck, and it's while he's patting down his face a second time that Jake slips in from who knows where and lands a second strike to the chest. This one catches Bob on an unprepared right pectoralis, and while there's ample flesh there to prevent the possibility of being seriously hurt, he can tell right away a bit of breastplate's going to be bruised tomorrow.

Come on Bob, hit me! Jake says.

Bob reholsters the towel and glances over to get Alyssa's take.

Certain of the wraith contingent will spend some long hours in the aftermath of what's next, debating at what point Bob was really going to hit this guy, like was he ready to do it in response to the sucker punch—didn't seem like it, you might almost describe the initial look he shoots at Al as "wry"—You believe this guy?—only there's very little sympathy in her response. And a point the wraiths will further debate is whether she can really be held accountable for reacting a tad unfairly here, in the sense that Bob never asked to be hit, since she may at this point have intuited the unfolding action without Bob's having made it all the way down the decision tree, but at any rate, what she says is:

Jesus, would you two knock it off already? Could one person at this party attempt to act his age?

And meanwhile, Jake has streamlined his masochistic request into a kind of chanted incantation: Hit. me. Bob: hit-me-in-the-chest. Hit. me. Bob: hit-me-in-the-chest... aaaaaand: Bob goes ahead and hits him, only he doesn't just sort of pop him on the pec a bit, but—and this is the *mistake*—gathers full force, which is actually a lot with Bob, and heaves whole-body in and hits him, and Bob's a big boy, so logically it shouldn't come as the shock it does to him when flattened Jake, on his back in the adjacent room, with a few hacking coughs makes his own personal liquid contribution to the beer-pool he's created with his fall, viscous material coming out with each hack, stuff that's of an absolutely more elemental hue than beer, and the whole thing just not an encouraging sight.

幕間

(前年)[1]

And now this same triune of office warriors comes at a wamble in unsteady correspondence from the Snack Gold Value's moschate gloom. Arms actually linked. No bills left in Bob's plastic fold save for the one *sen yen*. Some kind of cryptic incantation that's not quite thought because he cannot either shut it down or train its course, that isn't speech because his tongue roves insubordinate—as it will sometimes on the amphetamine arc's earthward plunge—but that's mostly English, plaited with an ornamental thread of the Tagalog he's been trying to pick up, and therefore seems to be his own, evokes obscure dark portents for the evening yet to come. Nonstandard English on the decayed marquee indicates Snack Gold Value's operative hours and Manila theme. A Family Mart *konbini*'s green-and-white effulgent beacon casts imbrex-and-tegula of single-story quarters in brackish luminescence; a single *sen* would stretch to several cans of low-malt *hopposhu*. But then there goes the cab-ride home.

Rudimentary Tagalog in the augural weave perhaps denoting Bob's tarrying urge here *ex post facto* to exchange notes with plump cymotrichous *Concepción*, whose professional ministrations he'd apparently misread—*really* misread—though she's still in the "snack bar" and he's alone out in the darkness draped like some discarded sacerdotal robe over the stucco parapet's terminal post, his woozy vigil shared with unseen feline life whose ceaseless mewls' intensity

[1] The Previous Year

bespeaks some kind of mass communal heat, a scant few dozen meters from the SGV from which he's as of just this evening been debarred *until the end of time.*

The salarymen have paused a ways down the pedestrian arcade, arrayed before the low protective wall, and soon three healthful spurting jets of micturition belie the pricks from which they've issued's unimpressive girths, the three currents of liquid waste converging to be subsumed as one into the weak flow of the creek below. Decision trees sprout and spread tangling limbs more quickly than do *actual* floral specimens pass from seedy infancy through stripling youth to responsible adult citizenship in the botanical community in many of the natural-world themed cable-television broadcasts Bob once favored as a younger man. And the catenary lines are surged to life as asterisks of sparks foretell the coming of what must be the evening's final Fukuoka-bound Express.

The little fucks continue with their lasting pee. Bob unsteady, rising aid-less in *his* wamble, mere months into his Japanese campaign, the rumble of these tons of steel's approach obtruding into brief dread-freighted impressionistic brooding on the coming day's Augean face-off with some five hundred *ichinensei* writing journals waiting for him in forbidding stacks—a thriving realty of paper development that has expanded sprawling onto the adjacent properties of Yogi and Kubota Senseis' desks, these accommodating neighbors to his own desk's north and west not directly *asking* Bob to either find some other site for his high-rises or just finally fucking grade the things, but gently emphasizing the vexation of having to relocate to some other workspace for certain tasks demanding a whole desktop's worth of space with histrionic groans anent the weight of whatsoever matériel his lack of consideration has forced them to transport, or accidentally dropping outsize reams of papers as they founder under the burden that his ungraded compositions have imposed on them, profusely sorry with a slew of *Shitsurei shimasu! Gomen!*s when Bob gets down on hand-and-knee to help collect the scattered sheets—which inexpert compositions he must correct every last one of by the end of work tomorrow, in light of some poor time-administration that was itself probably a consequence of some decision trees assessed without the scrupulous attention that in hindsight they each patently deserved, beginning two-and-a-half-weeks back, when his students had begun handing in work according to the strict rolling submissions policy he'd devised and implemented expressly so as to avoid a very bad workday and possibly late-evening-and-beyond spent scouring the devastation wrought upon his native tongue page after brutal page when these edifices had first started to go up, but now he's kind of got to grade them, can't be helped—or as the Japanese say, *Shoganai*—except just now his own grasp of English mechanics, to say nothing of the finer flourishes of usage, idiomatic verve, &c., is not what any fair observer would describe as sound and isn't showing signs of rallying within the next four hours or so, and the concentration-aiding diet pills he snorted the very last ground-up three tablets of some eight-odd hours back in the so-called "Language Lab" during his open 6th have now been taken off the table cognitive-performance-enhancement-wise, and he's trying—though it's hard—to give wide berth indeed to the decision tree pertaining to advisability of secreting an augmented liter-bottle of Coca-Cola into the mountaineer's pack he hauls his teaching gear and supplementary equipment in to work each day in as he'd done last Friday to calamitous results he's still not sure he's seen the final repercussions of, or else maybe the last six packets of the codeine that he'll need to find some further way to swindle more of from the increasingly skeptical-seeming *Nihonjin* doc who already last time seemed right at the cusp of being unable to accept as plausible the sequence of ineptitude whereby this young man bright or at least *organized* enough to put himself through whatever bureaucratic fun-house was involved in applying for and actually obtaining teaching work in a country not his own could nonetheless misplace his prescribed painkillers on the Nishitetsu train, then presumably drop them from a coat pocket while trucking down the station escalator to board a different incident's ultimate car (a vignette Bob's enthusiastic ex temporis improvisations on the spectacle of aerially dispatched Japanese might've undermined the vérité of), then sans explanation in the subway, and then while blundering from a bus on three separate respective occasions—but these powdered narcotic treats he'd meant to save for some more festive date.

—The fuck's so funny, wonders Bob, in English, quiet at the footbridge.
The urineworks all but dried up. Pecks still unsheathed in open air.

Bob once had a pal pull diagnosis for ergophobia: nothing current pharmacology could do, prognosis bleak: Life's hard, you know. But Bob is not averse to work *qua* work. More like he's put off by the ever-present specter *of Bob* struggling to do work that haunts him when he tries to get things done. He sits down, for example, to a stack of student papers that by all rights should be no more than a mild discommoding, ready to just bang this fucker out... and then forthwith he's floating somewhere in some near but other region like an eidolonic echo of himself witnessing his own piteous ineptitude and paltry seeking for some Bob-enjoined emancipation to not only act but Be, and though he tries to stay engaged as possible with whatever task's at hand it's thus far into his no-longer-quite-so-young adulthood proved very difficult to withstand this self-but-other-seeming perpetual *witnessing* of the Bob approach to taking care of life. The reason that he knows *his* problem's something vaster, more character-encompassing than his pal the ergophobe's is that there aren't really *any* circumstances in which this unflattering dissociation isn't more or less predestined to take place.

Three Shochu-woozy *Nihonjin* sharing a smirk. One Bob.
「I'm fine sank you」 says one.
—Brah, we can do this anytime.

Concepción! Sacred name! Our Lady of the Intercession between God the Father's spotless wrath and fallen man, whose gross transgression Righteousness must not abide—the Incarnation, Word made flesh, I bring to you good tidings of great news, through Grace eternal liberation from the binds of Law far too immaculately obdurate for infirm humankind, and if not Grace what is it that Bob seeks this early Thursday morning in the ill-lit warrens of Futsukaichi's less well-trodden streets?

For whosoever stumbles down his archaic *jutaku*'s spiderweb-encrusted stairs clutching two cans of lemon Chu Hi seeking evanescent succor in the night, deliverance, who seeks to pay in darkness of the shoddy exurbs of Japan's southernmost major island's largest urban hub (though Fukuoka's not exactly Tokyo or Osaka) some enigmatic penance for crimes against the celestial seat, crimes he cannot name yet must be perpetrating still—else whence this retribution handed down, this sense of obscure reparations to be made, punitive measures justly meted out to him, due recompense for unknown breaches of the Law, the incorrect behaviors, habits, patterns of thought and feeling, this unpardonable trespass of *just being Bob*... the night is long, and whosoever lives alone among the cunning Japanese with whom even the most earnestly undertaken effort to establish some cross-cultural rapport is bound to be rebuffed, witness Bob's students' energetic reproductions of his imprecise *Nihongo*, special attention devoted to idiosyncrasies of tone (the language of the Japanese takes as its phonetic bedrock just the five vowel sounds—a̱, i, ɯ̂ β̱., e̱, o̱—fronted by a small sampling of consonants, creating phonemes such as "Bo" or "bu," and foreigners may *think* they pass these speech components through their lips as musically as do the Japanese but usually they sound as if they've got some kind of vocal-fold deformity, which naturally the detail-oriented *Nihonjin* will note), as for instance when Bob, rising to resume his station at the musty classroom's head, disengages from a private consultation with this first-year student—a baseball player, as betokened by his number-two buzz and battered Nike-brand duffel bag of gear—via gentle shoulder-squeeze, an educator's gesture of support, his spirited *Ganbatte yo!* (Hang in there! Do your best!) played back for him an instant later in aural pantomime of Western twang and drool, the excess volume humorously emphasized, each vowel-based phoneme distended to a nasal high noon drawl and he is given then to know *just what a monster* he must loom before his youthful charges as, sopping up clavicle-concentrated sweat with the three-towel set he cycles through per fifty-minute class, white button-down a sodden linen wrapping for the XL package of his gut, these young citizens of Japan he'd like to inculcate with just a glint of interest in his native tongue, let's face it: he's an obese harlequin to kids in his Oral Communications class and a humorous diversion for the faculty and staff, and there are no other foreign residents of Futsukaichi, and it's not all that hyperbolic to say this genial *hostess* Concepción was his only friend before the business with these outdoor urinators back inside the bar, and whosoever, in witnessing himself squander an undeserved or -looked-for one last chance to start anew at twenty-eight, quit fucking up, finally get right, in this new country a chance to make a new Bob, who sees he can't, who sees he never will, and thus perceives *the shadow of death*, rears out enshrouded in this black penumbra clutching Chu Hi in each fist to head downhill in seek of shelter in the arms of *Concepción*, blessed woman from the open fore of whose leather-strapped wedges protrude two sets of perfect *maron-* (chestnut-) colored toes, pristine unpainted toenails compelling argument for existence of a loving God, walking with some discomfort one of a small number of career paths available to diaspora Filipinas of her station there at the SGV, and who thenceforth fucks up again: *this man has sinned* against Heaven or Earth, probably both, and the amercement is beyond his means and will no man come forth to aid him in his settling of accounts?

The anuran one says something else amusing to his friends in Japanese, but Bob's not not even bothering now to hear or try to comprehend.

—That's funny, he asks, hauling back his sleeves.

四

Bob looks up from his research on contemporary stylistic applications of the gray blazer to see Anna, the other new girl from upstairs and across the hall, whom Bob just hasn't done a great job of getting acquainted with (her wraith confirms she's been in Fukuoka the same three-and-a-half months as everyone else but is unforthcoming regarding her activities during this period, save to note that she's never struck it as especially important, almost more like a figurant than a character of flesh-and-blood), a development that seven train stops together will be a great first step toward rectifying, passing through the open automatic door and into the train at the other end of his car.

Hey Anna, he shouts. Several Japanese stir from lolling slumber or raise eyes from electronic displays to stare. Small world! If any of these *Nihonjin* had retained more from his near-decade-long compulsory pedagogical tussle with English than the ability to pose that inquisitional standard of American greeting, How are you?, or respond to this same query with rote assertion of high spirits and gratitude for the interlocutor's concern, or else name certain varieties of fruit, he might be able to follow at least part of the subsequent conversation, if not apprehend the nuance of every development or turn, as Bob lumbers over to join her in the little vestibular open space between the doors on the car's either side. But in this compartment the only comprehending eavesdroppers are wraiths, who are no more citizens of *Nihon* than they are of Earth. Always nice to encounter a familiar—Bob hates to say non-

Japanese—face after eight hours of all the teachers' gentle harassment and the kids' stares and what not, you know?

What do you mean by "gentle harassment," Anna asks. They pass a high school that is neither Anna's nor Bob's—there really are a lot of high schools in this country—and whose baseball diamond's right-field abets a section of Nishitetsu track, prompting Bob to lend brief credibility to a scenario whereby some left-handed slugger's best deep shot comes crashing through a northwest-facing window's glass, possibly injuring an inattentive passenger, or at least startling the shit out of the whole car, since you have to admit that this is a remarkably easily-startled race. Granting the profound unlikelihood of such an occurrence, since the conditioning modalities employed by athletes in this country lag behind the rest of the First World's by a good forty years, particularly when it comes to the cultivation of upper-body strength. To the point that Bob, who'd be the first to come right out and admit that he's absolutely not in his life's finest shape, for instance this semester he can once again get away with donning the soft-pornographically embossed belt buckle that was basically the only thing the old man passed on when he went some years back and that the Vice Principal'd had to ask his supervisor to suggest Bob maybe not wear to school anymore, at the very least on days when he was teaching classes—probably Anna can't even tell he has a belt on—due to its being tucked up behind the overhang of his bulging gut, which distension Bob attributes primarily to Chu-hi, plus—this is embarrassing—there's also been a certain ominous new bite to his recent sweat-output's bouquet that compels panicky speculation about some kind of organ-decay—you sort of have to suspect liver—yeah, sorry: it's gross— the smell's

closest analog Bob can come up with off the cuff being actually
natto, that famously ghastly native dish of rotted soybean paste, but
so strength-wise Bob estimates ninety-percent of them he could
probably take, in, say, an arm-wrestling contest, bench-press max-
out, or one-on-three drunken brawl in the street—assuming in this
final illustrative case that the heat didn't suddenly show up en masse
right when the three little fucks were poised to break ranks and flee,
and with the grim Aspergerian but not unjoyful focus that your
Nihonjin male prides himself on applying to all tasks deploy the
truncheons and the Pershing boots and special threat-neutralizing
martial arts regimen Japanese cops are required to master before they
can be dispatched to maintain civic peace against Bob alone, who
perforce without a weapon of his own would eventually be subdued,
while the three equally culpable limpdicks in their tailored suits
cowered and whinged about damage sustained and threatened civil
suits. Though he'd naturally give them the advantage on the judo
mat, judo being a matter of almost pure technique where physical
strength only peripherally factors in. (Good fun though, getting
your ass tossed over some midget's shoulders and sent tumbling
across mats redolent with the sweat of ages, if you're not too uptight
about feeling like somebody's bitch.) And, again, it's not like Bob's
Captain Planet or anything back in the United States, which speaks
volumes about how you don't even have to have a background in
physical conditioning or sport to be able to tell from just looking
at these guys' arms that you'd need to commission a whole team
if you wanted to transfer something heavy, for instance a piano
or grandfather clock. Take for example this character with the
elaborate cellular phone here, Bob says, indicating the individual
whose cerise-and-steel-toned *keitai* is rather involved, even by the

lofty standards of *Nihon* high-tech: Just look at the lack of any kind of muscular definition, he urges, and keep in mind all the men in this country were at one stage in their lives just high school-age boys, who you have to figure weren't exactly going to be more formidable in terms of as physical specimens back then, in their *koukou ji dai*—"high school days," or more accurately high school "era"—probably weren't being asked to pose for shots in so-called "muscle-mags," those glossy ad-rich panegyrics to steroid abuse and whey protein, considering that they train every day of the week, bar none, except for maybe during *O-Bon*, which is when they take time off to honor the deceased. Which relentless workout pace with no time for beaten musculature to recover would be condemned by any personal trainer worth his consultation fee back home in the States, where we might without question have our own set of entrenched limitations on athletic achievement, particularly in the domain of cardiovascular conditioning and health, as well as questionable methodologies, but definitely know how to build mass, the forerunner of power and speed.

Bob encourages his fellow ALT to recollect the debacle that recently threatened to annihilate the moral legitimacy of American professional baseball, in which members of our national pastime's time-immemorial MLB tainted the legacy of the game by making use of so-called "performance-enhancing drugs," which, and here is Bob's point, how did these drugs enhance performance? Did they improve batters' capacity to counter whatever the professional hurler might select from his nearly bottomless bag of deception and skill? Certainly not. They made these legacy-indifferent sluggers' bodies bigger, because increased size equals increased power, if we're talking about muscle-size, and one look at the *Nihonjin's* upper arm should be all you need in terms of reassurance, as concerning why passengers commuting past the high school baseball diamond that's several stops back now are probably safe. Though Bob does wonder if there's ever even once been some kind of anomalous incident. Would have been something to see.

But now he wants to know all about the book Anna'd probably been planning to read before lucking into her jutaku-mate here on the train: Any good? The author's quite famous now, she replies, but this was his first book, written in Japan, actually, while he was doing the same job as us, just an ALT, while he was still a very young man. He wound up marrying a Japanese woman, with whom he went back to his native UK.

Figures, Bob snorts. He squints at the paperback's cover: What, so the deal is it's actually written by a ghost? Like a fucking poltergeist? Or is this an arty figure of speech. Bob offers to borrow it after she's finished, give it a good peruse. Maybe the two of them can get a little reading circle going. Or it wouldn't technically be a circle unless they brought some other ALTs into the fold, which they can cross that bridge when they get to it. Does Anna also write? Not Bob: way too much solo time in the old echo-chamber for—hang on: gotta take this. Bob flips open his *keitai*, shouts he'll have to call back in a few because he's riding the train and you know how they revere the Silent Commute, already half the train is glaring at him side-eyed like he just upchucked in the middle of the aisle, yes, Hello there, I realize I'm ruining your afternoon, Bob shouts, Anyway, gotta run. Oh, but he did finally try the fucking cheese platter. Right on, brother! Ha! Ha! Over and out.

Bob turns to Anna, winks, and posits that fundamental differences between Japan and the West are ripe for observation in artificial social circumstances like the one they're privy to here, public spaces, in other words, where, Bob indicates, you'll notice how nobody actually talks on his cellular phone, this despite nearly unilateral possession of that felicitous modern device as evidenced by the parallel columns of black-haired heads bowed in quiet concentration, fingers negotiating tiny consoles. In other words it's not for lack of opportunity that they rarely, in Bob's experience, can be witnessed deploying their phones for an audio chat. No: it's the humorously-illustrated signs imploring them not to do so, since the noise would unsettle fellow passengers (who in the pictures have index fingers thrust into their ears, eyes abulge beneath epicanthic folds, or are clutching their heads in what looks like migraine-caliber pain) because, and this is Bob's insight, which he stresses is only the result of a year and a few months of being for the most part the only foreign resident in this semi-backwater, which is why he continues to feel truly blessed by the sudden influx of fresh ALT meat—not that he considers Anna "meat," per se, it's an expression—even if it's true that they haven't quite gelled as a social unit to the degree Bob'd envisioned yet, and there've been the inevitable bumps in the interpersonal road—Jake's rib being at ninety percent fyi, or so Bob's overheard while listening in from out on his balcony the other night when it sounded like everybody'd gotten together for a probably spur-of-the-moment pizza-beer-and-movie-type thing at Fondu's place one floor below Bob that Bob'd been down at the supa picking up the evening's Chu-hi when they probably knocked on his door to invite him to and so wound up only hearing snatches of from his balcony whenever they opened up a window or door, which was no big issue with Bob since he'd just picked up all that Chu-hi anyway, and the weather still being clement here for a couple of weeks he'd figured what better way to spend an evening than out on the balcony sipping Chu-hi, enjoying the fresh air and chatter of frolicking *Nihonjin* kids, since winter is dark, cold and terrible here like you wouldn't believe, plus the Japanese pizza tends to be sup-par and overpriced at best, and's often topped with shit like mayonnaise, squid and corn. Oh, the *ketai* insight being just that his personal perspective on the Japanese is what you have here is basically a whole race of people who all just do as they're told.

I'm not so sure I'd be comfortable making that kind of claim about the whole country, Anna objects, and—ok, weird question, but… was there actually anyone on the line a minute ago when you were saying the thing about the cheese? Somehow I didn't hear any ringtone or buzz, as Bob deploys the towel—a necessity until winter tightens the knot on its gi and gets down to its annual business of cutting off citizens' serotonin-and/or-dopamine supplies so that by late January or so the whole country's locked in a choke-hold of anhedonic despair—to mop up face and neck. A quick wraith-consultation confirms that Anna hadn't found the pizza—just plain pepperoni, tad expensive, but so what?—that bad at all.

五

Bob invites any interested parties to come have a look at his new bike. It's a mountain bike. Probably won't see much mountain action under Bob's stewardship, but if called upon it absolutely could. Anyway, what kind of music is everyone into? Anybody partial to hip hop? Bob is—but he wonders whether you mean the same thing when you say the words "hip hop," because Bob's assessment is that what you're basically looking at is two nearly parallel universes of taste that coexist in much the same way that scientists hypothesize actual parallel universes coexist—in other words utterly unconnected, except for in the incredibly rare cases of wormholes, which if you've done even the most cursory independent research into space-time you'll appreciate are such an incredibly rare happenstance as to constitute a kind of exception that proves the rule of how never the two shall meet except under extreme duress. Which is exactly how you ought to view the anomalous cases of rappers who both Bob and your typical multinational-corporate-media-conglomerate-hoodwinked "fan" of what he mistakenly considers hip hop ("fan" being delivered in those effeminate scare quotes that Bob declines to physically provide but are conveyed via vocal modulation) can vibe with. So, that said, anybody into hip hop? Just please for god's sake nobody say "Lil' Wayne." Et tu, Dwayne? Hypocrite! Ha ha—Which by the way reminds Bob of something he'd maybe not even like to be reminded of tonight, since the emotional damage is still somewhat raw in the way he imagines Jake's chest must have felt like in the days immediately following the blow Bob still deeply regrets having floored him with but that he just couldn't come up with the proper way to apologize for face-to-face during either month of convalescence, as a man would have done, a will-failure of which he is likewise profoundly ashamed, which is why he'd like to take this opportunity to come forward and just say he's sorry, Jake, for probably ruining a good two months of your first half-year here in Japan, or at least hampering them somewhat, depending on your capacity to function through pain. Not that Bob is suggesting anything emasculatory in this direction whatsoever, seeing as how people simply vary remarkably in their separate capacities to countenance pain, it's one of the truly scary things about being alive when you think of it, this sense that no one can ever know the degree to which somebody else suffers—you might be a pain-exhibitionist, theatrically playing up the slightest disturbance in comfort for pity and love as easily as you might be more or less dying and seem totally fine, it's like how two people can look at the same cloud and perceive dramatically different forms.

Anyway, Bob doesn't want to go into details, but what happened was Bob's been studying his *Nihongo* hard this past couple of months, apparently unbeknownst to his native colleagues, and while he hasn't demonstrated much improvement on the speaking front, he's actually understanding more and more of what he hears being said, and what pained Bob today was to discover that his beloved co-worker, one Akimatsu Mirai, whom up until this very afternoon he'd counted his very best at-school friend, who frequently spoke to him in her adorably splintered English and leaned in over his desk most mornings to chirp Good Mahning! with unconscious punishing charm, might not think as highly of Bob as Bob has led himself to believe over the fifteen months of their burgeoning friendship, if his admittedly still middling comprehension of *Nihongo* is to be trusted, since what it sounded like she was saying to and laughing about with several other *Sensei*s was in no way flattering to Bob, and seemed as far as he could tell to make numerous pointed references to both the new scent-development and the entirely Chu-hi-to-blame ballooning weight, and these observations were just by no means all she had to contribute to the project of belittling Bob. Very few things rattle Bob's cage worse than hypocrisy, and as far as he's concerned this country's awash in the shit. Of course, everywhere else is too, he suspects. This just happens to be the particular nation-state in which Bob tries his hardest—and it usually doesn't feel like enough—*gagner sa vie.*

Anyway, speaking of clouds, Bob avails himself of the opportunity to fill the newbies in on this quintessentially Japanese linguistic touch, whereby, unlike how in, say, the U.S., where a common-to-the-point-that-it's-practically-a-cliché feature of your ordinary American person's fond recollections of childhood is those times when said American and his or her mother would sojourn to some bucolic haunt like a neighborhood playground, or publicly-accessible beach, if, like Bob, you grew up in a place with numerous beaches close at hand, and spread out a blanket or military-surplus poncho or what have you and lie supine and attribute—often dubiously—the shapes of, say, farm animals or geological features or figures of popular legend and myth to the slowly mutating cumuli forms, that one looks like Sonic the Hedgehog, and so forth, the point or purpose obviously being to indulge the child's whimsy and imaginative ignorance of the way shit really is, and maybe simultaneously allow the parent to reminisce back to a probably nonexistent time when such flights of fancy were not delusive indulgences but the way things might in some idyllic unworld actually be. So now on your other hand the Japanese, it transpires, have approximately several-hundred prefab designations for cloudshapes built into the language, so that in what Bob identifies as an archetypal Japanese move, the goal of any such parent-kid cloud-observation excursion here in Japan would basically be to inculcate the kid with another list of terms he's supposed to memorize and learn how to apply with precision in appropriate future circumstances—That is a "horsecloud," son, and so on—which is just so depressingly typic in Bob's view of this automated place, but also makes Bob feel sometimes—and is he the only one who feels this way?—that there's actually maybe something fundamentally wrong with him for not only failing to know and be able to apply the appropriate cloud-shape nomenclature, but then also to have ever even allowed himself to believe in things like whimsy or chance and the possibility of spotting a cloud with no agreed-upon name.

One noteworthy feature of this somewhat free-associative discourse being that, in theatrical parlance, it is what's known as a soliloquy, a monologue undertaken by a cast member alone on-stage, with the unseen wraith-contingent filling in nicely here for the dark-shrouded silent audience looking on as Bob struts and frets from one *tatami* to the next in his *jutaku*'s gloam, nursing the tallboy of lemon Chu-Hi he fortuitously encountered behind a tray of *sashimi* that no longer looked safe for consumption, thus postponing the switch to the more potent and dangerous shochu that will inevitably come next, delivering himself of his lines. And "lines" is also appropriate here, as he is in fact rehearsing: tomorrow's the Big Day of the outing he's proposed via social-network mass-invite and flyers posted conspicuously all around the apartment complex. It's a habit Bob's fallen into lately, wanting to make sure beforehand he knows exactly what he wants to say, because he so often seems to wind up saying things wrong, all wrong, it's always wrong, and there's nothing like a little advance-preparation to ease the performing artist's nerves when at last he takes the stage, and he will be ready tomorrow, when it's time for everyone to gather out in the jutaku lot and saunter as one over to the Nishitetsu stop for the train ride to Daizenji, that justly renowned garden temple they're all lucky to live so close to for what Bob's enthusiastically envisioned as One Last Group Outing, some sake and bonhomie before the weather turns vehemently bad, and as he rehearses his lines one last time, not even the wraiths, whose powers of insight fall short of prognostication, can discern—though, being intelligent wraiths, they might of course very well guess—that what will happen is no one will show.

六

There's legitimate cloud action coming in from what looks like due north, if you judge by the nearly-down sun, but Bob reassures all present, as they spread out the blue tarp they'll be spectating from and settle in with the footwear-removal and begin to produce and distribute *bentos* and bags of the promisingly-labeled but generally not very good local snack products, that the weather forecast, which in Japan is reliable on the level of Swiss-designed clocks, is for clouds but no rain. Fortunately so for all at hand, since firework festivals in Japan are nobody's notion of a joke. The backing is corporate and intense, with different prominent *kaisha* squaring off to see whose sponsorship will generate the most scintillating sequence of blasts. Kirin took the crown at this past summer's display, in Bob's assessment, with a closing enfilade of swanworks gliding on an iridescent golden sea through a flame-gate somehow finagled to imply spacial depth, the swans fading softly off into a distant night tableau having passed beneath the arch inscribed with that globally familiar brand-defining slogan: Ichi-ban. Wish everyone could have been there to take it in with him. But the *michi*-level word he's got upwind of holds that this loosely winter-themed affair (note for instance, the vast makeshift presence of heavyweight U.S. pressure-fried-chicken purveyor KFC in the form of booths set up at numerous points alongside all the usual *yakitori*, soba, and *okonomiyaki* stalls in the byzantine sustenance arcade, because Japanese couples and families traditionally consume the famous Colonel's enigmatically seasoned crisp drumsticks, breasts and thighs on Christmas Eve; this custom's origins [actually the result of an ingenious '70s campaign so revered among marketing types that it's still taught in business schools today, sort of your anti-New Coke situation, according to a friend of Bob's back at UH who's just finished his MBA] can't be traced as far back in the annals as, say, the Samurai Code, but it's still considered quite important, to the extent that actually if anybody wants to take part in another facet of the native way of life, you'll need to place your order at least one month in advance—already missed your chance this year, but if anyone's re-contracting, just a head's-up) is up for grabs. Monolithic Coca-Cola naturally figuring to muscle into the upper tier. And he hears good things about Honda. *Michi* means street, as at this point everyone ought to know without Bob having to step in, though anyone still in the comprehension-dark might want to give a little thought to the still-standing offer described in those handbills Bob'd personally deposited in each *gaijin* postbox a month-odd back of weekly, bi-weekly, or even nightly conversation practice sessions, which he's still, as advertised, willing to provide free of charge.

No takers yet, although Dylan, who's brought along the classy semi-acoustic acquired with one-third of his paycheck last month, does commence a brief michi-themed refrain over a couple fingerpicked self-penned bars, in his tender country-mountain drawl. It's true that no one technically invited Bob to come along, or even mentioned the Bob-excepted consensus that this festival held along the bank of the river Kurume would be worth getting trashed together and taking in, but the Futsukaichi foreigner community is sufficiently small and self-contained that all it would take for a person to catch wind of plans from which he'd probably been unintentionally excluded might be, say, a surreptitious slip out to the balcony, with inside-lights shut off, while other community members confabbed and batted back and forth logistics, together out in front of the *jutaku*, milling around by the square concrete benches below.

As practically everyone knows, firework display spectation is made measurelessly better by the sensory enhancement brought about by bong or joint or blunt or pipe. Any marijuana delivery system will obviously do, even a one-hitter, though Bob's always been partial to the so-called Lung, which he could explain the complex architecture of any time, but only to pupils with a genuine enthusiasm to learn, as the engineering is somewhat involved.

Of course, good luck procuring here. Roughly ninety percent of outdoor music fest attendees in Bob's Aloha State home base will be in possession of felonious quantities—we're talking ounces, not grams—and will happily provide any paying consumer, with little to no concern about potential legal fallout, Five-Oh contingent, many in mufti, notwithstanding, assuming you didn't want to just drift along with the contact-high that envelops all comers by the second or third act's taking stage. But it's tricky in Japan. However Bob lets it be known that he's relatively deep in discussion with certain extremely reliable and solid-seeming potential local sources, in case anyone else is interested in testing the acquisitional waters with him. The relentless admonishment not to take the risk at just about every new Assistant Language Teacher Orientation he'd had to sit through last summer had put Bob off the pot for this whole past year, with the somewhat dire repercussions associated with a swap-in of that legal CNS-depressing poison for what ought to be a legal mildly psychoactive herb. But it might be worthwhile now that he's made this whole batch of new foreign acquaintances, many of whom he feels comfortable already calling close friends, you know who you are, and all of whom have felicitously joined him in the apartment complex where he was the only non-*Nihonjin* resident all last year, a situation that wasn't so bad, really, Bob made the most of his time, but that did once in a while, particularly during the winter months when it was cold and got dark so fucking early and the only warm sector of his apartment was beneath the kotatsu heater under the low table, which set-up Bob imagines might facilitate a kind of cozy intimacy with a *koi-bito* (i.e., beloved: important word) or even a brood of little half-Japanese kids, but gets to be a drag some nights when you're the only person at same table watching incomprehensible television programming and trying but mostly failing to memorize the *kanji* characters that are at least part of what renders this language so darn near impenetrable to foreign folk like Bob, who had always seen himself as quick to pick up new things, but, he's kind of embarrassed to say, still isn't really satisfied with his development so far, which shouldn't discourage any prospective Conversation Session participants from at least popping by the Residence du Bob and giving it a trial run; language-acquisition is a

cooperative endeavor, and there will inevitably arise situations wherein
the designated teacher can be taught.

But if anybody's got an interest, Bob figures he might as well be the
point man in terms of trying to sniff out a little herbal recreation for
the group, particularly in light of the psychic devastation long-term
dipsomania is known to wreak. Granted, just about everyone seems
to agree the stuff you'll find here if you do manage to find any without
getting snitched on and tossed into the legendarily draconian Japanese
penitentiary system is crap. It's just he's lately been wondering how
many times in one lifetime a body can bounce back from benders that
terminate nightly in black. Besides: all you have to do is keep your eyes
peeled and be on the lookout for potential sources in the right kinds
of spots, for instance *izakayas* off the beaten path, if you're for-real
about procuring this so-called contraband, is Bob's revised current
position, because no matter what you might have had rammed down
your throats by the shitbags at Orientation, it's a well-known fact
that there is no accessible geographical coordinate on this perishing
planet whereat you can't find fellow enthusiasts for the green, if you
know how to maintain the previously indicated peel-eyed state, at all
times, which is what Bob intends to make it his business to do, in case
anybody's keen on jumping in. Probably even in the few remaining
non-accessible locales, Bob reflects, such as parts of what's left of
the Amazonian rainforest, your more intrepid cannabis-sniffing-out
type would most likely come across a healthy bud-smoking primal
community. Though why the hell these explorer-type morons you see
on popular reality television programs broadcast on a certain variety
of premium cable network that Bob no longer has access to but used
to watch a fair amount of, evenings after work, eating frozen French-

bread pizzas (which are really not half-bad), hands faintly redolent of feet, back at his most recent bachelor pad Stateside—why these clowns want to go roving around the last remaining ass-cracks of total non-civilization is a mystery that's entirely beyond Bob. Your thrill-seeker is at heart a man who won't admit he's basically running away.

Anyway, who's in?

Nobody leaps at Bob's offer to get in on the ground floor, which is fine: if Bob has learned one thing in life it's that the weed'll still be there, long after we've reverted to dust. It's time to hike down to one of the many kiosks erected along the riverbank, catering to nearly all imaginable Japanese culinary tastes. Plenty of beer, but Bob's hoping he'll find further Chu-hi, even though at these festivals it's shamelessly overpriced. This is his third or fourth trip downhill—nobody's counting but the wraiths, who confirm four and were privy to a certain ill-advised last-minute imbibing of a certain prescription grade sleep-aid that Bob has lately discovered can be taken recreationally if you're constitutionally-sound enough to fight through the drowse and probably didn't work through the old decision tree as carefully as he might have been advised to do, had wraiths been serving in an advisory as opposed to strictly observational capacity—and we're witnessing an eruptive facial pigmentation that would hold its own against any of the crimson-hued blasts in the forthcoming pyrotechnic display. During this brief interval of Boblessness, the conversation applies itself to a number of uninteresting topics, and Jake keeps requesting songs that Dylan either can't or wordlessly declines to play. Anna's looking over her pink-rimmed glasses at it looks like Dylan's deftly-working hands. John Fondu can't read a word of Japanese, but might or might not be amused to discover that the flavor of synthetic-potato-chip he's already polished off half the bag of is in fact "The Richness Cheese Fondue." Jake withdraws to the blanket's southwest quadrant, next to Alyssa's handbag, which she's entrusted the group with on her way down to the food stalls, in search of fried squid, and takes an enormous hardcover from his messenger bag and begins to laugh at high volume in little belches of private hilarity that if anyone were giving it a thought, which no one is, they'd probably suspect is some kind of nebulously-intended thespian display, to plant precisely what seed of insight into the Jakean condition it would be anyone's guess, and the wraiths, themselves sounding a touch weary of Jake, confirm that he hasn't read an actual sentence yet, even though he's hunched close over the open tome, mechanical pencil poised for marginal commentary a few millimeters from page.

Bob returns and spills three-quarters of a Chu-hi on Jake's head (luckily he's got three more), which development Dylan has just begun to work thematically into a new acoustical improvisation when Alyssa also returns and an apologetic Bob settles in next to the shoe-pile along the blanket's eastern rim, running fingertips nonchalantly along the strap of one of Anna's open-toeds.

The five members of a Japanese family seated placid amid *bento* boxes and a few cans of fake beer for Dad on a pretty cherry-blossom-patterned quilt to the *gaijin* contingent's starboard side all wear surgical masks. Bob reflects on the cognitive dissonance inherent in such a rigorously logic-oriented race of people so readily donning these flimsy barriers to infection that any airborne microagent worthy of dread will zip right through in ninety-nine cases out of a hundred like salt through a sieve. Though it's sometimes the case that they're worn to ward off allergens, of which, by the way: Bob notices Jake's been sniffling and rubbing his eyes as if they itch. It's hayfever season, fyi, and as Jake surely doesn't need to be told by Bob, you can develop an allergy at any season in your life, so who knows, maybe some mutation in the Japanese strain is triggering this multi-symptomatic response. Which possibility calls to mind an experience Bob had with frozen processed vegetables.

As a youngster Bob was a hearty consumer of this affordable produce, and might eat an entire bag at any given meal. Carrots, broccoli, green beans, peas: you name it, excepting lima beans, which no one on Earth actually likes. Then one evening he found his system had abruptly reversed its position on frozen processed vegetables. After supper he threw up for several hours, at first in a kind of lurid all-color revisitation of the offending mixed-vegetable bag, then eventually a graying paste as the hues began to drain until finally all there was was stomach bile, which, if you've never experienced it, feels terrible to puke. And this happened once again some few weeks later at a friend's house, during the dinner phase of a sleepover, when the friend in question's mother served as a side dish frozen processed peas, and Bob, caught up in both the thrill of recreation time to come, and a never-quite-gotten-over zeal for frozen processed vegetables, forgot himself and ate every pea that wasn't on another diner's plate (and actually half of his friend, Jose's, who ludicrously didn't care for peas) and so what was to be an evening of ice cream sundaes, frightening movies, Mortal Kombat, was quickly transformed into several hours spent purging himself of probably three-quarters of a bag of frozen processed peas, which just makes it clear in the event that it wasn't already that you never know with allergies. He has plenty more to say on the subject, however: Behold: the first firework has scraped light and sent sound splintering the skies of Kurume.

終

Maybe you've heard of the famed Japanese track-jumpers, famous in the sense of their interchangeably nameless deaths, collective anonymity. So frequent an occurrence that they mainly make no more than annual news, numerical contributions to the yearly tally of self- and public-transportation-inflicted death, a stat that, with the odd anomalous dip, is for the most part on the rise. So commonplace that the Japan Rail customer-assistance counters include on laminate English-language placards listing common causes of service interruption, to be produced preemptively and offered to the frequently impaired foreign passengers before they can work up enough indignation over the delay's impact on their personal business or recreational itinerary to get unpleasant this placating communiqué: CAUSE OF DELAY: PASSENGER FATALITY. There's a moment of intense eye-communication while the JR employee searches your expression for some sign of comprehension, perhaps spurred by his own seven-year stint of blanket incomprehension to doubt the capacity of these strange ugly symbols to convey sense or meaning to anyone, even large pink-faced foreign businessmen with sweat darkening more than half of the cheap material of their ridiculously poorly tailored suits.

In other words they're cleaning up the tracks. You can imagine the particulars of this custodial task with whatever degree of specificity you wish, but your train is not going anywhere until the situation's been addressed. It should be noted that this entire procedure is not without its attendant costs. Not just the immediate material consequences of a blood-, bone-, organ-, skin-smear-spattered track and chassis, presumably the front and undercarriage of at least the first several forward cars, though scouring this human residue is by no means cheap, but the considerable loss in revenues the Company incurs during the period of inactivity, which can be and is calculated with that tenacious *Nihonjin* precision the Japanese apply to everything they do. Given the frequency of track-jumping suicidal events, it's only natural that official Company policy is to abide by the contract implicitly binding potential patrons of JR services the moment they set foot in any JR station, or on any JR-affiliated track or Company land, which holds that in the event said patron elects to make use of JR-controlled company machinery in any non-sanctioned manner, such as availing himself (the perpetrators of these transgressions against the common transportational ease being predominantly male, though not exclusively, of course) of a JR passenger train's velocity and mass and precision-engineered nigh-indestructibility as a means by which to destroy the freight car carrying his mortal vessel and perhaps even soul via voluntary collision, it will be incumbent upon the deceased deviant customer's immediate family or closest solvent kin to defray the as-noted not-inconsiderable costs. So that, in light of the material costs piled onto the presumably not-inconsiderable emotional expense he'll be leaving his loved ones to pay, your Japanese track-jumper really needs to be in a bad way to go ahead and jump.

And yet they do it all the time! Reside in any backwater shithole of cicada swarms and rotting teeth for six months and you'll be incommoded thus. Any metropolis of decent size: forget it—you could be platform-bound and late for work on just about any day of the week. And why are the Japanese so suicide-prone? What makes these men so keen to die? We should resist the foreign resident's intractable impulse to engage in La-Z-Boy anthropological extrapolation. The reasons may be complexly interwoven with the whole socio-cultural tapestry so seemingly every-citizen-inclusive that it presents as a kind of uniform national psychopathology. Perhaps it's as difficult for the foreign observer to analyze or comprehend as are other, less thanotopic characteristics of the Japanese. For instance, the fucking relentless bowing. The sugar in practically every dish. The uniform requirement that participants wear what amount to uniforms for every conceivable activity, be it conducting a Nishitetsu train, cleaning the high school lavatory, going out for a jog, purveying "goods." The idiotic staring. The maniacally tedious explanations that even I don't need more than half of to get the gist of, and I barely speak elementary-student-level Japanese. The ludicrous misuse of a language the entire nation is taught to speak from an age young enough that its average citizen ought in adulthood to be able to do more than name the apple or point out that "I am Japanese!" Maybe they can't bear to follow orders anymore. Maybe decades of fourteen-hour corporate days have finally dripped them dry. Maybe it's something that no mere expatriate should dare presume to comprehend. Perhaps there is unparsable complexity, but perhaps the explanation is not so complicated as all of that.

There are as many strains of sadness as there are hearts to provide them with rhythmic support, and there's a huge supply-demand imbalance, a surplus far in excess of what would suffice to fill and burst the several billion hearts that each mark time in keyless penitentiary cells designed to hold one member of the human diaspora each, within which each lone detainee waits to face the thing that can't be known, and if the sadness doesn't stop when it's too much to contain, if it flows on from its ruined vessel like some miracle water source without relent, a room-filling deluge of pain, then for the drowning man who knows there is no surfacing from this, only the long slow asphyxiating death, what's the terror and uncertainty of a micro-second's rendezvous with some streaking late-night steel, the whole horrifying prospect obliterated in an instant's intercourse between flesh and super-express?

A sloppy trainward trek from the Kurume River's bank. Retinae still retaining optic memory of the marathon pyrotechnic display, gaits unsteady, carriages not exactly what you'd call erect. Laughter without pinpointable source. Proposals for a pre-ride konbini-run for further beer and snacks. Rampant hilarity at the idiosyncratic host nation's expense. Five young frolicking ex-pats, uniformly in the tank, giddy with the understanding that they'll have to clock in tomorrow, in all likelihood feeling like ass (to degrees varying from one reveler to the next according to precise volumes of intoxicant consumed, constitutional heartiness, long-term patterns of consumption, and so forth), get suited-up and mouthwashed and generally abluted no matter how potent the aftermath of tonight's free-for-all and be at their respective desks in their assorted teachers' offices for the 0830 start of their respective high- and junior-high schools' morning meetings, where it's their duty to show an as-much-as-possible jovial, smiling, easily-approachable-seeming friendly foreign face—and that's pretty much it.

I.e., no one present can think of a single work-related task, language-instructive or otherwise, that he or she will be expected to carry out tomorrow beyond being present and it goes without saying properly dressed and genial at their desks at 0830 to show face. Well, Fondu's wraith breaks with protocol to remind him he might have to teach a ten-o'clock, but still. After the unintelligible meeting they probably ought to stick around in deference to the remote possibility of a Japanese English Teacher actually wanting their assistance with some paperwork, or in class, but since none of the Japanese English Teachers can converse in the language it's his job to teach, no one is likely to want this lack of expertise demonstrated in humiliating real-time for a class-full of forty ordinarily too-sleepy-to-give-a-shit young-adult *Nihonjin*, who you'd better believe would find the presence of their tall-nosed huge-foreheaded horror-film hirsute and odd-smelling native speaker's in-classroom presence more than compelling enough theater to restrain drooping eyelids and raise heads from desks so they can witness their already strongly held convictions re their supposed English Teacher's utter incapacity to use the language he instructs get confirmed firsthand.... So they'll probably have plenty of time to sleep off the damage in some remote unused classroom, for which contribution to the Japanese educational programme they'll continue to receive a considerably higher monthly wage than what many of their native colleagues (who are assuredly not at liberty to sleep off their hangovers, though the entire male contingent of faculty members appears most mornings to be dehydrated to the level of spiritual pain) pull in. It's a sweet gig. Hence the whooping and hollering here at going-on-midnight as the drunkards lurch toward the station hoping to snag one of the last northbound trains.

A massive crowd spills down the station steps, immobile, pure logjam; no one's boarding any trains. The *jutaku* crew'd expected a wait, but this? Official *Nihongo* booms from unseen P.A.s, there are gendarmes at hand, but the crowd mostly seems befuddled and confused, an edge of unsober annoyance to the polite milling around, it's as close to anarchy as you're likely to find in this self-policed, obedient state, but the foreigners are considerably less patient when it comes to interruptions in the smooth functioning of public-serving systems they've already come to presume as their inherent right, only nothing seems to be happening here: What's the hold up? Why this massing passenger presence, how long are they expected to wait, can anybody at least make a little sense of what the station guys are trying to say? Jake would be the logical interpretive choice here, since he does legitimately speak some Japanese, but Jake is not in a very good way, and is being more or less tugged along by a Dylan who doesn't look much worse for wear but doesn't speak word one, and what Jake tries to say the Japanese are saying is roughly as comprehensible to the others as is the actual Japanese. None of the other newbies has picked up enough to decrypt the encoded pageantry that is official Japanese, which really only leaves one option, so:

Anyone seen Bob?

Under Joe's Volcano

In the beginning was the Word, and the Word was the light that would shine in the darkness, even to the ends of the Restaurant, but the darkness did not comprehend the light, nor the Restaurant the Word nor I the Restaurant, nor could I speak the Word.

Through the loading dock's night-shadows, my steps clocked weak percussion to the traffic's thrum. I saw seven garbage bags stuffed with sauces, cheese, brownie, ice-cream, caramel scum, ketchup, swirled mashed potatoes, blackened grease, French fries, your gold locket, chunks of chicken, burgers, steak, sodden napkins, stray utensils, melting ice; I saw silhouetted forms, hunched before floating embers, beneath smoke curling skyward in the semblance of a face:

and the pavement shuddered—crackling, rose, breaking as pebbled foam over the crest of a great gold whale. Its eyes were rubies; its tail rose from under the earth and thrashed up at an orange moon—

Those who had gathered for smokes or cocaine now broke into opposing camps: the cheering and the afraid, or so I'm told.

(And, within, the telephone rang.)

I ascended the stair—to the landing with the abandoned register under dusty photos of Volcano Joe's once-favored surf spots.

Fear rimmed even the leaky tea-vat, trickled out over plains of cracked and unswept wood toward me; it was also my job to mop and sweep.

They will wonder how much I could have seen.

This should suffice:

We know that when the warriors swarmed naked from under the upended canoe that had hung from the wall between the yellow crossroads-semaphore and old Trystero's horn, the night was not yet far along and we who were living were not free, either to shrink or disbelieve, even as the canned sauces and torpedoes fell from wall-shelves like aluminum rain.

And that ancient maple choir—velvet-robed, viscous-voiced, spangled with flower and ice, studded with points of wet silver light, stuffed into the Restaurant's retrospective telephone booth, mouths splayed howls against cracked amber glass (as I'd always pictured them)—revived:

and wept and prayed, wept and prayed.

It was then that I, small in my voluminous apron's soiled black, thought I saw you at the glass table, eating eggs, which we both know are not on our menu, from a silver bowl that could not have been ours either, opposite a fat man with a wooden sled on his lap and a newspaper dividing the space between you.

"Those roses," I shrieked, pointing for the table-center's tin vase: "those will never bloom!"

But you saw or heard nothing; my demon, idiot love;
the spears began to fly.

Company tanks came down the spiral stair. Volcano Joe Himself,
wild-browed, sinistral, skin a cruel leathered tan, grinned at the
procession's head—
he was goofy-foot on a gun turret beneath The Restaurant's colors
of Red, Black and Fun, the raised standard whipping high above
his head.
Only the glass that was already his eye, deactivated by some surface-
breaking reef in '68, spared him lost sight
when a stone-arrowhead struck, spraying glassblood down the
wreck that had been his face,
but there was no time to exult or to grieve;

blood of an impaled Guest's rare ribeye steak juiced from a Section
30 2-top's checked plastic tablecloth, puddling with the floor's
gentle decline
and I got the mop again.

From the telephone booth a creaking banshee hymn:
I am the Truth and the Light concealed between stacked clipboards
cataloging clean dispensations of tasks—

A trapdoor opened beneath the storeroom's floor, and, Lo, a crystal
tide swept out along the channels, flooding the graveyard behind
our Store, where the dying whale flopped on cracked asphalt, its
great golden tail carving swaths through regathering tourists who

crowded, relentless, for photographs.

You gave me your job, or something like it; they called you the "hyacinth girl," a sobriquet I could not understand, but which revived my suspicions, particularly when I saw the leers on certain swarthy Servers' faces. I hated them then, I hate them now.
I should have taken you away somewhere, I should have trusted no one—

In the parking lot one night not long after the event, when I came to pick you up from a double shift so that you would not have to take the bus, we discussed:
—I'm so sorry.
—So am I.

([Sung]:
"As the deer panteth for the water
so my soul longeth after thee.")[1]

In the storeroom I saw the Devil, eyelids stretched over his face, crouched between halflit shelves, wheezing a Word I couldn't bear to hear; I covered my ears with my apron, closed my eyes—
worse.

Over intercoms and hollow spans swollen with grief, my inbox chimed—
but I was forbidden to go or even to think of you, Sweetness, Lover, Womb.

_____
[1]c.f., Jon 7, 33-31: Pain.

"From the heart of the parking lot next to the Restaurant at the end of nearly all things, I write to you, my love. Stop."

In a vision of wet limbs and carfog I saw your hair grow damp, rope-like, and swing between sweaty faces, one perfect, one
I hate.

"Stop!?!" I typed, in a rage.

<* Stop *>

Here is a joke that T-Rex, our bartender, told—a tasteless, insulting, unfunny, racial slur that I will now reproduce without emendation or irony:

What da local boy wen tell da haole when he wen take one giant lead off turd base?
What?
What, brah, you give up? You no more one guess?
Nah, what he wen say?
"Das right, haole: go home!"
Ha ha ha.
Shit, brah, I fucken hate haoles.
Yeah.

<* Stop *>

In the women's bathroom rumor holds a ghost but I have never seen her.

O, Honolulu night.

In dreams I walk with you, in dreams I talk with you, in dreams it's me alone that gets to peel your shimmering skin away and swallow what's—

"How now," she said, "How now? Have you lost the sense with which you were born?"

(The ringing phone rang ringing, ringing it's ringing ring, I couldn't help a single Guest, not one)

Enough, quoth the Happy People Greeter, who was studying to be a marine-biologist and who would shortly be dead, and who also pole-danced at her uncle the Viscount's dive, down Sand-Island way, but it was too late:

warriors stormed back through the heavy wooden doors that I and Tommy, balding ex-shift-leader (caught doping down pre-shift; demoted) held open most Friday nights—

"We need a sub-HPG asap, folks."

In dreams I have your body.

In dreams I have your touch.

Your warmth, your toes, your sweet embrace.

It's you I love so—

XXXXXXXXXXXXX

We watched them recede into the night as they chanted traditional war chants—with some irony, I thought—and hefted our Greeter above their heads.

I saw seven shot-glasses empty at the bar's four corners,
tiny contests on television screens,
a wrinkled regular,
withered limes,
dust—

You, my only love, my cherished, alone, in candlelight (but the
Restaurant does not provide candles!), the book I wrote of proverbs
quips and psalms,
clutched open in your hand, frail white fingers quivering, as you
remembered me—or else the fat one, my enemy, cheap devil.

"Unto thee, oh Lord, do I deliver myself up."

After we'd collected the blue-books and tallied up responses,
after we'd sent purple taro-mash tonics (complimentary) to tables
that hadn't fled,
after we'd listened to the squashed sparkling choir sing the usual
midnight anthem (penned by Corporate [i.e., Joe, before he was
dispatched]),
after a certain amount of sighing lamentations (more or less assumed
at that hour after any busy weekend night),
after all of these things,
the Finale descended as a cloud of sweet-potato light:

1) At the center of the bar-pond, the geese became swans and T-Rex
fell into the trough of ice I myself had brought in buckets.

2) Trick-or-Treaters swarm the gates!!

Third):
From The Restaurant's far corner I heard a voice, crying out of our
Store's own wilderness:

I don't love you anymore, you said, and I need my check.

Beneath bins of dirty plates, utensils, cups, sizzle platters all acrust
with cheese, I dumped our offal into still more plastic bags, dragged
these out for the whale-demolished dock, glittering now with
golden innards, and slick quivering chunks of what had been within
(plankton, puppet, harpoon, Jonah, rust),
sifting through which (with spears, canoe-paddles, a palm-
switch) the warrior Chief and certain of his men to whom
he called out (in a tongue I interpreted by pitch alone):
"Men: relieve him of his brain, his heart, his balls, his eyes,"
indicating, with an outstretched arm: me.

And they moved as if to obey, so that I foresaw—and in truth
embraced—
the end.

But your voice—

Your voice,

Sugar, Plum, Honeyfuck, Balm of my Life:

You sang in a voice so sweet that even the rocks cried out, and cracked themselves and the warriors sheathed their spears in their own black and crumbling hearts and I saw the whole of that monolith collapse, suck itself down into a sinkhole of cement and wood and glass and food (cooked and un-) pulled down into pooling cess—

Over an incessant intercom the voice of one Store-Manager breaking as through stone:

WE HAVE SEEN THEM SMOKING BATU FROM THE GLASSPIPE

THEY ARE GONE.

HERE ARE THEIR APRONS, ONLY THE WIND'S HOME NOW.

And it was as if I'd never had you to lose the memory of the last time you traced the troughs of tear-drenched hollows beneath my eyes, as you leaned in to kiss me goodbye.

(Before the war.)

A horn's blast; radio; cries.

Do we meet them at the gates? Are there gates to meet them at?

The list of those who died a thousand bloodless afternoons in our Restaurant's wilted gloam:

T-Rex, Tony, Justin, Heather, many more (the names go just before the faces.)

How I needed you the night the ice vaults cracked and yielded glaciers, solid as bone,

the night the hordes spilled from the opera-house across Ward Avenue

and I could not Greet them fast enough, could not, could not …

O city city I sometimes hear the yowl of waiter-wraiths

who bear platters down boneyard alley

where the dead men lost nothing

only the mops' home—and also buckets and sanitizer—

In the grill-smoke, where the men who have no words cook sterile food,

the secret notes in gesticular code,

the scents:

tomato, lemon, oil, garlic, meat, coffee, Tropical Tea, cigarette,

vodka, ganja, batu, mushroom, powder, needle, pillcrush, sweetness, lover, home,

o, god, release me from regurgitated air

(Your name the Word I no longer dare—)

In cold steam we lock the vault behind us and waltz down cellar-stairs

to the treble thump of a lavender heart

that glows at the basement's core,

our aprons stripped from our bodies,

round the bathing light we dance

a duet of shadows dispatched from the body's thudding chorus
of thunder and fried heat, fear.

Here is what they can take from me:
A highball shatters—
The rest is silence.

A Few Thoughts in Closing

<u>Oct. 12</u> (cont.)

All of which is to say I've basically decided to go ahead and kill as many as I can at school tomorrow, assuming I do go to school. As noted above, the old man actually seems to think, or, since "think" is probably too strong here, seems at least to assume for some reason that I don't know he keeps the Berretta, both semi-automatics, plus the bazooka in the "hope chest" under some rotting blankets and old family photo albums in the shed out back. Which: what the hell does he need a bazooka for? I don't know. Actually I don't know why he has any of them. Ours being the extremely safe and relatively well-off upper-middle-class suburb I've also previously described in some detail. But he does have them. When I say "as many people as possible" or however I put it a second ago, I don't mean just spraying bullets sans discrimination like these clowns you see on network news from time to time, necessarily, though it's true that on the whole since there are far fewer people I'd prefer to save than continue to let suffer, this method would, in my case alone, as far as I know, be the more moral one, as the selection of those condemned to life will be as it were "natural," random as opposed to some manifestation or blueprint of my petty gripes. Simple arithmetic. When I'm honest with myself, which isn't as often as I've tried to pretend in these notes, very frequently even going so far as to lie brazenly, to myself, as I write them, though I'm not lying now, I admit that of course a very cruel part of me would prefer to see that bastard Rick Victor live into his nineties, but this is the kind of savagery I intend to eliminate in toto with tomorrow's work. So, no, I don't have a list of people I'm going to go out of my way to avoid. Which means it is going to look a lot like the so-called "tragedies" you see lighting up the news-cycles between soft features on panda bears or sprints for division leads. Which is why I've gone to such lengths in the preceding pages to "take stock" of my thinking here, on the eve of my benefaction, which will of course be baptized a "massacre" or "tragedy," or I suppose "spree," not so much to explain myself—and certainly not to anyone else, since I'll be bringing this journal with me and these notes will therefore presumably burn with whichever school building winds up being the final "resting place" of my ashes and bones—as to sort of clear up some confusions for myself, this not being the sort of undertaking you want to undertake in a state of anything but the highest, the absolute utmost clarity, I think, though I certainly haven't finished sorting it all through yet.

To be one-hundred percent honest, assuming such a thing is possible, which I naturally doubt, most of the people a person like me would want to make suffer are already suffering more than enough, so that it's more a reflection of some kind of moral failure or weakness or insensitivity to others' pain and difficulty with the kinds of things that we all have to face, in high school, of course, and, I can only assume based on the very little I am able to infer about the quality of our adulthoods to come, from partially illustrative examples such as, for instance, my father's nightly fifth of gin, his consumption of which is of course generally begun in the form of elegantly concocted cocktails, such as the so-called "smoky martini," "salty dog," "bloodhound," and so forth, but soon thereafter devolves into long miserable sucks or "quaffs" of

90-proof straight from the bottle—it's an inability to wrap your head around the kind of grim brutality that's just about everybody's life. For instance take Brett, whom we've obviously seen quite a bit of in these pages: yes, his behavior towards me but of course not only me has been by just about any standard you want to apply of decency or regard for others' physical or spiritual well-being nightmarishly grotesque, and we certainly don't need to revisit in anything like the foregoing's detail or depth the humiliation he authored during the now-locally infamous New P.E. Uniform Orientation–assembly, though I will note one last time in passing that it seems almost cosmically cruel that of all the days I might have elected to don the crotch-torn crimson boxers which were the only pair but one left in my undergarment drawer, it had to be that miserably frigid bleak late-December morning when the gymnasium's heating had gone haywire and no one on the administrative staff surmised the potential counter-productiveness of refusing to cancel or even postpone the month's second so-called "spirit assembly" in lieu of conducting it in the soul- and genital-shriveling cold—but what I mean to say about Brett is, who's to say I wouldn't have done the exact same thing, if I knew I could get away with it? Brett having probably gone through most of his life knowing he could get away with it. I mean more or less any "it," within reason. In all fairness, it was probably a lot of fun, I too no doubt would have relished the foudroyant glory as the whole shivering student body howled with schadenfreudeal glee at the outcome of my sudden antic inspiration, and of course then the person I'd pantsed and exposed the entirely-temporary-but-no-less-humiliating-for-that private personal circumstances of to the entire student body would have wanted his revenge on me. This is why specifics are so dangerous. If I want to be entirely honest about this, which, again: unlikely, I can't really point to a single thing anyone's ever done to me that I wouldn't entertain the idea of doing to somebody else, if there were anybody I could get away with doing it to. At the very least I could imagine that if I were one of the dicks behind one of the various deplorable things done to me over the years I might be more inclined to want to give one of those dickheaded gambits a test run on someone like me. Part of the problem therefore of course being that there really isn't anyone I could think of being able to get away with doing this kind of stuff to, at least not without the added leverage of weaponry, but I say part of the problem because I think that while there is an aspect of this that could essentially come down to sheer souring wrathful grapes, Raskolnikov, Nietzschean Will-to-Power, all that stuff, I think it's also true that there's a much bigger problem that contains this problem in it, which I want to try and explain here before I go ahead and shoot myself out of it, I mean the problem, with my unceasingly soused dad's small arsenal. On the other hand, I'm suddenly feeling like I might be too tired to do the explanation justice just now. Speaking of sleepiness: don't think it hasn't occurred to me that I might just need some good old nod. Since I haven't slept in a long time. I mean, I go to bed. I lie down, I close my eyes, but then I just sort of lie there all night, or until I decide to get up and do some homework or brew coffee or siphon a few more bullets from Dad's stash for eventual use, or else just lie there, wondering how I'll ever get upright. I do wonder sometimes if I might not be less like this with just a little more sleep in my system; if so, we're all even stupider than I'd thought.

Oct./14

Yesterday's so-called attempt having obviously been a failure. I mean of the Will, in the sense that I never even smuggled or "lugged" the weaponry in lieu of books and my supposed guitar—I don't even own a guitar, just the absquatulated case—in to school with me in the first place, not that the war-machinery malfunctioned or my aim was off, or some analogous comedy of ineptitude ensued, though I wouldn't rule this out as an eventual possibility, in fact I'd forecast it as fairly probable should I eventually surmount this clearly more formidable obstacle to doing the job, my "Will." Actually, I didn't even go to school. I called the Dean's office and told Ms. Flinkelgrath that I was sick—I *was* sick, obviously, but no more so than I'd been any other day I'd gone to school without complaint, or at any rate with only minimal complaining. Actually I complain a lot, come to think of it. Longtime readers will no doubt concur. It's not clear what I hope to accomplish with my complaining, none of my grievances, or very few of them, are ever redressed or even generally so much as acknowledged in consequence of my "bitching and moaning," as people say, an inaccurate idiom, I think, as most people only rarely moan, I almost never do, although I'm moaning at the moment, as I write, as a kind of trial or test—maybe I haven't been moaning enough—and I also generally don't feel any better afterwards, i.e., I don't even take any kind of carminative pleasure or joy in airing the congested displeasures oppressing my mind or emotional core, or "soul." And yet I continue to complain. To the extent that I'm not sure my mother—once the chief auditor of my myriad nitpicks, grouses, bemoaning lamentations, abjurations, metaphysical bones to pick, protestations that I can't possibly go on—even heard me anymore, while she was alive, as she never seemed to respond. Which makes me wonder if I ever actually did my complaining aloud. This disconcerts. She almost certainly doesn't hear me now, addressed as she is many mornings via apostrophic plaint. What I did yesterday on my day of convalescence was I lay down and stared at the poster on my bedroom's south wall. I've already described this poster elsewhere, no need for repetition, I'm nothing if not fierce in the face of pleonastic excess, but yesterday's contemplation seems to have thrust me into a kind of time-lapse or even a trance. At any rate it was no longer light enough in my room to make out the features of the professional basketball player I admired with a probably pathological ardor a few years ago when I was under the impression that interscholastic athletics would function as an escape hatch from or portal out of my pain and into the dimension of glory and amenable wisdom and perhaps the sweet mysteries between a pair or two of cheerleaders' legs, when I realized I'd been staring at the poster for a while, in other words that night had "fallen" and I hadn't noticed, and I'd begun by peering in the clear morning sunlight directly into the German's strain-contorted face. I didn't and still don't consider it a lost day, though I was suddenly starving, and crept out of my lair, slunk downstairs at the behest of a kind of ravening need to the pantry, from which I selected an entire "family size" package of double-stuff Oreo cookies, which my father stockpiles as a kind of sadistic concession to the increasingly tubby Tom's appetites for gunk and which I secreted back to my bedroom, ripped open, and polished off the full contents of, no milk—I frankly would have liked some milk but there was no way I was risking the stairs again, so that I wound up viscerally incommoded all night and was unable to sleep even the hour or two I can occasionally manage if I can endure plainsong enumeration into the low ten-thousands.

Obviously I didn't want to go through with it today then, either, not only because of how physically ill I felt on account of the Oreo overindulgence I'd capped my sick-day with, but also because I wanted to make sure nobody's violent death could be even tentatively attributable to bloating, constipation, anemia, or cramps. Which reminds me: last Tuesday or maybe it was Monday's episode of note was when I latched myself into the downstairs boys' bathroom's farthest stall and dunked my head (fastidious to the last, I flushed beforehand), tried to force myself to breathe in the swirling second vortex, but it turns out the lungs have been about their business for just far too long, I mean evolutionarily, to fall for this kind of puerile ruse. It really was pure buffoonery. I was playacting at misery and lunatic rage, clowning, to be honest, but for whom?, aspiring to a pain more metaphysical and clean, when in truth my insides were just punishing me for the previous evening's sin, which in this case had been my consumption of an entire bag of off-brand and ostensibly "nacho-cheese" saporous corn tortilla chips, assuming gluttony or any of the others can be counted a sin, which is also dubious. After all, I only ate the exact quantity of speciously seasoned snack product that I wanted to eat. No more than I wanted (granting that I stopped only after capsizing the bag over my open mouth to harvest all remaining crumbs, so that perhaps you might argue I'd have continued to consume tortilla chips from a larger-sized bag, though I've never seen anything beyond the 11.5 0z., which doesn't mean it isn't out there, somewhere, of course, a principle that applies, generally, to just about everything we haven't seen, I assume, though of course here, too, I might be wrong), and it isn't as if I *wanted* to want all those chips. Right? Your Honor, I now call the Author of these vile urges to the witness stand—fuck it, dead end.

      After the unsuccessful felo de se Ms. Kim wanted to know why I'd missed two thirds of her class and also how my hair and collared shirt had got so wet. In response I suggested she go dig up the dead parakeet she spent half of last Friday's last period telling us she and her husband had buried in a cardboard shoebox the previous evening after having come home from a presumably tedious night on the town to find themselves not entirely unexpectedly bereft of (the bird had apparently been suffering from some kind of avian cancer or flu, which one I forget) but still plunged by the loss into a strange kind of grief that can only be really understood by a particular type of person predisposed to fall in love with his or her pet, to take this perished avifaunal specimen and cram it up her too-inquisitive cunt, leave me the fuck alone, for Christ's sake—kidding, haha!—that's just an approximation of what I'd wanted to say. All I actually said was I'd been washing my hands and slipped forward into the basin, klutz that I am. In any other class this would have been the occasion for some lively commotion at my expense, but they tend to stock AP English with all the spiritless eunuchs and hags who haven't been siphoned off by Fine Arts and Film. Kids like me normally drink promoted liquor and escape into narcotics, art, literature, tattoos, film, is the impression I get from the relevant literature and handful of films I've bothered to read or see. Or skateboarding. Comics. Tomorrow being Saturday, the plan for now is Monday, although this could obviously change, again. This whole Oreo episode has fucked with my composure. I'm starting to wonder, how to put this, I'm starting to wonder about my own particular infirmities. How do I mean. Well, so for instance, I don't really want to pay anyone back. Or actually I don't want to *want* payback, because I don't want anyone to want to do the kinds of things to me that I'd want to make them pay for, and I don't want to know deep down that a big part of the reason people like me feel this unquenchable need to make them pay is that their doing these kinds of things to me (which, granted, are any way you look at them, for the experiencer not so pleasant) reminds me that I'm being deprived of the obvious fun they get to have at my expense because they're taller or stronger or prettier or funnier or have richer dads or better hops/court-vision, or all the other advantages they might bring to the playing of the game, that they're basically just better at life and more potent than I am—so that what I'd really like is a situation where I didn't feel like I was missing out on the opportunity to do to other people the kinds of things I hated them for doing to me. But just being realistic here, it seems pretty unlikely that people are going to stop wanting things that the enjoyment of, if you follow the thread all the way down to the spool, is probably coming at someone's expense, obliquely or indirectly in plenty of cases, for instance how I'll never get to enjoy any of the recherché (to make use of yet another lexical entry stockpiled in the short-term registry during preparation for the variously-acronymed college entrance examinations that Monday's adventure will obviously render my supposedly superlative performance on superfluous) imagined postures and poses or diverse locales (including weirdly and kind of embarrassingly, the beige vinyl settee in the lobby of my Mom's office, dredged up obviously from the fairly distant past, where I've, as noted elsewhere, also actually entertained some Oedipal enjoyment with the good old Dearly Departed herself) in which I've balled the fear of god into just about every available opening or orifice or even concavity of Jessica S., but will never actually get to even prosaically approximate or indulge in a scaled-back, moderate, reasonable way, thanks to the bastard Rick Victor, whose name's grim aptness I've addressed myself to in any number of previous entries, as the attentive reader will no doubt recall, but who I'm attempting to say here can't strictly be accused of *doing* anything to me, directly, with respect to Jessica S., since I've naturally never had anything non-vigorously-onanistic to do with her, not a single conversation, not even a smile or "Hello!" to tell you the truth, as a far as I can remember, though I can remember spending entire Latin and macro-ec periods perusing her legs on days she wore the merciless cut-offs, in a kind of whole-body-wracking pain, the somatic authenticity of which is verifiable by, I'd imagine, a pretty sizable segment of the male adolescent population, and though I spent hours literally or at least practically panting over the non-possumus cruelty of her thighs, I'm almost certain in this case that the hoary She doesn't even know I exist actually applies, at least I've never seen her so much as see me, i.e., register my spatial-temporal presence as ontological fact, and so old Rick Victor can't strictly be blamed for my not getting to enjoy a particular enjoyment that, to be fair, I never had any say over whether or not I'd frantically, violently, wrackingly ached to enjoy, I was never consulted on this instinct-initiative, frankly would have shot it down if granted the executive veto—but on the other hand his getting to have all the fun it's sort of impossible for me not to elaborately speculate about him having after basketball games he's scored forty points in, in somebody's bathtub at some dithyrambic house party I'm obviously not invited to and can only venture speculation on the miscellaneous particulars of based mostly on depictions of high school life I've seen in films and on TV, but assume do exist (and would probably be driven absolutely mindless with envy and pain by my presence at, so I certainly don't cite these speculative parties as another instance of me "missing out"), but as I was saying, on the other hand, his getting to indulge this particular carnal inclination does more or less rule out my getting to do so, right? Assuming she's not a real goer, which actually I've heard tales, or technically overheard, since nobody bothered to tell me.

Anyway, it's not just the sex I'm not having, though I guess my failure to break up the preceding several-page speculation into slightly less frantic separate sentences doesn't really testify too persuasively for the accused against the charge protests too much. But the fact is, it isn't the sex but it is the much bigger thing the sex winds up being a kind of synecdochical symbol for. Do I mean metonymy? This is the kind of thing I can't ever remember. Meanwhile I can quote from memory all of Macbeth's final Act, as we have already seen on I believe several prior occasions, during none of which did I require recourse to the text. Ditto on Hamlet's better sallies. Anyway it's some kind of symbol for what I want to try to work out or name here, whatever it is, exactly, that I'm trying to talk about, if for no better reason than that I assume you don't want to be dealing with second thoughts when you're pausing to reload between rounds in some spattered hallway down which the screams of unlucky ones the bullets missed or scared away continue to echo and merge. Look: judging from the above-referenced and a handful of other books they let us read in our so-called literature classes, I'm not the first person in history to mull through some of these things and come out concluding that it sure looks like the meaning of life is death, and I don't mean that poetically, I mean literally, like the point of life is to kill off as many urges as you can—which by extension also means killing off the chances of other people whose urges might overlap with yours to have the things they're urged to want before the grave takes care of whatever you haven't gotten round to killing off yet (it would seem, incidentally, the number of these urges actually grows by exponent with each one you dispatch: I wouldn't know for sure yet, since most of mine are elusive needle-pricks I haven't been able to salve, but this seems like an unfair, not to mention ill-designed system) by annihilating all of them, for good. I'm probably not even the only person to think this way at my own school, and yet somehow people seem to forget. At least I always do. But if the meaning of life is death, then how is it that people *smile*, is what I'd really like to know. What the hell are they all smiling about? I always feel when I see people smiling that they're lying on one level or another, it's entirely possible they don't *know* they're lying, but they're still nowhere near the truth, and this is not something I'm just being a prick about, I legitimately don't understand how you could smile for a single honest second in this miserable hole of shit, but maybe I'd be smiling if I were the one dunking the basketball in opponents' faces while crowds approved loudly, probably I would smile, but this, this is getting closer to what I wanted to talk about—yes, the smile's the problem, the smile is a real fucking problem, because basically it's the fuel that keeps this whole hell-cycle spinning on repeat and repeat and repeat, repeat—

Relax. Inhale. Swore I'd relax. Well, I'm a liar too. I'd never affirm the contrary. No, that's a lie, too: see? What I mean is, the smile is what keeps the machine spinning, right? Because, see, okay: as long as we've got these assholes up top making it look like there's some exclusive echelon above, a kind of country club, the first- or second estate, I forget which: whichever one isn't the priests, I mean aristocrats, nobility, a top tier where there's little or none of what would appear to be troubling me in terms of the whole litany recorded, in perhaps overly emotive but never embellished with respect to the facts, in these very pages, the whole miserable rigmarole, the occasional fisticuffs—wrong, "fisticuffs" require two or more combatants, what happens to me is I get my face punched in—the rigorous teasing in all of my classes except A.P. Lit (which, it's kind of astounding to me that not a single one of my classmates in that cesspool of bad posture and skin hasn't beaten me to the punch or trigger or grenade detonation, but this I think would actually support what I'm trying to say here) and obviously never getting laid and hating my pop in an entirely petty way that has nothing to do with any of this, in that the man is just the kind of shitfuck I'd probably like to see succumb to some long-suffering organ-rotting disease even if I were doing okay—but as long as they're up *there* smiling and really almost literally glowing, last year at homecoming Victor honestly did glow, marvelous! I have no idea how he did it! ... but then I wouldn't would I?—then what's always going to happen is, you basically figure: Fuck, I'm the problem, if I could only figure out how to get up there things wouldn't feel like such a fucking plague, I might actually want to get up earlier than I'd like each morning, perform menial mental tasks for a cadre of grim, underpaid, overworked, generally unattractive "teachers" classes, I might enjoy striding the hallways at dusk after practice, ferreting out the unsuccessful fucks and bashing their faces into lockers' grates, and so forth, and I just find this fairly insidious, because we're all pitted against each other in this death match to see whose example can best incite the next round of adversaries to engage in the same smiling bloodfest when meanwhile, jeez, hasn't just about everyone read Macbeth? What am I missing when I read or revisit the passages I've committed to memory and conclude, Yep: this is about right—especially when you consider this is a work that justly retains its immense popularity even today?

Anyway, for the foregoing reasons I've tentatively determined to target the lowliest possible. Which means the Victors aren't going to get it. It annoys me to imagine him giving teary condolences to the families bereft of sons he probably fired spitballs at at some point, or drunken daughters he urged to lick his perineum in that special way, pledging that tragedy will draw together and strengthen our hearts, but there's nothing to be done, it's out of my hands. So to speak. As much as possible I'd like to take out only the poor bastards who will never rise to the occasion of taking out themselves, though obviously I might aim for one or both of Victor's legs, and a handful of the more mean-spirited girls may catch a stray bullet or two, or the post-explosion shards from an ill-deployed grenade. Ideally these latter would be only disfigured or -membered, though I'm not as much of a stickler as I seem. I'm not looking forward to this, by the way, in case that's how these notes are starting to make it seem. Fuck it, I don't need to explain, why should I even

Forget it. Something ridiculous has taken place. A ridiculous occurrence. Occurrence being not exactly the right word for what's happened as I am in point of fact directly responsible for it occurring. It would be more accurate to say I've just done something ridiculous, and were accuracy a matter of the slightest concern to me in the so-called composition of these turgid notes, I would have dispensed with the prevaricating hedge and resumed not by implying my passive or peripheral involvement in a ridiculous sequence of events, but rather by asserting forthwith my direct responsibility for the ridiculous thing that's just transpired and interrupted the rapid conclusion of these no-longer-necessary notes, thanks to my own imbecile agency.

I've done something ridiculous—let it never be suggested that I am not a ridiculous young man, and therefore not only capable of but wholly likely to achieve new heights of comedy with every undertaking or "act," which is to leave aside altogether the ridiculous things I say, when I'm foolhardy enough to hazard human speech, or my ridiculous appearance, documented in prior pages with a thoroughness I wouldn't hesitate to applaud and even call brave were I not fully aware of the intent purely to shock and dismay the reader and shove her away from anything like compassion or pity, terrorize her to the extent that in the end she has no choice but to crawl back to my side, realizing her complicity in this grotesque spectacle, ashamed of her humanity. The texture of these notes seems to be undergoing a subtle tonal shift. Why? *I'm* certainly not the right person to ask. The other day when I sat down to write it was with the idea that I'd briefly establish the basic parameters within which my terminal action—that is, the "killing spree"—would ideally be considered by those not fortunate enough to have wandered into the extremely narrow brisance-frustum or "blast radius," those for whom my liniment will never salve the lugubrious agony of hauling around this unhealthy contraption of slick squishy organs, decaying sinew, rotting bone, rot generally, decay, wheezing vital intake, flaking skin and failing teeth, those left unrelieved of this need. Considered according to *my* terms instead of being subjected to the kind of tedious post-facto speculation for which I've always had an acute distaste, though it's true that even at the outset I more than half-imagined I would burn these notes, or the notes would burn with me, surely the explanation is in the action, the action glosses itself—only it doesn't of course, witness the general tenor of newscasts and punditry, the stentorian outrage, the howls of infatuated fulmination, funeral parades, the celebration of death, the cavalcades of denouncements which rarely go even so far as to mask or disguise their raucous function as a cheering section, erupting with maniacal relief in the wake of the massacred someone else. But I didn't want to get into this, the whole shit parade spectacle of overjoyed grief being better left implicit as the necessary impetus for my need to draft these idiotic notes, but I just get so mad, I really do.

I've been lying this whole time about my father's ostensive grenades. Obviously he doesn't have any fucking grenades. Ditto the "bazooka." He does have an assault rifle, however, which I guess isn't strictly that much farther downtrack on the line to preposterous, but the gun exists, he keeps it in the coffin-like chest my little brother the imbecile's lately taken to calling the "hurt locker," god knows why, at the moment it's lying lengthwise across my lap, the rifle, not the fucking chest, and, munitions permitting, I will indeed use it to annihilate as many of my so-called "classmates" tomorrow morning, wait, I mean the day after tomorrow, or perhaps the day after that, if I continue to dither with these "notes," your guess being equal to my own in terms of why. I don't have a list of preferred targets or anything. In terms of specific names. Nor do I have a counterlist of the non-preferred, contrary to what I may have previously claimed, i.e., the students and faculty and members of the administrative and custodial staffs whom the news morons et al. would no doubt refer to as the fortunate ones who miraculously were spared the "cruel" "misfortune" of their "mercilessly," "slaughtered" fellows, getting everything exactly backwards, as always—wrong with a kind of grim adherence to error so perfect in its counterfactuality that you almost have to stand back and hat-tip the straight-faced constancy. Not that I'm not cruel. Which is actually what I wanted to talk about before I got interrupted by the ridiculous thing I—oh yes: I'd almost forgotten the ridiculous thing. That's two topics to dispatch.

I was lying about the assault rifle, too. Not on all fronts, for instance there is a rifle, though I don't know that it can properly be designated "assault," an embellishment intended no doubt to analogously embellish or intensify fore-images of the coming carnage, and this rifle, assuming it's a rifle—maybe it's a musket? I wouldn't put it past it: it's certainly old, not to say antique, though I'm told by my father it does still fire powder and stone, so to speak, and this rifle or whatever it is does belong to D.o.D., the dipsomaniac failed diplomat, and he does store it in a long dusty chest of shaggy-grained wood, but this chest has never to my knowledge been referred to as "the hurt locker," which fraternal anecdote I inserted solely to make use of the opportunity to further shit on Tom, I really am a monster to the end. "The Hurt Locker" being actually the title of an underwrought film we were shown and then urged to reflect on in the venerable scholastic praxis of the short essay (which, parenthetically and perhaps obviously, bears precious little resemblance to its eminent progenitor's collective namesake, though I obviously wouldn't dare claim Montaignian resonance for my own rough "assays"), in Ms. Kim's class on composition and lit. Speaking of whom—I mean Ms. Kim, who, leaving the dead parrot out of it, or whatever the hell kind of bird it was, is actually pretty good at her job, to the extent that such a repugnance is something a person can actually be "good" at, analogous in my opinion to being good at, say, tooth decay, and I'm not ready to admit that you can, leaving aside altogether the question of why the hell anybody would, but she generally gives us books, some of which granted aren't very good, but they're considerably better than the so-called "discussions" we are subsequently compelled to conduct about them, which always begin with me urging myself to contribute my own thoughts on or personal insights into a given story, poem, short novel or play and end with me furiously scribbling these same down in silence as further contributions to these notes, as we have seen in entries on any number of previous days, though this is not her fault unless you want to blame the woman for an entire generation's incapacity to think, but meanwhile she's not without a certain kind of slanted perspicacity, I think, and we do get to read sometimes during class, which is anyway better than breaking open frogs… regardless, good teacher, Ms. Kim, might even go so far as to admit she sometimes makes me think, at the very least she's small enough that I don't find her terrifying as I do my other "teachers," she's actually so small she wears what look like large twill men's button-down dress-shirts as a kind of muumuu or frock to school each day, she has about a half-dozen of these she cycles through, a charming touch… so these days Ms. Kim also had been having us write up responses to selected poems once or twice a week, the frequency I assume varying with the declining parrot or parakeet's fluctuating health's impact on her emotional life at home of late, and its impact on her capacity to concentrate on sifting through these landfills of syntactically disastrous composites of received opinion and cliché, though now she's been giving us a lot of stuff in a decidedly more macabre vein,

Dickinson etc., as if the fucking bird's going to feel gratitude for this propaedeutic memento mori down in its decomposing shoebox, underground however many feet.

I've always hated writing these responses. But the other night what happened was, I was at my desk drawing spirals in the lower margins of my foolscap—yes: the selfsame helices we've seen proliferate over so many pages of this journal, preceding these concluding thoughts—thinking about hanging myself with a belt, I mean thinking about specifics, wondering if I could pull it off, running through a mental inventory of all my belts, trying to decide if any of them would support my weight long enough for my body to exhaust its stored reserves of oxygenated air, or else snap my neck, I didn't particularly care which—pain is pain and Time's for chumps—when I suddenly hit upon a truly stupid idea outstripped in stupidity only by its colossally stupid subsequent execution, which essentially entailed my drafting an original poem and then writing my response to that, and claiming that the poem under explication was the work of an anonymous author. The poem was a diagonal slash running left to right down a blank white page. In the bottom corner under the slash's terminus in the smallest font my word processor could manage, I typed the word "no."

My response to this flight of fancy—a mere imaginative lark—wound up running to something like thirty pages, handwritten, granted, but each page front and back, a practice Ms. Kim doesn't encourage, and normally I do toe the line, why make things worse for the woman, and besides, what the hell do I care (have I mentioned her wall-eye?), only I was in such a gurgling rage, eventually going so far as to weep and even superimpose luminous trails of snot over the smudged ink of freshly scribbled lines as I raced on in a horrible trance, toward what, I don't know, that it was impossible to break the hypnosis long enough to bear this page-skipping injunction in mind, turning the things over when I had to was torture enough.

Well, the ridiculous thing I just did a little while ago is I interrupted my attention to this preamble, in order to idly page through that pathetic composition, which now on revisitation yielded meaning from its handwritten signs just about as readily as I imagine would any of the scripts and tongues my provincially circumscribed, brief but naturally not brief enough stint here on Earth would not have afforded me the opportunity to acquire, assuming I cared to speak to the natives of any foreign land, which thankfully I have never had any desire to do, "communication" with my countrymen having been considerably more than sufficient imposition on baseline equilibrium for me. I.e., I couldn't really untangle much of what I'd had to say, but, in a handwriting that wasn't mine and in the red ink customarily forbidden to all but the keepers of the gates to secondary-educational "knowledge" rammed down the craws of enrollees at our pedagogical institutes, appended to the bottom and flowing onto the back of my inscrutable composition's final page was an additional or supplementary composition, a response to my response, which unfortunately I could parse, all too clearly.

I decline to reproduce a word of this personal address, which I had not seen until it struck me dumb a few minutes ago, when I ought to have been wrapping up these ridiculous notes: decorum or even a kind of tender respect—I refuse to say "love," reason absolutely forbids it—but its effect—and it did stun me—was to reproduce the earlier tableau, that is, of me once again bent over the manuscript, crying, again, albeit no longer scribbling with stupefied rage, once again leaking considerably onto the paper, so that it's not clear I'd be able to quote more than a few disjointed phrasings and bits of unbridled compassion from that earnest note, were I inclined to embarrass my teacher here, which, as I have said, I am not.

We now turn to the problem of my cruelty. Directly. Or indirectly. Indirection being more in line with my general approach. Misdirection, really, you could even go so far as to say. Though I think we can safely begin with a bit of straightforwardness, entirely out of character, perhaps: Where do I get off killing all those kids? We've established with some clarity how I feel in broad terms about this misery pit, so that from a certain perspective— that is, *my* perspective—every successful shot with the rifle—if it is in fact a rifle, certainly "automatic," was taking things too far, if I ever said "automatic," I can't remember, no that's wrong, I'm always taking my embellishments too far, possibly as admittedly meager compensation for my inability to take anything else far enough—every kill, I'd begun to say, not only can't be considered cruelty, in light of the miserable circumstances from which it will extract each harvested soul with no further obligation imposed, but really ought to be cast as a gift of mercy, the closest I'll have come over the course of a markedly pitiless life to what I assume people mean when they use the word "compassion," though I doubt they understand the word any better than I ever have, which is to say not at all. Yes, homicidal mercy—the only possible mercy, considering the conditions under which we subsist, or the only possible directly compassionate act, though I concede the potentially palliative analogous effects of suicide on those for whom the eliminated soul's ongoing being would have continued to cause vexation and grief. Anyone unfortunate enough to flee the premises at the first round's reverberations will be depriving herself of the author's last great gift, the only gift he's ever given, in point of fact. But the cruelty question is as follows: If we trace my thinking on the subject to its logical end—an admittedly burdensome, not to say hopeless task—it's difficult not to conclude that the least cruel course of action would be, not a single day of altruistic slaughter, but rather a whole career undertaken on these imprisoned creatures' behalf: in a word I'd need to take up the mantle of what's known as a "serial killer," and while the prospect is not without a certain romantic—perhaps jejune— appeal, I honestly don't think I have in reserve whatever amalgam of stamina, cunning, mental acuity, and practical wherewithal is required to pull off more than the one day, and even that will in all likelihood be a bust. I imagine it's hard work, over the long haul. For which I just don't think I have the heart. Which—I swore we'd eventually get here—makes me wonder if deep down I might not be kind of selfish and cruel.

You don't think it's a bit greedy of me in the end, to finish what ought to be the prelude to a long, arduous career as a genuine public servant by taking the so-called rifle to my own dubious head? Certainly such a finale will demand considerably less of the kind of heuristic brainwork I've always particularly abhorred than would the need to elaborate a reliable exit-plan plus long-term scheme for future strikes from some shadow lair against mortal indecency and pain. To start with, where would I acquire the reliable firearm, for instance, with which to carry on my work, or at least additional ammo for the antediluvian one I've got? From this vantage I'm starting to look like an inconsiderate brat. And I've never been able to disentangle torpor from cruelty. Yes, for the few fortunate recipients of gifts from my father's gun, tomorrow's programme will constitute quite the radiant revision of situations otherwise rather intolerably bleak—but from the perspective of literally everyone else, perhaps leaving aside the terminally afflicted for whom sunny Fate has marked on its calendar tomorrow's big day, or the various beneficiaries of aleatory Same's inscrutable mercy—for instance, those destined to die in wrecked cars—life will, as they say, go on, nothing will have changed. If I really wanted to make a difference, and it isn't clear that this has ever been the aim, I can think of very few less efficient paths than the auto-obliteration. But it'll be such a relief! Sweet, sweet release—I'm almost tempted to drop the pen and administer the mortal dose right now, it's time, I can't wait to die!—and yet all those suffering morons without the means: am I not cruel? There's incidentally a good reason I switched from the red to the black, a few pages back, you'd be surprised to discover just how many—who the hell cares. Pointless palaver. And there we have a redundancy, the superfluity of my thought rears its— no, no flourishes, though the thought naturally needn't be mine to achieve needlessness. But in these pages we're concerned with me, assuming we're concerned with anything. We? Yes we: We return to Ms. Kim. The woman won't keep out of my head! And the perished pet bird. Rest in peace, dead parakeet! Madness and death. Last night I watched Zapruder over two thousand times. Why? Is there perhaps something I'd like to say to the woman? I mean Ms. Kim. Hello, Ms. Kim. You are a little Asian lady with that queer taste for pseudo-sackcloth, an ill-aligned left eye locked into perpetual peer a touch skyward and to the right—I mean house right, of course—through which I assume nothing is ever seen. Unless it's the left eye you look with. In which case I don't think we've ever met eyes. Unlikely, but not beyond conceiving. Or both eyes see something, separate things, neither seeing its allotted sight especially well. This too seems unlikely, but then it would account for a number of things. The devotion to the dead bird, for one. How account? I don't know. Well, all right: the dead bird, before it was dead, when it was the cherished creature friend, was never strictly visible, was it, Ms. Kim? you never truly saw this chirping or short-spoken-phrase-reduplicating, depending on the type of bird, object of devotion, had to rely on your husband's pretty descriptions, assuming the man shares your dexterity with words, which, given the common—and it seems to me misguided, but what do I know—desire to pitch the matrimonial tent on shared turf, doesn't seem unlikely, so that perhaps it's less the parrot, I mean the actual bird, than it is your loving husband's loving renditions, now lost for all time, whose loss you truly grieve. Something in that. A touch tender for my taste—anyway you could have just closed one fucking eye, so forget it. I really hate it here. Certainly can't stick around for another whole year. Question is, who's coming with me. Thoughts, Ms. Kim? Why the hell do I keep coming back to you? And yet, here's an admission, I really hope we don't cross paths tomorrow (assuming etc.)... but why, why, why, why not?—doesn't this run counter to everything I've just fucking—stop! Stop! STOP! That way madness—

I've just thought of something, something's occurred to me: I've imagined fucking—I mean while whacking off—every female teacher (and, yes, all right, many of the males) over the course of my illustrious—shut up—except for you. Still time to rectify that, of course. Except I don't think I want to, never have—it isn't the exotropiaic eye, well, hmm, okay, it is the eye, honestly, I guess, but it isn't *just* the eye, the eye is not exclusive. Do I stare at you during class? If so, and the chances seem good, since who knows what I'm looking at half the time, I certainly don't, but if so, I apologize, I'm sorry, but it isn't lust, well maybe it is lust, but not the carnal kind. It's longing. What did you think of my poem? Your response, from what I can still make of it through the smear, while thorough, thank you, not to say kind, thanks again, would appear to address itself strictly to my notes on the poem—which, frankly, from what I can still make of them through see above, strike me as strict havering hogwash, no offense, I mean to you, I'm not likely to be offended, or defended, but here we've begun to veer—you responded to the response, not the poem. But the poem's the thing. Isn't it? I still quite like it. Perhaps the slash is lavish, a touch of my characteristic decorative bent, but I don't think it excessively detracts, do you? Do you? Wait, I've hit upon a revision. Here it is:

Hmm. Still leaves a little something to be desired. Well, that can't ever be helped—corollary to the first postulate that nothing can. Anyway, fuck poetry. Tomorrow's the big declaration. I've always preferred prose. I've decided. I'd address my final thoughts to Mother, if Mother weren't dead, Dad: no chance, you fucking dick, so the doubtful honor falls to you, dear Ms. Kim. I can't say I'll miss looking up at you—strangely toy- or birdlike in your pseudo-sackcloth gown beside the towering rostrum at the head of our nerd-crowded class, holding forth on Act III of Hamlet, volume perched open on your palm, or speaking of the perch, peering with equal quantities of elegiac need into separate sectors of the middle depths, each eye betraying a glimmer of wet, as you recount for the class still further happenings in the brief but joyous life of the dead fucking bird, "miss" would be obscene, plus, obviously, after the action there won't be a me to miss things or give thanks at last to be set free from the rank abomination of everything—but there will be a number of scenes on which tomorrow's brief excitement will slam a terminal door that I guess I would miss a whole lot less.

Well. So long, Ms. Kim. If you never get the chance to read these notes, I might have gone ahead and done it.

History

Not the lynchings, nor the first indigo dawn behind a nuclear-gnarled skyscape, nor the self-anointed tyrant's decree that a third of his sudden subjects be cast into the purgative flames; not the chanting blood-faced demons carving the figures of virgins preserved for future delectation, nor the war-sparrows' song, shrill and sweet in the mornings they were loosed to pluck insurgent captives' eyes, not the bonepile ziggurats over which waves of withered vagrants—the history teacher's own forebears among them—scuttled and picked with frail fingers, nor the winedark river from which these ancestors drank, having no other water, the unspeakable hunger, its unspeakable antidote, the wastelands' desolate chill, the deep caverns' crushing heat; not the frenzied rituals of the elect, dancing round the new ruler's throne, not the improbable culmination of a generation-spanning war in frail survival, peace, gradual restoration of the oldest order (though now under this sunless sky)—

No:

What the teacher sees just before he kicks the chair from beneath his tip-toed feet (his eyes closed against the dim lamplight that might spare him this last pathetic vision), is the flimsy little student he has often seen: surreptitiously shouldered, laughed at, shoved into the hall-tunnels' crumbly walls, last-picked for burrow-ball, alone at mess, presumptive author of a host of lugubrious poetic lines left in palimpsestic evidence beneath the scrawl of a rather poorly-written paper on the Fathers of the Underground Revival;

the child's small blue eyes peer into his, in the moment after classmates append to the jeering appellation they've already been forbidden to apply a few new, loudly-whispered threats of innovative violence, while he, the teacher, empty at the end of another afternoon of unheeded disquisition on the world of light and wind that once was, long ago, overwhelmed, again, by the brute stupidity of his scoffing charges, these hardened tiny monsters to whom he's supposed to be passing on the flame, pretends simply not to hear, the boy's eyes a plea from which he silently looks away—

The Point

Middle of the night I wake up hot and damp, an actual pool of sweat gathered in the hollow of my neck, a warm shallow pool like the sun-cooked remainder of a puddle hours after the rain—or like one of those temporary little wading lagoons beached in the rolling sands of Sea Isle City, on the New Jersey Shore, where you might splash and play with the bucket and shovel you'd salvaged from the bottom of the netted bag the unfavorite uncle would haul from the rented beachhouse's garage each morning, preferring the island of lukewarm water over the gray and thunderous frigid Atlantic where there were waves like the end of the world and older boys with mayhem in eyes hurtling wild down each cresting rampart's face, the shrieking a reedy cacophony, girls in the shallows thickets of slick bronze legs, and lifeguards who'd blow their whistle and shout at you—at *you*, you would realize slowly in the face of a great and rising awful Dread—before swimming out to retrieve you from the high and treacherous seas you'd swum too far out into after the plastic yellow boat your favorite uncle had bought at obscene mark-up from a little toy-stand on the walk over from the rented beach-house this morning but that you could only, as the lifeguard towed you back in to safety and admonishment ashore, watch be taken far from you by the endless expanse as you looked out and tried not to cry or cause the glossy stern lifeguard much more trouble than you were already causing, in terms of him having to paddle with just one hand as he towed you with the other, and to listen well as he chided that the deep water was no place for a little dude with only orange floaties at his elbows and no Adult Supervision; the lagoons, then, in which you'd shovel sand from the sea-floor beneath a half-foot of uterine water with bright plastic tools and try not to think about how much Atlantic lay between Sea Isle City and England or France, the rocky cold shores of which ambiguously distant lands represented the only hope of safe harbor for a small plastic boat borne off on strong and invisible currents away from shore, to sea—a shallow pool, but still a pool, of sweat, into which I can actually dip a fingertip, disgusting and unprecedented but also so incredible as to hold a brief and sleep-muddled fascination for me.

Three-thirty-ish, I'm thinking. Far as time goes. A clock being right up near the top of the list of things I'm going to have to summon the energy or task-organizational art to compile and then go out and purchase soon as I get around to making this garret a home. I do have a cell-phone that keeps time quite well, but one of my last sentient instincts—a good one—was to turn it off so that in the event anyone decided to call he or she would be unable to interfere with the decent night's sleep I'd sensed I was right on the brink of not being able to get through a single subsequent day without getting—is six hours too much to ask?—as my feet fumbled for purchase against the still-tightly-laced shoes I needed out of before I could strip off my jeans—which are inverted and crumpled over next to the nearest stack of large cardboard boxes I haven't unpacked yet, I notice, so the shoe-shucking would appear to have been a success, though I don't see them anywhere—and pass out. Not that I necessarily expected anyone to call. A precaution.

But so three-thirty seems about right. There's a kind of familiar texture or hue to the stage of post-alcohol swelter, the reduction discernible in sludgy stupor from under which I seem to have oozed into waking. Plus the spectral shadowwork across the ceiling.... Around three-thirty, way more alert than I'd choose to be. One reason I can't slip softly right on back to sleep being the room's tumid stench. Robust effluvium oozing from under my sheets, which are clammy and cling to my frame, a whole cavalcade of nasty stuff that needs out, not too much I can do to hold it in, not that I'd even want to, gas expulsion being brief relief to your chronically backed-up frustrated young man.

I turn onto my side, spilling the sweat-pool onto the exposed pages of the book that lies open, even tonight, spread beside me in bed, yes this is probably a theatrical touch, a bit of an excessive devotional display—for no one, since no one knows I do this—but it's what I do. I sleep with your book. I curse, try to dry the sodden page with a sodden corner of sheet, close it, sad. Set it down beside my second-favorite (because April is always cruel), the front cover's pale clouds glow orange in a faint light whose source I'm suddenly curious about.

The darkness seems to shudder, breathe. Weak fractal light-patterns (I think they're "fractal"; not one-hundred percent sure what the word means, mathematically, but I've seen it used to describe streaking proliferation that resembles what I'm seeing) strobe ceiling and walls—source, again, obscure. I have a look around:

On the small nightstand, i.e., the discarded office chair I found abandoned on the curb the other day, at roughly one o'clock w/r/t my position abed, on the seat where I'd left, I'm pretty sure, my purple-velour-covered journal, towering even on his ass, sits David Wallace. No shit. He's smoking what looks, and, I now notice smells, in aromatic counterpoint to my own stink, like a joint.

He's got a stapled packet of computer paper up close to his face, a plain old #2 twirling through meaty fingers as he reads whatever it is he's reading by the burning coal's faint orange glow. He nods and smiles and narrows his eyes once in a while, drags on the clip. Mostly looks serious and committed and engaged.

I cough. Rustle the sheets a little. Prop up on my elbow to look right into his ember-lit face, but he reads on—chuckles at what I assume is an amusing line. I glance around the room, a little self-conscious about the boxes I'm using as makeshift desk, dresser, ottoman—one's open but only half-emptied of my non-favorite books; the laptop I neglected to shut down or at least throw a shrouding tee-shirt over, pulsing the white cone of its operating light up onto the opposite wall at intervals; the laundry scattered without pattern on the floor. Which is to leave aside altogether the problem of my farts. I'm wondering if maybe the weed's smoke hasn't canceled some of that. Maybe he hasn't noticed. Yellow smoke curls out over my bed and I clear my throat.

He flips a page, sighs. Another hit.

Hey, man. I pat the book that's back in bed with me on its front cover. I didn't conjure you. You just sort of showed up, didn't you? Not that I'm not happy you're here; just love to maybe get in a word or two, you know? Hey: David. Buddy. Uncle. Dad. You listening? I'm in here.

I start to hum, stop, sigh at high volume.

Not a glance. The man's concentration really is a force. I roll back over and close my eyes, fart yet again—toke on that you uncaring fuck—and consider:

David's incredibly tall. You can see just from the way he

has to hunch over himself in the little misplaced desk-chair. It's somebody's story he's reading, I'm almost sure. Or I'm not really sure, obviously there's no way of verifying without asking, but it just seems like that's probably what he's doing. You get a sense for this kind of thing in the middle of the night sometimes. I do, at least.

Why not ask him, I ask myself. Start a dialogue. Interface. Well but if he'd only look up, if there were a way to catch his eye and hold his gaze, plus if there were even something to tell him, I mean, what do you say to your favorite person when he pops up next to you one foul pre-dawn in the flesh? What's the protocol here, if there were only someone to tell me—if I could just think of a way to tell him, press it all down to something small enough, transmittable... my throat itches, if there were only a cup of water in here I might swallow a long deep cooling draught and work up the nerve or coherence to at least catch the eye, draw the gaze, Yo— then he might breathe a yellow mist out and up into the polluted air we share, beneath the cannabis-fume cloud we'd hang silent a few seconds before he reached up, scratched the famously formidable chin , narrowed his eyes and asked in a rich kind patient voice: Hey, so listen: What's your story?

(The Father)

See there, the guitar in the corner (Fender, American Strat—$1100, birthday, sixteen, next to the amplifier (Line 6—$850, Christmas, next year), gifts from the Father, both—the Father who, if what his son wanted to do was devote his whole self to the elevation of guitar-play from mere technical prowess to a kind of metaphysical quest for the One Holy Note, then he was absolutely all for it.

Son, he would refrain from asking, in response to the

latter's labored attempts to verbally reconstruct the spiritual Place at the peak of his most intense and full-souled disintegrations into the divine sweetness located dead-center in the heart of the light, those special koanish, consummating Moments of pure communion with the music's absolute and sacred soul—Son, he wouldn't ask: what exactly are you practicing *for*? What exactly is the *point*, he never once wondered aloud.

The love inhering in which restraint the son was only much later able to discern and appreciate the full extent of, realizing with retrospective feelings of admiration, guilt, sorrow, and the full consciousness of a hopeless, unremittable debt, the degree to which the Father must have ached to provide his son with the basic human equipment called for to one day provide for himself both in terms of material and spiritual well-being, at the very least solvency, knowing full well the added hardship in store for any coddled and unprepared man on the day he must confront a capital-centric adulthood less likely to allow for the unmolested time that treks into the heart of the light inevitably required, and far less likely to grant the luxury of freedom from, say, utility bills, rent or mortgage, car-payments or subway fare, and a full- or even multiple part-time job(s) with which to pay them, and, as a Father, wanting desperately to anticipate and help the boy prepare for the pragmatic minefield stretching out before every young man—but persistently checking this constant urge to instruct or even sternly command, acceding for the time to a genuine sense that the son was not yet right and a heartbreakingly generous if doomed hope that he might yet one day become so, might get right, might follow his own path to wholeness, inner-stillness, maturation, manhood if he were only given a bit more time.... The Father having never foreseen himself

needing to stretch out over the rim of the well or pit or otherwise
very deep hole into which his firstborn son had plunged and peer
down, helpless, unable to clasp or even touch the hand of the boy
who'd somehow fallen into this dark place, a sadness and despair
he (the Father) could neither explain nor combat with any of the
wisdom or practical tools he'd acquired over the forty-plus years of
his own by-no-means-without-adversity-and-hardship-but-never-
letting-despair-win-the-day life. The Father in fact having never
felt despair like the full crush of his own feeble inability to reach his
hurting son that pinioned him waking and often weeping, secretly,
through the long insomniac nights, weeping over his impotence—
impotence manifested most horrifically in the paradox that he could
tell the boy a thousand times that a whole world of shimmer and
chance awaited the moment he managed to haul himself out of his
dark place, stand again and face the day, the Father'd of course help
in every way he could—but he couldn't make him do it: Get up,
Son, please get up....

   And he would praise the perplexing music his boy produced,
rave about the beatific songs the son recorded in anticipation of the
day he'd meet a group of other people he'd feel comfortable sharing
his work with and possibly forming a band—songs that were, even
in these rough nascent stages, precociously masterful, the early work
of an obvious prodigy whose late-blooming had only to do with that
lode of precious talent lying unmined for the first seventeen years of
his life, the Father'd generously discern: he could tell him just how
apparent it was that he (the boy) was in line for very big things, the
very bigness of which would only be limited by the extent to which
he was willing to work for them. He could tell him that he was
as moved and paternally amazed by the boy's new manifestation

of musical genius as he'd been by the discovery some fifteen years back one evening just before bedtime-for-bonzo, as he completed the night's last diaper-change, after the young family'd watched its favorite network television show during repast, as was their wont, that his little boy was *humming the theme song to M*A*S*H*; he could even listen to the rough and naturally underproduced demo the boy'd recorded, bring this disc to work and broadcast it incessantly from his office desktop's inexpensive speakers as his personal daily score for a stretch of many months on end and advise patients or other docs in the ward, who never asked, that what they were hearing was not an album one might purchase in stores—yet: but was the creative output of his oldest son, who was rapidly—where does time go?—transforming into a man, You must be proud, the more tactful might mutter—*I am*, for his son would make him proud even if he weren't such a gifted guitarist, singer, songwriter (plus developing keyboardist); and the father could foresee every deserved good thing that his boy had coming his way, soon enough—
but could do nothing to make these things come.

All his life he'd needed only to apply himself when a problem needed solving, to act, this Father was a man of vigor, decision, vitality, grit: but for his boy's powerlessness, there was nothing in his power to do. He solicited psychiatric assistance, counselors, shrinks, sought various prescriptions, not to mention copious quantities of son-focused prayer, but nothing seemed to work: for the first time in his life he was impotent. Bleakly and wretchedly impotent, unable to quell a seething psychic pain felt on another's behalf, his firstborn son, from whom he could not look away. So that an added ferocity accompanied his struggle to withstand the cancer of the lower bowels that methodically laid waste to his insides and eventually confined him to bedrest and feeble, croaking snips of pain-choked speech... to the last he refused to let his spirit succumb even as his body underwent one long dismal gradual succumbing, on his back in a featureless room of just the sort he'd once strode into, eased anxiety and suffering and fear of his patients with a wise fair honest voice and calm confident hands, how many had he saved?—but he couldn't save his son. The Father.

Flipped and contorted under the cooling (but still wet) covers, I settle on a dispensation of limbs that is novel and vaguely hieroglyphic. Face to pillow, I try to reject the shame this mini-narrative has dredged. And I'm laying on the sentiment a bit early and thick here, no? Tugging at the old heart strings in earnest, notwithstanding how I know my auditor here feels about irony? (I share his distaste.) Yes, well, David will perceive this. He'll see right through all my flourishing bullshit. Who wouldn't?

But David! Wait! Have a heart! Listen, I'm trying to tell you. I need to tell you: there's more! Of course there's more.

(The Son)

Leaves still on-tree scale down the spectrum from a few pinpricks of blood through jaundice down to ash, getting ready for disintegration, falling. As is the temperature. The foliage was gorgeous just a week ago; the Japanese word is he believes *yuuge*, which translates roughly as "the melancholy of beauty's fleet passage to death," in a basically Keatsian, High-Romantic sense. He knows or suspects this because for, oh, seven years, give or take, he'd entertained notions of acquiring this exotic language of the East, soaking up the culture, grasping the history, the nuance of a whole

Oriental way of life, mainly in the hopes of seducing a few Japanese girls. Except learning the language and ways &c. hadn't really helped, as he'd pretty much known it wouldn't from the outset, since females from all manner of background and ethnicity in the Aloha State of his adolescence tended not to respond too favorably to the mumbled advances he might work up nerve to attempt once every several months or so, when a particular classmate or neighbor or girl on the dance floor he'd been watching for several hours from his cornered folding chair's charm had proven too enticing even for his own sense of the effort's destined failure to restrain him from the humiliating sequence to come as he tried yet again against hope. Which lack of hope had sort of conduced to the lackluster if prolonged effort to actually learn *Nihongo* as an undergrad, penultimately spawning the egregious ambition of sojourning for a season in the Land of the Rising Sun, eventually becoming a Professor of Japanese himself and winning or wooing an adoring native Japanese whose own language he'd help her to appreciate the finer syntactical points of while she coached him culturally, but ultimately (if you were to take the present as the end) resulting in him being able to remember, from all his years of study, little more than his two favorite words: *yuuge* and *sabi*, which sort of corresponded to the "autumnal melancholy" described supra, and "wintery despair,"[1] respectively. He never did get to Japan.

He's presently foreseeing how he'll feel one glum December morning when it hasn't snowed but the trees are leafless, frail, it's very cold and he's alone under a pallid sky—because he'll know exactly what to call it. The feeling. "*Sabi*."

If he were a poet, he would put it into verse, if he still wrote

[1] C.f. Lear, Act I vs. Lear, Act V.

songs he'd paint it over an arrangement thick with soothing minor sevenths; but he no longer writes songs, and he is no author, of verse or anything.[2] And it's of course more than a little ridiculous to conflate the motion of pitiless Nature with the nature of a personal inability to meet someone to love and be loved by or at least bone.

He's naturally thought about maybe trying his hand at men—but men have cocks, which are, unfortunately to him, nearly cockroach-level grotesque. Therein lying that particular rub.[3] And,

[2]Let's avoid altogether the excruciation of the song lyrics he used to compose in the middle of the night and awake to the mauve absurdity of in the AM.

[3]Hoho. No but the special pertinence of this particular reference being that, while sabi is technically supposed to be a Learish sort of All-is-vanity, Oh-god,-we-really-are-all-only-dust;-only-now,-too-late,-do-I-see Cosmic Despair coming crushingly down as a spectral, twilit epiphany that alights on and brutalizes the enfeebled despairing consciousnesses of once-great men, like Lear, Macbeth, circa his "brief candle" phase, or Hemingway or Johnny Cash, right before the cataclysmic ends of volcanically-lived lives—at least in his interpretation, which admittedly might be wildly off-base—he doesn't see any real problem in grafting it onto a more immediate sort of soul-level despondence or angst in the tradition of, e.g., Hamlet, Prufrock, Munch's Screamer, himself, &c.; although the Bard's implication does seem (to this reader, at least) to be that the Prince more or less has shit together before the nefarious patricide, at the very least he has a beau, making him a bit harder to relate to for the Son than he'd've been if, say, as the unimpressively-statured soon-to-be Prince of Denmark he just couldn't get any play with the ladies at court, or had a hard time getting anyone other than his Dad to really appreciate the Danish Sonnets to Longing and Despair that he'd consequently labor to compose in his gloomy and copious free time, or got cut from the Varsity fencing squad but persevered on the JV in spite of the slings and arrows and general derision hurled his way by the rest of the adolescent courtesans who were contemptuous, vindictive, without heart—all in the hopes of earning for himself what he hadn't been granted at birth (basically the equivalent in fortune of a few extra inches of height)—and for the rest of his life sucked at fencing and got jittery and upset at the mere sight of a fencing strip, but could never resist the sick allure of an empty dueling space into which he would surreptitiously sneak with his equipment and gear, thence to dance a solitary sequence of flawless lunges, parries, glides, ripostes, the difficult-to-master moulinet, blade flashing through its loops and arcs and arabesques down the Piste, envisioning Victory, sweet and total, the noise he'd almost hear a million people cheering his name as he flourished through a deep-swept bow; only when the actual fencers showed up he'd slink back to the shade of the spectator bleachers and watch, thinking he could beat these assholes, he just knew it, plus write better

anyway, *who could learn to love a beast* like him? And I could tell David this crap and more, pour my leaky heart out on the poor guy,

But none of this makes for much of a story. Which is what I wanted him to ask for.

And I do see it. It's true. In the bedroom, in the miasmic haze of swill-and-General-Tso-scented post-colonic gas, mixed with marijuana smoke, under the brown-red fog beneath my coverlet, sweat-soaked and cocoonish, I'm having a hard time convincing even me that any of this means much of anything. Was it always this hard for you, Dave? Answer me!

Sleep would probably be best. Sleep, some unconscious digestion. Tomorrow, lots of water, fiber, the battery of stomach meds, and then: who knows? If I could only get some sleep. A bedtime story. My favorite children's book up there on the mantle (not really a mantle—just a taller box): David might think to read it to me if he weren't such an unfeeling asshole.

I try to drift back off, since there's no point discussing any of this with David, some hero, only there won't be any sleep just yet; in its lieu dreamy sublevels of consciousness begin to obtain and lurk at the unholy edges of shit.

And... oh by the way: no one stays a virgin forever! All you need to do is meet someone even more lonely than you:

Sedan interior already close with sweat, heat, bodies in each other's space. Nestled into the backseat's seam, the husk of a stray

sonnets than any of them, only their girls and their fathers and their friends would never even know, because here he was lurking in shadow, shame; and who most days didn't even get dressed and out of his boudoir until mid-afternoon, after he'd read all the fencing-related articles on Cnnsi.com, Espn.com, Foxsports.com, and Yahoo!Sports.com and had consumed at least a pot of coffee, and how this might be seen as a privilege deserving scorn, not pity, by most of the rest of civilized Denmark, but was actually a mighty mortal Curse. O that this too too solid flesh would melt, thaw, resolve itself into &c. &c. &c.

sweetgum seedpod, brittle dry spikes' tips minutely bent. Every Christmas, at his parents' house a few of the same, encrusted with red and green glitter, are dredged from the bottom of an old battered box filled with ornaments and holiday relics. The son believes he can remember drizzling glue on husks, pulling free of his mother's guiding hand so that he might make one all by himself: sprinkling the fine sparkling powders from separate plastic canisters and leaving the ornaments to dry on the cracked white windowsill and hanging them later from the boughs of the Christmas tree beside the hearth in a two-bedroom townhouse as a boy—a craft undertaken together during December afternoons when lunch was finished and he'd risen from his nap and they were all each other had for company while the Father worked long and hard to complete his residency—but maybe he's imagined this scene? Grafted it onto memory, that artifice of reconstructed time?

It makes no difference here: the lone and unexplained husk wedged into the crevice of a Cavalier's cramped backseat is not a Christmas ornament but an anomaly and a potential discomfort that might disrupt the fun: she plucks the spiny thing out from beneath her and smiles at him as she flicks it back onto the fuzzy expanse beneath the rearwindow's tight slope. And who is this girl we come upon in media res? Does it matter? She's long-discarded now. He smiles back, sort of, looks out over her shoulder, where harbor and cityscape shine lacteal through body-fogged glass; she tugs loose of shorts and panties with a practiced unfurling of long white legs.

Soon, hunched over her knees, neck craned, she looks back up at him, reluctant but ready to please: Really? He nods. She looks away, he reaches down, strokes her, ass, thigh, calves, toes, squeezes assurance, smooths her like an animal, and she sighs, nods, dark curls glitter in the streetlight's slant. A little spit. Some fumbling: inexperience. Her every muscle tensing, he sees her wince, grimace, bite her lip. Squirming, more probing manipulation. When he finally pushes in, she gasps, sucks in the pain as he slowly, gently but not relenting, presses deeper, grips neck with one hand, ass with the other. In a moment he chokes on an upsurge of full-body-shuddering joy. He grunts, grips her tight to himself, presses her face deep into the dirty seat-cushion.

Soon as he's shot his consciousness recoils in horror. Watches the body that is ostensibly his withdraw from the other quivering body and looks down in repulsed fascination on the thing that is his and would appear to be stained in places with thin blotches of what must be, well, hmm. Wipes himself clean as he can using the boxers he'd been wearing, his own hands the trembling ones now, the girl turns, tucks her legs under sits beside him in the manner of the Japanese. A lightshaft spears darkness before them, he feels her lean towards him, she lays a hand on his thigh, squeezes softly, says she loves him. His gaze, stricken, alighting, as it obviously must, on the brittle husk.

Poor girl!—surely just as hurt in her own way as our guy (hence, perhaps, her delusory "love"), a girl for whom he might feel great pity and sadness, might be moved by to something like real compassion, if only he could stop fucking her to consider, let alone feel, but whose tender little body he has, against what little remains of his conscience's persistent counsel, not only used to work out all of his long-thwarted lusts and carnal eccentricities &c., but whom he has convinced—and even convinced himself once in a while, at least in the moment's supposed "heat"—he loves. Until he leaves her, as he'd more or less intended to do all along. This not being one of our hero's more admirable spells... but what's the big deal? Everybody's got a little romantic disfiguration hidden on his body somewhere, right? Maybe so! Maybe so! Does a convention's familiarity mean it can't also be awful?

All of which is to say, you're right:

There's no story here—really, who cares about a lost plastic tugboat not discernibly linked to or symbolic of anything; or a Dad whose failing wasn't a real failing like alcoholism or rage or neglect of his kid, wasn't even his failing at all unless you count the abject failure of the thing you've created to do whatever it is it's supposed to do, since you're the one who made it, as your own—and even if you do count this, who cares?—And plus it's unmanly to over-grieve the passed-on father, a fault to nature, whose common theme is death of fathers... and fetishistic longing for an Orientalized Other? Big deal! So what!—Wait I can go smaller:

(Ghost)

Tomorrow afternoon I'll be standing in the rain outside the shit office I supposedly work at, smoking one of the shit cigarettes I bought not realizing they were shit—because I know nothing— smoking this cigarette I don't even like because it goes well with the pill I'll take, guiltily, from the bottle of prescription amphetamines I stole from a friend months ago after the M.D.s finally cut me off, and I'll be standing there wet smoking in the cold rain, feeling the fat drips come down, looking through puffs of cigarette smoke out into the street where cars splash past under a sodden canopy of soaked trees, everything gray, dead, dying, sabi &c., and I'll be contemplating another pill since the first one's effects have already begun to wane wishing as I contemplate that I didn't need unprescribed stimulation just to "get by," debating whether to take the pill now or in another hour when I'll probably really need it, except I really need it now—and what happens when the pills run out?—and as I'm standing there soaking up the premature *sabi* of everything, a car pulls up and stops at the red, windows half-down despite rain, releasing a few flaccid measures of that stupid song, "Against the Wind,"—this will be the actual song—before the light changes and the music fades, and as I'm standing there smoking the cigarette I won't like, contemplating the pill I'll wish I didn't have to take, and somehow really desperately needing to hear the rest of the old song, a dead sodden gray leaf will plop to the muck at my feet and what'll happen is, I'll look down at that leaf and the understanding will erupt within me that a leaf falls, dead, a leaf just falls and lies there, morte, in utter filth, sopping up its own rotting sog,—loneliness, I'll think—only that's somebody else's fucking story and it's already been told with more panache, skill and of course concision than I could ever even hope to bring to bear, meant more than I can ever hope to mean, and at this point I'll just give up. I've got nothing left. In the freezingcold, my unenjoyed cig smoked down to the hilt, I'll take the other pill.

Big deal, I know. No wonder you're not listening.

And since these explanations don't seem to be accomplishing much why don't we reverse time a bit?

One Saturday morning when I was sixteen I watched various members of my immediate family[4] pile into our enormous white cargo van, the backseat stacked with foam "boogie" boards in assorted shades of neon and pastel, my father herding passengers in

---

[4] Have I mentioned my five little sisters? They are beautiful and kind.

like one of those circus clown acts in reverse, botching the words to a popular radio hit of the day that he'd probably only heard secondhand via one child's unaccompanied impression, since he himself listened to nothing but 95.5 FM, The Fish—"Today's Christian Music"— and if he'd actually known the words of the song he was also getting the tune of entirely wrong he'd almost certainly have disapproved, but my father was an abstracted man, and may well not have even known that he was singing, let alone lending paternal credence to contraband. At this point the ingressing figures blur in memory, perhaps out of naturalistic faithfulness to the actual tableau's shifting features at the time—I was crying, tears were, as they say, streaming from my eyes, while I attempted to watch the people I both sometimes loathed and burningly needed affection or compassion or pity from pile into the oversized unwashed conveyance with its temporary graffiti art finger-sketched by neighborhood ruffians into the chassis' dust, revealing the original paint job's brighter shade of white—as I'd just decided (the occasion for these particular tears, although tears were not exactly rare or even occasional during this epoch), out of my life forever, since before they'd returned from their day at the beach I would be dead.

Not that I intended to commit suicide, or at least "intend" seemed superfluous, irrelevant, moot, more than I could manage. I'd refused repeated entreaties to join them on this Saturday outing, citing an array of unconvincing reasons that I needed time alone; I wanted to be left alone so that someone could come rushing in at the climactic moment having apprehended just in time that I actually needed not to be alone—but at the threshold of that moment I was still alone. I brought down the bottle of pills—prescribed for my depression, to be taken in tandem with the therapy sessions I was

supposed to be attending every other week but frequently skipped—
my hand shaking with the knowledge of what I was destined to do,
and I took several more pills than I was supposed to take but not
enough to kill me.[5]

Of course, I was afraid to die. I never told anyone I'd taken
all those pills, and though my folks—particularly my father—surely
must have been concerned when they found me sleeping fitfully on
the living-room sofa several hours later, I was able to persuade them
that I hadn't been getting enough rest, and was just very much worn-
down. The subsequent quasi-bedrest lasted for several days, me mostly
sticking to my room, until I suppose my liver had done its extra work.,
and I was "clean."

Not my only attempt. One time I had the noose around my
neck, you know, I had it secured to a ceiling pipe, I was ready to do it.... .

But hang on: Recall the guitar over there in the corner to
which I first called your attention some while back, David. Around
this time, or soon thereafter, is when I realized I wasn't really
interested in making music; I wanted to *use* the music I made to
accomplish what I truly wanted to do, which was something like
channel or expel or pass on or dredge up or I don't know the best
verb for what's anyway a pretty fucking well-understood conceit—
i.e., that the music was not there for me merely to be music, but to
act as a vessel, to carry something precious or toxic or maybe like an
admixture of dark matter and holy broth. And for this reason the
music was never very good—or maybe it was extraordinarily "good,"
maybe it was intensely, immeasurably, obliteratingly, good, in the

---

[5]Any amateur flirter with auto-inflicted death will of course know
that it's more or less impossible to kill yourself with most prescribed anti-
depressants—you have to take a lot—but I was sixteen, knew even less then (in
some ways) than I do now, and anyway probably didn't really want to die, as noted.

sense that it accomplished with naked straightforwardness the task that art seems to me most well-suited to pulling off—the expression and, much more important, pure communication of *pain*—only I know this isn't most other people's view of art. In fact I'd argue they believe in something close to this definition's opposite: art as beauty, as prettifying scrim, as pain-concealer, or at very least transformer of orderless, entropic, unrelenting hurt into something possibly affirming, infused with meaning or sense: a distraction, balm, maybe even offering a measure of redemption—rather than sheer communion with pain....

This may merely be a roundabout way of suggesting that my music wasn't all that technically accomplished. I fretted chords, lumberingly learned the pentatonic scales plus a few others (Mixolydian? I now forget the names), recorded versions of derivative self-written songs, overlaid leads I tried to mask the blandness of behind sound-cascades of multi-tracks. But you must know what it's like, David, to sense there's something massive and awful and perhaps even *pure* inside of you, with maybe even the power to move someone else—only, no outlet, no effective means.... Or maybe you've never felt this way. I bet you have, but one never can tell, can one?

I was only just beginning to understand that art existed and that, at least as perceived through my own narrow interpretive lens, it might represent the expurgation and curating of something the artist, the creator, the former human harbor of the sickness purged, had needed to transfer from within to without, and to frieze or statue or in some other way hold fast in the world so that it could not seep once again back into him, at least not in its original form, and that what you were doing when you read the poem, saw the film, heard the song, was witnessing the manifestation, the substance, communing with the material incarnation of some suffering soul self-transformed into music through an act of courage and will....

What I was responding to was pain. I never once heard my father use the word "depression," evasive of him, I suppose—we all knew what was going on—but I didn't hold this against him: I didn't want a diagnosis, name for my disease; I wanted him—and everyone—to know the pain itself. To know the me.

And I don't know that I ever could articulate what that pain was really like, and maybe anyway I wouldn't need to, it's certainly been done (by you better than just about anyone), and then too I wonder if any of us need to be told what suffering's like: I share the same anxiety I once saw you work out in a story about the potential vanity if not full-blown inbent solipsism involved, or at least risk of it, the risk that I appear to be condescending to you, Reader, whoever you happen to be, from some exalted anguish-peak.... Yet another sad part of this being that I can't get inside your pain any more than you can mine, so that it's even possible I know nothing more of pain than anybody does. Maybe I'm simply more inclined to scrutinize the finer contours of my pain, to relish and luxuriate and dwell in it, which means I'm basically an asshole, or at least I'm not really in the human race, since everybody knows the first condition of participation is acceptance of the need to suffer more than you feel you have it in you to possibly stand or fight through, on a pretty much daily basis, so that monitoring or acknowledging or even taking note of, let alone complaining about (let alone "dwelling" in) the sense you sometimes have that you're just not going to get through this, whatever "this" may be[6]—is just entirely bad form;

[6] an exam you need to pass in order to have a shot at graduate school;

because even if "this" as you define it is a feeling of exquisite dread, terror before all human beings (including but naturally not limited to: your "friends," family, significant other, colleagues if you work, students you teach, customers if you keep a store, patients if you care for the sick, opponents and teammates if you enjoy or formerly enjoyed or believe or at least would like to imagine you once enjoyed participating in competitive sports), even if "this" is a sadness so devastating and complete that it's embarrassing to try to compress it into a single signifier or whole pages, reams, piles, mountain-caves crammed with them, but if you were to take one last whack at it you might say it's something like not only feeling hopelessly unhappy about every imaginable aspect of your own life, your own frustrations, failures, terrors, loathings, &c. &c., but also about the sense you begin to get that everyone who doesn't feel exactly as awful as you for every second of his or her life is somehow deluding him- or herself and that (this is one way you know you're really deep down in it) this sense isn't a cause for scorn on your part, the sort of sneering supposed "knowing" that shakes its head and smirks and inwardly anticipates with a kind of happy schadenfreude the day when the whole cardhouse will come collapsing down without

a sixteen-hour double-shift washing dishes when you're brutally hungover and running on less than two hours' sleep; inconclusive but pretty damning evidence that the girl's been telling lies and that the truth is really going to be pain; the slow succumbing to cancer of a father who had heretofore been so hale and vigorously full of life as to be almost obnoxious, overbearing in the sense that his very vitality made you feel comparatively feeble and scarcely alive; several years of solitary detention in a prison camp run by enemy combatants who may or may not be any more inherently cruel than your own countrymen conducting their own camps, but who have certainly not demonstrated any particular concern for your international "rights" as a prisoner of war, in terms of refraining from say, breaking and rebreaking your legs when you refuse to divulge certain choice bits of information about the position of the regiment or battalion or platoon you happened to be reconnoitering from when you were captured, or shooting your scrotum full of electric shocks... .

much sound or fury... nor is it outrage, a desire to hold the heads of a whole race of hypocrites in a vise, grip them in place before the only accurately reflecting mirror they've ever been forced to look into and, for the first time, really see... it isn't even envy, the sort of broken wishfulness of a man who'll do anything to push the pain away, even if it means burying his head and sucking in mouthfuls of sand and willing himself to believe that the granules working their way down his throat are pure, sweet water—which is to say it isn't coveting your neighbor's happy inability to see... no, even if the really horrible thing you think you may perceive when you're forced for whatever reason to leave your apartment or home and edge out into the updraft of people on the move as they go about their business or pleasure is neither smug contempt, indignation, nor even a self-pitying pining for the human touch, or for just one chance to finally enter the race, none of these but rather an awful, fathomless foreboding that every one of the people behind these faces is doomed at some point in his life, before she dies to feel exactly as you feel, the same agony you've been suffering through, it certainly feels like alone—it is alone—you're suffering singly, but not singularly, and that maybe for these poor people it'll somehow be even worse when the horror finally hits, because you, miserably self-pitying pain-obsessed pariah that you are, are at least willing to accept the prospect, the reality or truth of this pain; whereas the man who's been running from it fifty years without even knowing he's been running, or maybe occasionally catching a glimpse of the ground flying beneath his feet, occasionally hearing the thud of his overbeaten heart in either ear, but not letting himself pause, let alone turn and look back—this guy will never know until the day he's finally forced to slow down (everyone slows down) and hauled bodily around and head clutched in hideous gnarled black-yellow claws and forced to look the pain, the sadness, the horror, the unspeakable, It in the face—and what will it be like for him then?—but even if this is what it's like for you every time you shuffle out your door, trying not to look folks in the eye, terrified that something awful's bound to happen (but what could happen? What could be worse?!), if every bit of contact with what everyone else seems to consider the real world is for you an exercise in looking away from a numberless host of pursued people fleeing not merely their pursuer but the very fact of their pursuit, trying not to glimpse the sagging faces of those who may be on the verge of knowledge; even if "this" is an entire way of being, an abyss you are dismayed to learn every day is miraculously capable of hauling you down deeper into—and that it is worse the deeper you go—even if "this" is the surface or tip of what you mean when you want to make somebody, anybody, for christ's sake, *see*… it doesn't matter:

Not because any of them are necessarily callous or cruel or unfeeling or secretly pleased by your suffering or even because they simply can't conceive of how awful it must be to be you—though all of these things may of course well be true, there's just no way to know—but because you can't begin to imagine whether what they're feeling isn't in some way wholly unimaginable to you, or actually hundreds of, thousands of, infinitely more times worse than what you perceive as the absolute nadir of your suffering (granting that you're still on the way down); so that you can't ever know whether your inability to communicate the sheer horror of what it feels like to be you during every millisecond you're forced to be conscious (and also during all but the dreamless REM-cycles of sleep) and to some absurd extent in the world, is a consequence of imprisonment within suffering too intensely inhuman to be communicated to anyone walled off on its outside—or merely yet another indication of your obsessive indifference to all but the most self-sequestered facts of what you conceive of as life, your concern with nothing but what you need and can't have, your failure to bother to wonder whether anyone else is in need of more than what she can possibly ever expect to have, your fetish for your own pain—"weakness" is another way to say this—that is, *you're* the one who fails to see: in fact, the rest of the world is waiting for you to open your eyes or perhaps the better metaphor is to punch a hole through the cell walls of you and squeeze your way out, the monster is eating himself alive, the one without a heart is in here, and whether it's willed cruelty or congenital weakness doesn't matter, just as it wouldn't really matter if after all it turned out that it *was* their inability to see, you weren't a weakling, everyone else really *was* blind, lost, stupidly unconcerned—the critical, insurmountable badness is that it's impossible for you to know,[7] and all you can do is either push on, as you presume everyone else must be doing, or give up.

Pain is what I perceived in the first works of art that moved me. Pain that had slipped through some infinitesimal fissures in the wall between its victims and progenitors and me.

You will have noticed the scattered allusions to Eliot's Waste Land in the preceding discussion. It embarrasses me, a bit, to reveal that I was so moved by that poem, so sure he was speaking directly to me (I didn't know literature; what I knew was pain), that I recorded several variations on a musical adaptation of the song—a poor adaptation, naturally, as I was a poor musician, but an adaptation that

[7] "We live, as we dream, alone."

came, there isn't a better way to put this, from the heart.

What I was attracted to in art was the semblance or reflection or relative of my own self-suffusing, seemingly inescapable pain. I wondered whether the artists responsible for the art I loved had managed—even for an exalted instant, at the peak of creative fury— to escape the pain, or if not escape then perhaps abide within it, become consumed by their work to the extent that they momentarily lost touch with the pain they were trying to channel. I became a connoisseur of pain, David. So you see how I had to find you.

I wish you could have been there when I first encountered Hal, Don, Madame P, Kate, The Mad Stork. Nothing prepared me to receive the gift you would have no way of knowing you'd given me; I took it greedily, hungrily, messily, whole. But I did receive it, David, I knew you. We might have touched for a brief epoch[8] during which I was able to slip out from within me....

...and I wish I could tell you something like You saved me that day, that morning I stood up on the folding table and looped the noose around my neck and prepared to kick myself free... only a line or image—Don Gately risking his life that some asshole might live, e.g.—or that some insight you'd imparted to me leapt to mind before I could leap from the edge... but the truth is I hadn't met you yet, I was too young, too young to see much of anything: a scared boy senseless with inarticulate grief, in a lot of pain he couldn't understand but that even if he could or could see that he wasn't the first person to feel and surely wouldn't be the last it wouldn't have necessarily helped at that stage since all he wanted was to make it stop hurting so much.... I was seventeen, I stood there with the

[8](well, technically several months, is how long it took me to finish the thing)

noose around my neck, and the truth is that not even you could have saved me if I hadn't been too scared to go through with what I wished I were more sure I wanted to do.... And even after I had met you—do you know how many times I've read 'Neon'?—there's no guarantee it would have been enough, of course: We aren't ever saved but always in the process of salvation, sometimes it needs to happen every day, the saving, more often than that, which is how it's been for me, and how you've in this sense honestly saved me many times, David, there have been other nights like this, believe me, you've been with me through many of the worst of them, but I'll obviously never be saved—and that's I guess what being alive is, David, you helped me to see that, though it's something I for the most part fail or maybe just forget to see. Two nights ago I was sure I would drink enough to work up the courage to finally go through with it, you know? We have a high enough rooftop not too far from my place. And I did climb up there and peer pretty melodramatically from the edge for a long instant—and I guess I'm glad that I didn't step over, if only for the opportunity it gives me to tell you now, I understand: you never offered anyone a way *out* so much as a way further *in*, you wanted to live, not cheat life or beat it at its own brutal game, you showed me how to be alive, if you don't mind my putting it so nakedly, I'm reminded of this often when *in life* is the very last place I want to be, when I'm sad, I mean really sad, I want to go ahead and let go, only this impossible holding on *is living*, burning at the edge, and you knew just what I mean, so that I knew I wasn't alone... and so I'm grateful I at least get this one chance to tell you that, David, to thank you, to let you know you really did touch me, you really do, to tell you basically that you are loved....

I roll over and throw off the damp sheet, loose more of the stench I've produced over the last hour-plus of nonsleep and stare at where he'd perhaps by now have drifted off into a marijuana-dipped doze, only, yes, of course: the empty chair, only the wind's home, &c., only there isn't even any wind, in the stinking gloom, the shadows and the brownish fog of an autumn pre-dawn, beneath the spread of my own noxious waste... if I only once could have told you, David, just once.

I kick over the chair and stumble out into the hall towards water, the hallway unlit long, longer than usual, longer than I can ever remember it being, and I've walked for some time before I pause to turn and see only pure shadow behind me, shadow before me, beside me too. Head clearing, clarity stark against the flat empty darkness, I walk—because I'm thirsty—and walk on. Down the sprawling length of unfamiliar corridor, out of darkness into further darkness, everything black... you get the idea. I'm starting to regret—well it's hard to isolate a specific object for regretting, but there's a general sense of everything being calamitously ill-advised. I'm wondering whether I ought to make an effort to remember this in the morning—when I walk right into something solid and huge.

I stop since I don't seem to have any choice, and tap against what's revealed by my touch to be glass. A massive sheet of smooth obstruction, unseen. I spread palms on it, press my whole body flat, and it is cool (like glass) and apparently vast. I try to look through to see if there's anything on the other side, and, it's true, I can't see anything, who knows what's in there, through the glass, but for some reason I want to find out. This curiosity, it's entirely out of character, and it's also true that I am strongly inclined to turn around and slink defeated back the way I came. But I don't. I press an open palm to the thick pane, sort of tap at it a little. Inspect it for holes, cracks, knobs, slits, &c. Nope. I look around: the whole house and probably the whole world has gone black. A glass pane between me and more black. Except something glints from inside.

With an awkwardly clenched and unsteady fist (naturally I've never done this) I punch through the glass, shatter it and carve up my hand, substantial bloodloss, but I somehow don't care, advance into the room or hall or further empty space and walk toward where I thought I saw that light-sliver. I open hands before me, step careful, light, and still stumble right into the big solid thing at-center, banging my knee. Nothing more in the way of illumination, but I don't need it to perceive that what I've reached is a piano. Grand piano. I run my fingers down the length of exposed keys. Sit at the little bench and rest my fingers on the ivory wishing I knew what to do with it. That I could deliver up more than the stuttery plinks of a pure hack. In the silence, in the still black space, the near-absolute, I hear myself breathe, am aware suddenly of the creaking action of my lungs, unoiled bellows laboring to take what they can get, making their unrelenting claim on the surrounding void. Feel the pulse of transubstantiation, life meted out in nonnegotiable rations to that insatiable brawl of throbbing need. Blood from the gashes over my knuckles, perhaps invisibly staining keys. I hear more breath.

Well: I play a chord—a C major, nice and easy, clean and white—and then I play another—a G sprouting one half-step down from its component B, as far as I know the oldest most beautiful motion in all of music—then another, down to the e minor, and I won't transpose the rest, but it's a three-step, a lovechain, a deathwaltz through empty time, only no one's dancing and the melody slides out of me, looping through the grid I've laid out for it—the oldest, simplest song there is—and it happens as it used to happen, it's happened a thousand times before, when I was a boy, when I was young, before:

I close my eyes and dip my head and drift and then I'm there, I'm in it, unleashed inside, the music swirling around me a torrent of sound and pure furious soul, and now as then, I float in a space at storm's eye, howling blackness streaked with light of the one song that forks and striates darkness and I'm taken up by a violence of feeling that would be embarrassing in almost any other context. The music, my music, is around me, in me, through me, is me, me alone.... I blink open and see that as expected everything's fallen away except the keys at my fingers, the brittle crude music, the motion a trance I might as well be watching on a screen, for an instant I wonder whether to give it up, let my fingers rest—only a *Hand*—touches my shoulder, squeezes, and I turn, still playing—and behind me, beside me, with me: a form, an eminence, figure of a man, somehow radiating light, and I *see* him in the darkness, all lit up from within, beside me, touching me, smiling down on me, and as the music swirls I see there are silver tears gathered beneath his glowing eyes, dripping, then quickening to a stream down his face.

He reaches out to catch the glitter as it slows to a trickle, the light fading, and just before it's gone, I see him smile and wink as he closes his fist. A great wind rushes up beside me and I hear woven in with my notes a shout, a voice I've never heard, but imagined and believed, rings clear, a galaxy of liquid sparks explodes above us in deep space, and behind him—He's still here, beside me—is every person I have ever wanted to love, mother and sister, my friends, poor sad girl, Dad!—shit, they're all there—and under a shower of white light they're floating in darkness as he smiles and throws his hands up and the throng *actually starts to sing*—they're singing my song, a song I've never written or possessed or given before just now, a melody sung to twine seamless and sweet with the floating chords I've lost all control over, like a mate for their incorporeal soul, and the music sparkles with the constellations of crying light that rain down on us for what might be forever, deep in the heart of a place way beyond wanting or time.

.

Thanks to the many people without whom I couldn't have written this book:
Alanna Schubach, David Hollander, Chris Makoto Yogi, and my uncle Mike, who've read material I've sent unbidden for years: if all of our work is composed with a handful of readers in mind, then I wrote every page of these stories for you; Ted Pelton: generous, committed, patient, himself a full-time fiction writer, academic, and parent as well as guerilla publisher, but never too busy to address himself to this author's abundant neuroses, transmitted more or less daily via electronic mail; Matt Bell and David McLendon, who ran some of my earliest stories and have continued to work with me for the past several years—it's always an honor to appear in *The Collagist* and *Unsaid*; thanks, too, to the editors of other venues in which pieces of this collection were first published: *Pank, Witness, >kill author, Underwater New York, Fringe*, and *The Lifted Brow*; thanks to Cynthia Franklin, Melvin Bukiet, Brian Morton, Paul Lyons, Daphne Desser, Rick Moody, all of whom guided a young man in need of a guide; Ian McMillan: rest in peace; to my family: Tim, Katie, Chris, Beth, Kimmi, Jenni, Mom and Dad and the whole non-immediate horde: 衷心深謝し、七重の膝を八重に折り礼を尽くします—particularly those who purchased copies of the book; thanks to my good friends, Kevin, Scott, Nicki, Connor, Jeremy, Robert, Akana; thanks to Tanaka San, and Senseis Tokunaga, Maeda, Do, Kawano, Noguchi, Takashima, Kakihara, Kobayashi, Kinoshita, Matsuo, Aihara, Tsutsumi, Hayashi, the entire basketball club, and Ogori High School, generally; thanks to Destiny, Ashley, Palani and Ron; thanks to the indomitable Sandra Allen at *Wag's Revue*; to LeBron James and Dirk Nowitzki; lastly, and most of all, thanks to my lady—the lovely, compassionate, compact and kind Yukie: you are loved.

Jonathan Callahan

Also Available from Starcherone Books

Starcherone Books, Inc., exists to stimulate public interest in works of innovative prose fiction and nurture an understanding of the art of fiction writing by publishing, disseminating, and affording the public opportunities to hear readings of innovative works. In addition to encouraging the development of authors and their audiences, Starcherone seeks to educate the public in small press publishing and encourage the growth of other small presses. Visit us online at www.starcherone.com and the Starcherone Superfan Group on Facebook. Starcherone Books, PO Box 303, Buffalo, NY 14201.

Starcherone Books is an independently operated imprint of Dzanc Books, distributed through Consortium Distribution and Small Press Distribution. We are a signatory to the Book Industry Treatise on Responsible Paper Use and use postconsumer recycled fiber paper in our books.